KNIGHT'S
Rescue

Book Two of Knights of KSI Series

BY SHELLEY JUSTICE

KNIGHT'S RESCUE

Copyright ©2020, Shelley Justice

All rights reserved.

This book is a work of fiction. The characters, places, names, incidents and dialogue in this book are products of the author's imagination or used fictitiously. Any resemblance to actual events or persons, living or dead, is completely coincidental and not intended by the author.

No part of this book may be reproduced, or stored in a retrieval system, or transmitted in any form or by any means, electronic, mechanical, photocopying, recording, or otherwise, without expressed written consent of the publisher.

The material in this book is for mature audiences only and is intended only for adults aged 18 and older.

CAUTION: This book contains references to abuse and rape. The details aren't explicit but should be considered sensitive material.

COVER DESIGN: CT Cover Creations
COVER PHOTO: Photography by CJC
EDITOR: Write Right Edits

ISBN: 978-1-7348725-2-1 (ebook)
      978-1-7348725-3-8 (paperback)

Dedication

"A good friend knows all your best stories, but a best friend has lived them with you." ---Unknown

I dedicate this book to my best friend and my forever encourager, Christie. You helped me to shape this book into the story I needed to tell. You encouraged me to be bold and chase the dream I've held in my heart for so many years. For all of this and for so much more, I will be eternally grateful.

Table of Contents

Dedication...Front

Chapter One 1

Chapter Two 9

Chapter Three 15

Chapter Four 25

Chapter Five...33

Chapter Six 41

Chapter Seven..51

Chapter Eight 57

Chapter Nine 75

Chapter Ten..93

Chapter Eleven...105

Chapter Twelve 119

Chapter Thirteen 127

Chapter Fourteen 137

Chapter Fifteen 149

Chapter Sixteen..157

Chapter Seventeen 167

Chapter Eighteen 179

Chapter Nineteen 189

Chapter Twenty	203
Chapter Twenty-One	213
Chapter Twenty-Two	223
Chapter Twenty-Three	237
Chapter Twenty-Four	247
Chapter Twenty-Five	259
Chapter Twenty-Six	269
Epilogue	281
Author's Note	291
About the Author	292
Acknowledgments	293
More from this Author	294

Chapter One

Sydney Reede felt the blood drain from her face. She retreated several steps until her back bumped against a ficus tree. Her only solace – slight as it was – was knowing she had gone unnoticed so far. She needed to disappear, but she was boxed into a corner in the crowded ballroom. She barely registered the people milling about her, save for the one person she never expected to see. The noise of music and conversation faded to an unintelligible buzz. Emmett wasn't supposed to be here. He was supposed to be out of the country on business. That was the only reason she agreed to attend the charity gala. After two years of him parading her on his arm, she always associated these events with the judgment and ridicule she'd received from her ex.

The irony was, this time, she actually looked forward to the event because Emmett wouldn't be at her side to degrade her. She had been able to walk into the ballroom, feeling pretty in her cocktail dress, confident she could be herself and enjoy the evening.

Then she saw him, devastating in his charcoal gray suit with not a hair out of place. She couldn't stop watching him charm the guests. They loved him, but then most people did. And that nauseated her. They didn't know him as she did.

She wasn't ready to face him. Dread welled up within her. She had to get out of here. *Fast.*

"Okay, don't be mad." Her best friend, Chloe Stephens, suddenly appeared at her side. "I convinced a friend of mine to dance with you. Since you refuse to mingle and get to know anyone here,

I thought I'd help you break the ice."

As the organizer of the charity gala, Chloe knew everyone on tonight's guest list. If her friend had approached her just a few moments earlier with the odd request to dance with a stranger, Sydney would have agreed. But now, drawing attention to herself, even in a small way, would place her in Emmett's crosshairs.

"I can't." Sydney's voice caught in her throat, making her words seem strangled.

"What's the matter?"

"He's here. Emmett's here."

"*What?*" Chloe's head whipped around, her dark eyes scanning the ballroom. Her expression grew fierce the instant she spotted Emmett Carter. "Oh, *hell* no. He's not supposed to be here."

"I have to leave before he sees me."

Chloe placed a reassuring hand on Sydney's forearm. "No, you should not be the one to leave. I'll ask security to discreetly escort him out."

Sydney shook her head vehemently. "No, please. He'll make a scene. Tonight is too important to you, and I'm not ready to deal with him again."

"Syd, calm down. I won't let him near you."

"I can't do this." Sydney struggled to hold back tears.

"Just breathe. That jerk can't hurt you anymore. He's not welcome here, so he's not staying. Let me handle it."

Sydney nodded, noting the determination and concern in her friend's eyes.

"What will you tell them?" Sydney hated the embarrassment flooding her body whenever others learned of her involvement with Emmett. She never wanted anyone to know how volatile their relationship had been or how long she'd allowed it to go on.

"Just that your ex is here, and we need to make sure Emmett

doesn't bother you. It'll be fine. This is what they're paid to do, so they won't ask any questions."

Sydney forced a tremulous smile. "Thank you."

As Chloe walked away, Sydney closed her eyes for a moment. Her heart beat a furious rhythm in her chest, but her anxiousness began to subside. When her lids opened, she felt more in control. Chloe was right. She and Emmett were long over, so it was time to break free of the hold he had on her.

She focused on the spot where she'd last seen Chloe, but her friend had disappeared into the crowd. She searched the ballroom for Chloe's familiar blonde head only to come up short in the sea of people. A tingling sensation prickled the back of her neck. As if an unknown force compelled her, she turned back toward the front of the ballroom. Her eyes collided with a familiar stare, one that held both surprise and contempt. Sydney's stomach plummeted to her feet.

Emmett cocked a dark eyebrow that spoke volumes to her. She'd invaded his social circle and posed a threat to his precious reputation. Emmett moved through the crowd toward her, but Sydney refused to give him the satisfaction of a confrontation on his turf. Since he knew just how to push her buttons, she needed time to prepare.

She spun around to search for the best exit. Because of the throng of people around her, her only option was to escape through the veranda doors at the back of the ballroom. She managed a swift retreat despite her high heels. She sensed Emmett closing in, but if she could beat him outside, she could hide long enough for him to lose interest and return to the party.

Reaching the glass doors, she startled when they suddenly opened. She lurched through them, the warm summer air hitting her in a blast. As she turned to hurry down the steps leading to the grounds, her retreat halted when she slammed into a wall – or what felt like a wall.

Her breath left her in a whoosh. Stumbling backward, she lost her balance and started falling to the stone floor of the veranda. Steel-like bands encircled her upper arms, suspending her in mid-air. She was righted to her feet by a strength that astonished her. Eyes wide, she lifted her head, craning her neck at an unnatural angle.

The sheer size of the man unnerved her. Well over six feet tall, his powerful frame strained the seams of his black trousers and matching, button-front shirt. The strings of lights along the veranda illuminated his rugged features. Narrow eyes, an unusual golden brown, studied her.

"Are you all right?" His deep voice rumbled through her, and she shivered.

"I, uh, I have to go." She pulled against his stronghold.

He released her but blocked her retreat. "Ma'am, are you okay? Do you need help?"

She leaned to the side to peer around the man's muscular build and into the ballroom. Emmett closed the distance between them. A smirk curved his lips, reminding Sydney of how much he'd always reveled in the chase - in forcing her to run just to catch her and prove she couldn't escape him.

Sydney skirted around the stranger and darted down the veranda steps. The hotel's garden stretched before her, dimly lit by solar pathway lights. She hurried into the array of blooms, shrubs, and trees. She needed a hiding place, but before she could find one, a hand closed around her arm like a vise. She spun around expecting to see Emmett looming behind her. Her scream died in her throat.

"Ma'am, I can help if you'll let me." The man she'd bumped into on the veranda had followed her and now stood in the shadows. Usually, a moment like this would put her on the defensive, but his tone was kind, giving her pause.

"Sydney!" A familiar voice rose over the stillness of the garden – a voice that evoked the worst memories to surface and shatter her peace of mind.

She turned pleading eyes to the stranger, the desperation in her voice was unmistakable. "He can't find me," she whispered.

The eerie lights along the path allowed her to see his nod. He led her into the darkness, to a cluster of trees just off the path. She felt vulnerable. She was entrusting her safety to this stranger, but she knew she had no other choice with Emmett so close.

The stranger placed her in the shadow of two trees. Then he shifted his body to shield her, his dark clothes providing the camouflage her royal blue dress didn't. The warmth from his body seeped through her clothes, driving away the chill that Emmett's presence had evoked. His musky scent swirled around her.

"Slow your breathing." His voice was hushed. "Even and steady. I won't let him find you. If he does, I'll protect you."

Something in his gentle manner made Sydney believe him. As he instructed, she willed her breathing to slow.

"Sydney. You know better than to hide from me."

Her body automatically stiffened at the proximity of Emmett's voice. Her hands gripped the front of the stranger's shirt, holding him in place. He could easily pull away from her, but holding onto him gave her a sense of control.

The stranger rested his strong hands lightly on her arms, his palms moving up and down to comfort her. Sydney had no idea how long they stood there. Shielded as she was between the tree trunks and his body, she couldn't see anything but the stranger. Eventually, she heard Emmett's heavy footfalls taking him away from the garden. Slowly she raised her eyes, seeking the stranger's face in the darkness.

"Thank you." Her quiet voice sounded odd in the stillness.

She unclenched her fists to release his shirt front, but her palms rested against his chest. She felt his heart beating steadily even as her own raced. A strange tingle started at the tips of her fingers and radiated up her arms, through her body and down to her toes. Electricity zinged between them, a pull she neither expected nor understood.

She sensed rather than saw his head dip, his lips hovering mere inches from her own. Her breath caught in her throat. She knew what was coming. She shouldn't want it to happen. The man was a stranger who just had a ring-side seat to the baggage she carried from her relationship with Emmett.

But what she *felt* refused to mirror what she knew. Anticipation swirled within her. Then his firm lips settled against hers.

The kiss began as a tender, feather-like touch. His tongue stroked the seam of her lips until they parted of their own volition. He deepened the kiss, drawing her even closer to him. The slow burn of desire made it impossible to resist him. A moan shattered the silence, but Sydney couldn't be sure which of them made the sound. The feel of the hard planes of his body weakened her legs, making her grateful for his embrace.

She had no idea a kiss could be so charged. Her mind was lost in a fog of sensation. She momentarily forgot this man was a stranger. A muscled arm encircled her waist to cradle her as no one ever had. They were fused together in their own intimate bubble.

The kiss ended as suddenly as it started. He released her, and she sank her weight against the tree trunk behind her. Several heartbeats passed before he stepped back. Sydney felt chilled after losing the contact with his body. He moved into the dim beams of the solar lights. He was back on alert, sweeping the garden to make sure they were alone.

Reality crashed into Sydney's psyche. She forced air into her lungs, her mind whirling. One moment she was avoiding a confrontation with her ex. The next she was kissing a strange man, one who made her feel more cherished than she had the entire two years she was with Emmett.

"The coast is clear." He seemed all business, not at all affected by their moment of passion.

Sydney's face flamed. The simple kiss may not have bothered him, but it knocked her off her feet. With a shake of her head to restore her good sense, Sydney stiffened her spine, lifting her chin high.

"I should go back then."

He didn't reply and never changed his position. He waited for her to make the first move, she realized. She stepped next to him on the garden path wanting to say something to ease the awkwardness, but her mind was blank. She finally walked away without a word.

As the hotel loomed in front of her, she threw a furtive glance over her shoulder to confirm what the goosebumps on her skin already told her. For his frame to be so muscular, he was light on his feet. He stayed just behind her and to the side like a paid bodyguard. His presence oddly calmed her. She stopped once she reached the veranda steps.

"I'm going around to the front to find my friend." She hoped he would stop trailing behind her, but she wasn't sure how to ask that without sounding ungrateful for his help.

"You can go back to the ballroom if you want. He won't be there to bother you. Security has him detained."

She almost asked how he knew that, but she decided it didn't matter. She didn't doubt he spoke the truth.

"Thank you again."

"You're welcome."

The gentle way he spoke warmed her. She smiled, and then raced up the veranda steps. She forced herself to go inside without glancing back, the feel of his embrace and their devastating kiss something she wouldn't soon forget.

Chapter Two

Sydney finally gave up any attempt to sleep after tossing and turning until she was tangled in a wad of covers. Her thoughts tormented her with memories of the night before. With a frustrated sigh, she struggled to free her legs. One solid tug on the sheet threw her off balance, rolling her off the bed. She groaned as she rubbed the spot where her hip connected with the hardwood floor.

That's it. She was done trying to function without some coffee jolting her system first. She scrambled up from the floor and headed into the kitchen. She kept her movements silent so as not to stir Chloe. The hour had been late when they eventually left, so Sydney had decided to crash at her best friend's apartment since it was closer to the hotel.

Sydney rifled through Chloe's collection of single-serving coffees before popping one of the strong roasts into the machine. The final drip barely plopped into the mug before she raised it to her lips. She breathed in the rich aroma and took a cautious sip. Warmth burned a path down her esophagus into her stomach. *Perfection.*

Her stomach gave a low rumble, so she opened Chloe's refrigerator to search for breakfast, not expecting to find much. Neither she nor Chloe cooked regularly. Sydney lived on frozen food, and Chloe ate out a lot.

Just as she finished toasting a grilled cheese sandwich, Chloe shuffled into the kitchen.

"Why are you up?" Her sleek blonde hair was piled on top of

her head in a messy bun that bobbed as she moved.

"I was tired of tossing and turning." Sydney started a pod of coffee for her friend. "Since I ended up falling out of bed, I figured it was a sign to get up."

Chloe smirked. "I thought I heard something, but I wasn't ready to wake up enough to check it out."

"Good thing it wasn't someone trying to break in, then."

"It's too early for that. Even burglars sleep in on Saturdays." Chloe's deep yawn cracked her jaw.

Sydney halved her sandwich and handed one to her friend, along with the freshly filled coffee mug. She placed the sugar and creamer beside it, and Chloe mumbled her thanks.

"I didn't mean to wake you." Sydney chewed a small bite of her sandwich.

"You didn't. The coffee did. The smell lured me out of bed against my will. Besides, I wanted to check on you."

Sydney sighed. "I thought I was finally moving on, but seeing Emmett brought all of those memories back."

"You're being too hard on yourself. Emmett abused you. Of course, you reacted like that when you saw him. I'm just glad those security guys took care of him before he could bother you."

"Oh, he tried. But I couldn't deal with that, so I ran and hid like a coward."

Sydney picked up her breakfast and motioned for Chloe to follow her into the living room. They settled on opposite ends of the couch.

"You're not a coward. You were avoiding a confrontation with your despicable ex, whom you haven't seen in months. It's perfectly understandable."

"Maybe. I guess I should be glad I haven't run into him before now with Grayson Cove being a small town."

"Do you regret staying after you broke up? Do you wish you had started over somewhere else?"

Sydney mulled over the question though she often wondered the same thing herself. And the answer was always the same.

"Where else would I go? Emmett saw to it I had no one in my life but him. I'm still surprised he didn't try to prevent us from being friends. If he'd guessed you were helping me leave him, he would have stopped us. Despite all of that, I couldn't give him the satisfaction of driving me from my hometown. I'd already let him take more from me than he should have."

"You have to stop blaming yourself. You didn't ask for any of it. Emmett is a horrible person. His actions are his own. Your actions were survival. Pure and simple."

"I know. It's just hard. I should've left him the minute he started being abusive, but I let myself believe he wouldn't always be that way. I let him convince me to completely change my life so we could be together. And I realized last night, rather than risk falling into that same trap with someone else, I've closed myself off from the world. I mean, I have a career I love, but other than work and hanging out with you, I don't do much else. It's pathetic."

Chloe's dark eyes softened. "You're not pathetic. You have to give yourself time to get over what you went through. You're living a good life. All the things that are missing will come when the timing's right."

"Maybe. I've just missed out on so much when I was with him. And then seeing him last night — I've thought of a thousand ways I would handle it when I saw Emmett again, and I did none of them."

"Where did you disappear to, by the way? When I came back from getting security, I couldn't find you."

"In the garden at the back of the hotel. Emmett followed me — the bastard — but eventually went back to the ballroom when he couldn't find me."

"I wish you had seen Emmett's face when those hunky security guys escorted him out. It was priceless. I've already decided we're using the same company for all of our events. They were great. And hot, so that's a bonus."

Sydney grinned. "I can't argue with that."

Chloe cocked her head to one side, a teasing light gleaming in her eyes. "You know, I'm sure I can get their contact information. If you saw one you liked, maybe we could arrange something."

Sydney hesitated. She thought she would hold the moment in the garden as a secret a bit longer, but the urge to tell her best friend was too strong.

"I ran into one of them as I was heading to the garden. He saw I was trying to avoid Emmett, so he helped me hide."

"Really? Now I'm really impressed. I need details."

"I was only around him for a few minutes. Plus I can only imagine the first impression he got helping me play hide-and-seek from Emmett."

"I texted Liam last night and told him what happened. He's trying to find out how Emmett managed to get an invitation. We were so careful with the guest list, I'm surprised he slipped under our radar."

Chloe's partner in Horizons Marketing, William "Liam" Conley, left much of the event planning duties to her, but with his societal connections, he often assisted with building guest lists. He was also a big help to Sydney when she left Emmett, so he was familiar with how violent her ex was.

"I guess it doesn't matter now. In a way, running into Emmett woke me up. I need to get out of my rut."

"How do you plan to do that?"

Sydney sighed after downing the last of her coffee. "I don't know yet. I do know I need more coffee before I head home."

"You could always hang out here. I have to go into work for a little while to wrap up some last-minute things from the fundraiser. I should finish by noon. We could grab lunch and spend the afternoon shopping."

"I actually have some work to do, otherwise I'd take you up on that."

After she'd broken off her engagement to Emmett, Sydney had decided to start her own cyber security business, working out of her apartment.

"Okay. I'll go to work. You go home, do your work, and then tonight we'll watch a movie. I'll bring pizza and wine, and you find us a couple of good rom-coms with super-hot leading men we can drool over while we stuff our faces and drink too much. Sounds amazing, right?"

Sydney smiled. "Sounds perfect."

"Great. I call the shower first. Then it's all yours."

Sydney chuckled. "Go ahead. I can shower at home. I'll just clean up here before I head out."

Sydney stood and hugged her friend before moving to take their dishes to the kitchen. She stopped in the doorway and looked back at Chloe.

"I love you, Chlo. You're the best."

"Stop it before I have to kick your ass," her friend grumbled as she disappeared into her bedroom.

Sydney laughed heartily, the events from last night already fading from her mind.

Chapter Three

To the casual observer, Coleman Atwood was the picture of cool relaxation. He settled on the waiting room couch with one leg resting on the other. His bulky frame occupied most of the seating space, but since he was the only one waiting, he didn't figure it mattered.

Though he looked at ease, his mind was on alert. His shifting eyes missed nothing. While he didn't know exactly what he was searching for, his gut told him there was more going on at Knight Security and Investigations than meets the eye.

Cole knew the company's owner, Tristin Knight, from when they completed BUD/S – the rigorous basic training for Navy SEALs. They were joined at the hip during their recruit days, but as they were assigned to separate SEAL teams, the two had lost touch until three weeks ago. The sudden call seemed strange on its own, but Tristin's offer set off Cole's suspicions.

"I want you to come work for me." Tryst, as his friend was known, didn't waste time sharing with Cole about his thriving private investigation and security business located in one of the smallest towns Cole had ever visited.

"I'm not a private investigator, man. I don't chase cheating spouses. I don't babysit wealthy CEOs. I'm not your guy."

Tryst countered by quoting a salary that had Cole's eyes bugging out, but it wasn't enough to change his mind.

"I can't go from serving my country to being a PI. It's not what I'm looking for."

Tryst had laughed. "Look, I get it, man, but don't dismiss it just yet. We're providing security for a charity benefit at the Regency Hotel Friday night. Work with my guys, get a feel for what they're like, and then we can talk. The event's drawn a lot of attention, and a lot of important people are on the guest list. We could use your help, and I'll pay you for your trouble. Come on, man. You can't tell me you aren't interested in us being sidekicks again," Tryst said.

So much about the phone call surprised the shit out of Cole that he ended up agreeing out of pure curiosity. A brief Internet search revealed Knight Security and Investigations employed some of the most elite soldiers to ever pass through the military to do some of the most mundane work known to man, and he wondered what appeal they found in the work, or if they did the job purely for the money.

Now that he was here to talk to his buddy, he was no closer to realizing the answers he'd sought than when they talked on the phone. Cole's eyes flicked over to the reception desk. The older woman behind it gave him an apologetic smile as she dealt with a customer phone call. He inclined his head slightly to let her know he didn't mind waiting. The time allowed him to observe as his mind replayed the events of Friday night.

He had shown up at the hotel expecting a quiet evening of watching rich folks drink too much and spend a lot of money for some obscure charity. What he didn't expect was working alongside tactically trained men who used the job to practice maneuvers.

The four guys handling the security detail included him in their training as if he'd been a part of the team all along, but they avoided any questions about the specifics of their work. They operated like a well-oiled machine, reminding him enough of his old SEAL team that he started considering Tristin's job offer.

"Mr. Atwood," the receptionist called, interrupting his musings. "Mr. Knight is ready to see you. Just down the hall, last door on the left."

Cole muttered a quick word of thanks before following the receptionist's directions. He rapped on the door and stepped inside when he heard a muffled "come in."

Tristin Knight rose from behind a large desk, a smile splitting his Hollywood-handsome face. He moved to meet Cole halfway before enveloping him in a bro-hug.

"It's good to see you, Panther."

Cole grimaced at the use of his hated SEAL nickname. "I'd like to be able to say the same, but I'm still trying to decide."

Tristin laughed. "Fair enough. How about a tour of the place before we sit down to talk?"

"I'd rather you just be straight with me. I don't like to have my time wasted."

"You never were one to beat around the bush. I know you have questions. I'd be shocked if you didn't. Just bear with me, and when I'm done, I don't think you'll regret coming."

"We may have gone through BUD/S together, but that was a long time ago. You want my trust now? You've got to show me you've earned it."

"If I doubted for a minute you were the right person for the job, you just erased it. Look, I know you have nowhere else to be. What have you got to lose by giving me an hour of your time?"

Cole gave a curt nod. "Fine. You've got an hour."

"Come on, then. Let me show you around."

Cole followed Tristin through the KSI building, noting the high level of security that was unique even for a firm that specialized in it. The maze of hallways primarily contained offices, but Tristin showed him a large conference room filled with flat screens, computer hookups, and a table large enough to accommodate a small army.

"This is our war room. It's basically where we plan our strategies when we take on complicated cases. We meet regularly to provide updates on what our agents are working on."

"You spared no expense on the equipment," Cole said leadingly, but his buddy just smiled and moved on.

At the back of the building was another large space, enclosed by glass doors and walls. A few work stations were equipped with computers. Monitors lined one wall with servers blinking at the back of the room. Cole noted the first group of employees that he'd seen outside of the lobby security guard and the receptionist. Tristin preceded him inside the room.

A beautiful woman with smooth olive skin and eyes that sparkled behind her glasses smiled brilliantly before sailing straight into Tristin's arms. The two shared a kiss that had Cole averting his eyes. The other two in the room continued working, oblivious to the make-out session going on in front of them.

"Panther, I want to introduce you to Katarina Knight, my wife."

"Sorry, I can't call you Panther with a straight face, so I'll just call you Cole if that's okay. And I'm Kat. Tristin is the only one who uses my full name, and since I love him, I let him get away with it." Kat gifted Cole with her wide smile as she stood in the circle of her husband's arms.

"Cole is fine. I hate that nickname, but in the SEALs, they follow you around whether you like them or not. Right, Tryst?"

Kat's laugh was light, sparking a gleam in her husband's eyes. "From what I've heard, he more than earned his nickname. Maybe you'll have time to share some of those stories."

"You name the time and place, and we can make that happen."

"No need. Those stories are in the past. I'm a happily married man now." Tristin dropped a kiss to Kat's hair.

Kat rolled her eyes. "Ignore him, Cole. We're glad you came by. I know Tristin is excited to have you work with us."

Cole raised a questioning brow. "So you work here too?"

"She's been here since practically the beginning. Kat heads up our command center. One thing our team members count on when working cases is technical support. The more investigators we added, the more IT techs we needed to handle the workload. Megan Granger has been here for five years now, and Nathan McCoy has been here eight. They're all the sharpest in the business," Tristin explained.

The other techs raised their heads at the mention of their names but went back to work almost instantly. Cole barely acknowledged them, instead studying the couple in front of him.

"Well, it's impressive, but that's what you were hoping for, right? You're going to have to do better than this."

If he thought to shock the couple with his words, he was wrong. Tristin just appeared amused, and Kat had her spirit shining in her eyes.

"You promised me an hour. I still have some time, and I'm not finished yet."

"Well, it was good to meet you, Cole. Regardless of what happens, I hope you'll join us for dinner one night soon."

Cole accepted Kat's handshake. "Just let me know when and where."

After kissing her husband's cheek, Kat went back to work, and Cole followed his buddy back down the hall to the war room.

"We're not going back to your office?"

Tristin shook his head. "You want answers, don't you? They're in here, but I need you to understand something. This is my business. This is the livelihood of my employees, and I'm protective of that. I wouldn't share any of this with you if I didn't believe you would respect that."

Cole's eyes narrowed. Tristin's cryptic statement confused him.

His gut churned, but he didn't walk away. He just nodded and followed Tristin inside the room.

"Well, it's about damn time. We've got better things to do than wait on your slow ass, Tryst."

The sarcastic voice came from one of four men assembled around the massive conference table, and Cole instantly recognized them as the same men he'd worked alongside at the charity gala.

"Have a seat. I know you've already met these guys, but allow me to introduce to you again to Jay Colter, Zane Wilder, Brennan 'BB' Bennett and Griffin 'Wings' Tyler, otherwise known as the wiseass who talks to me more like a drinking buddy than his boss," Tristin said wryly. "These guys are the Alpha Team. Guys, this is Cole Atwood, or Panther, if you aren't afraid of the dirty looks he'll give you if you use his nickname."

Cole didn't sit right away. He just stared at the men surrounding him as if he'd walked into an ambush in enemy territory.

"Now's the time to tell me what the hell is going on and what it is you do around here. Because you guys are not PIs."

"That's why we're here — to explain more about what we do," Jay Colter spoke up.

Though Jay had never identified himself as such, Cole got the impression he was the team leader. The others looked to him for instruction as they had worked the benefit, and now they followed his lead.

Cole lowered his frame into the nearest chair. "So explain."

"We do provide private security and investigations, just as we advertise," Tristin said, and Cole stared at him skeptically. "That part of the business is important. The last thing we want in a small town like this is for folks to begin to question all we actually do here."

"And that is?"

"I'm getting to that. We have a handful of folks on staff who handle the private investigations side of the house." Tristin swept a hand out toward the guys sitting around the table. "These guys do take some of those cases, but for the most part, they work exclusively as a covert ops team. We're hired to take on missions that aren't always sanctioned by the government but are not cases government agencies can handle because of the sensitivity of the case or because of their red tape. We also work on a contract basis to provide support for government agencies."

"Because of the nature of the cases we accept, we don't publicly promote the work of the Alpha Team or our other team, Delta. We fly under the radar," Jay added. "I was Tryst's first hire when he was building the company, and we hand-selected the other members based on their skill set. BB and I are SEALs."

"I'm an Air Force fighter pilot," the one called Wings spoke up, every bit the wiseass, cocky persona Cole knew most pilots to be. "Zane is an Army sharpshooter."

Cole and Zane exchanged a nod. The two had worked as partners during the charity benefit. The man had skills and obvious strength, but he kept to himself, saying little – exactly the type of partner Cole preferred.

"There's a lot of competition between them, but they work as a team. When they're in the field, their branches of service don't come into play. It's their collective training that gets the job done," Tristin said. "I think you saw that for yourself on Friday night."

"So what was Friday night, exactly? You said you only worked covert missions. That was anything *but*." Cole crossed his arms over his chest.

"Friday night was part of a case. It was supposed to be general recon, though I heard you did run into some trouble. Jay tells me you handled yourself well."

And just like that, an image materialized in his mind's eye of a woman who stood to just under his chin and fit in his arms like she was created for that purpose. He had been close enough to her, with just enough light on the veranda, to have her beauty emblazoned in his memory. At the oddest moments over the last few days, he would recall the fiery red hair, the porcelain skin, the hint of freckles that makeup couldn't cover, and a kiss – one damn good kiss.

"I didn't do anything special," Cole replied. "I'm not even sure what went down."

"Domestic situation," Jay explained. "You protected the victim, so we were able to remove the threat."

She was the victim. He suspected as much. "Who was he to her? Husband?" Cole tensed.

"Nah, man," BB spoke up. "Ex-fiancé. Used to beat her."

His fist clenched at that bit of information. He didn't trust himself to speak, but fortunately, Tristin saved him from responding.

"The point is, you worked well with the team. The Alpha Team is one man down, and we want you to fill that slot permanently."

"And the guy who's slot I'd be taking? What happened to him?"

"Sam Montgomery," Jay supplied. "He's still an investigator with KSI, but he decided to step down from the team after a tough undercover assignment. His girlfriend just gave birth to their son, and he wanted to focus on being a dad."

"Can't you pull one of the investigators to fill the slot?"

"They each have their specialties, and the last thing I want to do is break up the rhythm we have now," Tristin explained. "When I heard you'd left the SEALS, I knew you'd be a good fit for Alpha Team. All you have to do is agree to take the job."

Five sets of eyes regarded Cole expectantly. He supposed they figured a washed-up SEAL like him would jump at the opportunity they were offering. Another lifetime ago, he probably would have.

But what the Alpha Team did was not a new concept. He knew of other companies who employed specialized mercenaries for hire. Hell, he'd been recruited by one himself. Those companies typically condoned practices that weren't above board, going against the very code by which he lived in serving his country.

Cole stood, his gaze resting on his friend. "This is not for me. Thanks for the offer, but you need to find someone else."

"Not for you? Then what is? Correct me if I'm wrong, but you've been at your wit's end ever since you left your SEAL team. Give us a chance."

Cole quirked an eyebrow. "Last time I checked, you haven't seen me in years, so you don't know anything about me."

"I know more than you think. Give us a chance, and you'll see we're just what you've been looking for."

"Think on it," Jay added. "Take a day and just consider it. Tryst believes you are the fifth man we need. I agree."

Cole pierced each man with a hard stare. "A day won't make a difference. I'm not the guy you want." And he strode out of the conference room, letting the door slam behind him.

"Well, that went well," BB quipped to break the tension in the room.

"*That's* the guy you want to join our team? Way to pick 'em, boss." Wings' sarcasm dripped from every word. "Who the hell does he think he is?"

"Wings, let it rest," Tristin warned.

"He's got a point," Zane finally spoke up. "We've got investigators in-house who would fit in with the team, and they know what we're all about already. I'd be happy with Brick, Einstein or Isobel. Just pick one. We'd probably have better luck finding someone to replace one of them than convincing this guy to join the team."

"He's interested," Tristin said. "He just won't admit it. Yet."

"Then let me handle it," Jay returned.

The team appeared doubtful. Jay and Tristin exchanged a knowing look. Oh, yeah, Cole would come around. And Jay had an idea on how to convince him.

Chapter Four

Sydney tried to ignore the frantic pacing going on behind her but to no avail. Chloe was well into an emotional meltdown. No words could talk her friend from the proverbial ledge. All Sydney could do was try to correct the cyber problem that had taken Chloe's Tuesday and moved it into the "worst day ever" category before 9 a.m.

Just two hours earlier, Sydney had stirred from a deep sleep because of the persistent ringing of her cell phone. For Chloe to be trying that hard to get in touch with her so early in the morning, Sydney knew something catastrophic had happened. And in Chloe's corporate world, it had.

"Syd, my computer is possessed!" Chloe had exploded over the phone almost before Sydney could utter the word hello. "I think the whole system is locked up. We've been hacked or something! Help! I need you to get your scrawny butt over here ASAP!"

"On my way," Sydney mumbled in reply before she was fully awake.

Sydney had fallen into bed late last night, not expecting to rise at such an early hour. As part of her freelance cyber security business, she was able to accomplish a lot of the work for her clients from the comfort of her home, late in the evening when the businesses were closed. Security checks, system updates and computer maintenance were all handled with simple remote access to her clients' networks. Her work hours were odd compared to corporate standards, but she enjoyed the flexibility.

Of course, there were a few instances that required her to rise early to see to unexpected problems for her clients. When it came to her best friend's company, she did so without complaint or hesitation. Foregoing her usual morning shower, she plaited her flaming locks quickly. She dressed in her typical attire of well-worn jeans and oversized tunic, completing the outfit with a scuffed pair of sneakers.

With her messenger bag in tow, she set out for the brick building downtown that housed Horizons Marketing. The building served as home to a law office, a real estate agent and interior designer, but Horizons occupied a majority of the space. The firm was always a hub of activity, but today there was an energy buzzing around the place that put Sydney on edge. Chloe cornered her as she stepped off the elevator and ushered Sydney to her office without preamble. Sydney had been there ever since.

"If I get my hands on this hacker, so help me..." Chloe muttered as she paced.

"Chloe, it may not be a hacker. Someone opening a virus in their email while connected to your servers could have done this too. Just give me some time to track the source. Why don't you go to that coffeehouse you love and get a latte or something?" Sydney tried to sound calm, but her tone held an edge of annoyance.

"It's probably that intern Liam just hired. I swear that girl treats this job like one big sorority party."

Sydney stopped typing and swiveled the desk chair around to face her friend. "Chloe, I can't concentrate with you grumbling and pacing. Please, go grab some coffee. Give me some peace and quiet to work. I promise I'll get to the bottom of this."

Chloe halted her pacing. Exhaling loudly, she grabbed her purse. "I'm sorry. I'll go and give you some space. Can I bring you something?"

"My usual would be perfect. Thanks."

Chloe closed the office door behind her. Sydney sighed before focusing on the laptop in front of her. A few keystrokes and twenty minutes later, she realized the source of the network problems was indeed a remote hack. She shook her head in disgust as she used the tools in her arsenal to set the system back to normal. While she was at it, she enhanced the security protocols she already had in place. She was just finishing up her work when her stomach rumbled, reminding her she'd skipped breakfast. Chloe chose that moment to breeze through the door.

"How was the coffee run?"

"I turned it into a business meeting. Sorry, Syd. I couldn't just go for coffee. There's so much I should be doing but can't because my computer is possessed. So I surprised a potential client with an invitation to coffee."

"And?"

"I'm emailing a contract over to him as soon as you get my computer back up and running. And I have a date with him Friday night," Chloe concluded with an impish gleam in her eyes.

Sydney laughed. "You are a force to be reckoned with. Aren't you worried about mixing business with pleasure?"

"It's not a date that will lead anywhere, and let's face it – a girl's got to eat," Chloe returned with her typical dry wit. "Please tell me you have good news."

"Depends on how you look at it." Sydney rattled off the details of what she'd discovered. "You're good to go. I've checked with the other employees to make sure they were good too."

Relief flooded Chloe's lovely face as she set a large to-go cup of coffee in front of her friend. "I didn't understand half of what you said, but all that matters is my computer is no longer possessed. You are my hero, Sydney Reede. I owe you big time."

Sydney grinned. "I know. As a thank you, Liam can pay my bill without question, and you can take me to lunch since you put me to work before breakfast this morning. I'm starving."

"Done!" Chloe returned her friend's smile. "You seem to be in better spirits than when I saw you Saturday."

"I am. It comes from drowning myself in work and re-evaluating my life. I made some decisions, and I feel more in control than I have since before I met Emmett. It's…liberating."

"Wow. That sounds intriguing. Save the explanation for lunch though. Come on. Chinese food is calling our names."

Sydney did take a few minutes to fill Liam in on the cause of their network problems, effectively securing his endorsement of the friends' lunch plans. Sydney and Chloe chatted and laughed as they headed to the restaurant, their conversation light and fun. After their waitress met them at their usual table with glasses of water, the women ordered their typical array of dishes to share. Once they were left alone, the mood turned serious.

"Tell me about this soul-searching you've been doing."

Sydney took a deep breath. "There's one question that has been nagging me for a long time. Honestly, I've refused to let myself think about it. I just wanted to focus on building a life away from Emmett. But I realized I needed to answer that question before I could truly move on."

Chloe studied her. "What question?"

"How could I have let Emmett ruin my life? I wish you would have known me before I was Emmett's punching bag. I was someone who knew her own mind and wanted to find her own way. I never let anyone tell me what I should do or who I should be. Not even Emmett at first. But somehow, he managed to change me until I was nothing outside of him. We haven't been together in months, but I still don't know who I am. I'm no longer an abuse victim, but

I'm not the rebel I once was, either."

"I'm having a hard time picturing you as a rebel," Chloe said lightly.

Sydney's smile held a touch of sadness. "I know. It's hard for me to remember it. My parents always had this cookie cutter idea of how I should be. A straight-A student, the all-around good girl. They wanted me to study to be a school teacher, and the very idea of that made me want to run away. Did I ever tell you I dyed my hair jet black once when I was in high school just to prove to them I wasn't school-teacher material?"

Chloe laughed. "*What?* No way!"

"I did. I hated it, so I didn't keep it that way for long. But it made my parents freak out, and that's what I wanted."

"Your parents couldn't have been all bad. You said they hated Emmett, so that's something in their favor."

"That should have tipped me off about him too. I thought for sure they'd love him. He's polished and charming and refined. He seemed to be the boy next door they always wanted me to settle down with. That's why I resisted him at first. The idea that my parents would approve of him made me cringe. But I was in too deep by the time I took him home to meet them. Emmett clashed with my parents right from the start. My father actually tried to bribe Emmett to break up with me."

"Wow. Now I wish I could have met your parents."

"Me too. I can't believe I chose Emmett over them. If I had known that would be the last time I'd ever see them, I wonder if I would have chosen differently."

Sydney grew silent, shame washing over her. She'd never had a close relationship with her parents, and their disapproval of Emmett had been the catalyst for her to sever all ties with them. She tried to reach out to them after she left Emmett only to discover they'd died in a car accident. She never knew until it was too late to make amends. She'd actually wondered if Emmett had orchestrated their "accident," but according to the police report, there was no evidence of foul play.

Chloe reached across the table to cover Sydney's hand with her own. "Oh, Syd. I'm sorry you had to go through that. But you can't allow yourself to drown in regret. All you can do is learn from your mistakes and move forward. Now, you said you made some decisions to take back control of your life. Tell me about them. Let's focus on the positive."

Sydney smiled. "I love you, and your support has meant the world to me. I couldn't have made it through the last few months without you. But after running into Emmett Friday night, I realized I needed to stop relying on other people so much and start relying on myself. I want the Rebel Sydney to come back. I liked her. I think you would have liked her too."

The waitress returned with their orders, and Sydney allowed her memories to surface. When she'd first met Emmett, she turned down his invitation for a date. In those few minutes, she'd felt he was all wrong for her with his arrogant ways and demanding nature. Emmett didn't like to hear the word no. He had pursued her. He knew how to make her feel special one minute and completely worthless the next, but he managed to twist it so she always felt she needed him. By the time he'd proposed, she was totally dependent on him for everything – providing for her, telling her what to do or what to wear or how to be, giving her some sense of self-worth that wound tightly in her relationship with him. Though her parents had warned her about him, she refused to see their relationship as anything but just what she needed to make her life complete.

Once she agreed to marry Emmett, he convinced her to move in. The physical abuse started soon after. She had shut people out of her life, including her parents, because she was too ashamed to admit her mistake. By the time she'd left him for good, her parents had died, and the only person she had left was Chloe.

She shook the ugly memories from her mind as the waitress walked away. The friends began to tackle their lunch. Talking of all she'd lost being with Emmett left her with little appetite, but Sydney possessed a greater resolve to rise above the heartache.

"I signed up for a self-defense class."

Chloe sputtered, her food catching in her throat. Sydney made no move to help her choking friend. She only grinned at how she managed to shock the one person who knew her better than anyone and therefore, was rarely surprised by her actions.

"What the hell? A self-defense class? Don't you have to be in shape for that?"

Sydney giggled. "Maybe, but I don't care. I want to learn how to take care of myself, so I don't have to be afraid anymore. I know it sounds crazy, but I can't tell you the freedom I felt when I signed up for that class. The person on the phone probably thought I sounded a little too excited about it. I don't care, though. It was just what I need."

"Do you really think it's necessary? I mean I know Emmett tried to get to you at the benefit, but don't you think it was just a coincidence? He hasn't tried to make contact with you in months. Why would he seek you out now?"

"I don't know, but I want to be prepared if he does. Besides, this isn't just about Emmett. It's about my feeling safe again. "

Chloe studied her as if trying to figure out what was going through Sydney's mind. "Okay," she finally said. "I'm proud of you, Syd. Want me to come with you?"

Sydney bit her bottom lip thoughtfully, a telltale sign she was hesitant to share what was on her mind. Chloe shot her a just-say-it-already stare that was all too familiar. Sydney often said they were the closest of friends because they could communicate a lot without saying a word.

"I need to do this on my own. I've done nothing but lean on you since I met you. I want to prove to myself that I can do this on my own. It sounds crazy, but I feel if I can do this, then I'm taking away Emmett's control over me once and for all."

Chloe nodded. "It actually makes a lot of sense. But I'm here if you need me. You know that. When's your first class?"

"This afternoon."

"Okay. Then tonight, we have girls' night. I'll grab tacos. We'll make margaritas, and you can show me some of your moves."

Sydney grinned. "I'm not sure I'll have any moves after just one class, but I can go for the tacos."

Chloe returned her grin. "It's a date. Now eat up. You'll need your strength to learn how to kick some guy's ass."

Sydney laughed. The best friends continued with their lunch, enjoying easy conversation and more laughs. By the time Chloe had to return to work, Sydney felt empowered. She was ready to conquer the self-defense class and embrace the new outlook on her life.

Chapter Five

Cole thought he'd heard the last about the job the moment he strode out of Knight Security and Investigations. He didn't count on Tristin sending reinforcements.

He hadn't been back in his hole-in-the-wall apartment long before a knock pounded on the door. He'd only moved to Grayson Cove about a month earlier, and other than Tristin, he knew no one in the sleepy little town. He wasn't expecting any deliveries, so there was no reason for someone to show up at his doorstep. He moved on quiet feet to stand to the side of the door before darting to glance through the peephole.

He scowled as he threw open the door to glare at Jay Colter standing in the hallway.

"You can just go on back and tell him the answer is still no."

Jay leaned his bulky frame against the door jamb, his arms crossing over his chest. "Tell him yourself. But do it after we get back."

"Back from where?"

"Travis' place. I need a spotter while I work out, and you're it."

'I'm not going anywhere. You're wasting your time."

"You got something better to do than work out for free at one of the top gyms in the state?"

"Maybe. Why do you care?"

"Look, all I'm asking is for two hours of your time. That's all. You've got nothing to lose."

Cole stared him down, but to Jay's credit, he never flinched under Cole's glare. The truth was, Cole had nothing better to do, so he might as well see what the other man was up to. His gut told him Jay wouldn't leave him alone until he did.

"What is Travis'?" Cole finally asked as he gathered his wallet, keys and gym bag he kept packed for whenever he needed to blow off steam.

"A gym. We all train there as part of our employment at KSI. Free of charge. It's one of the perks of working for Tryst. Travis is his brother."

Cole processed the information as they left his building. All the time he served with Tristin, Cole never knew about his family, much less that he had a brother. Of course, going through BUD/S didn't provide many opportunities for swapping personal details. Any down time they did have was spent drinking, chasing women and harassing cadets. Yet Cole found it disconcerting that he didn't know more about his old buddy's personal life.

The trip to Knight and Day Fitness Center wasn't quite what Cole expected. The 24-hour gym catered to anyone, no matter what fitness regime they adhered to. Jay explained as they walked inside how the building was configured.

"The serious gym rats stay in that one area. They come to maintain their bulk and to tone." Jay pointed to his right as he spoke before indicating at spot at the back of the center. "Trainers work with individual customers back there to help them reach specific fitness goals. Then to your left is the area for those who exercise for health reasons, but aren't quite up to the same level as the rest. Travis wanted to keep each area separate so clients wouldn't compare themselves to others with different fitness goals."

Jay had scanned a keycard to gain entry to the gym. He stopped by the registration desk to sign in the computerized system and log in Cole as his guest. He handed Cole an electronic bracelet before putting on his own.

"The bracelets track your vitals and progress and log them into the system. Each client is given a personalized log-in so they can remotely monitor their progress."

Cole couldn't hide the surprise from his face. "That's a pretty high tech system for a gym."

"Kat set it up. She's scary good when it comes to programming and shit. Tristin hit the mother lode when he landed her. Smart and hot, she's better than he deserves."

Cole chuckled. His thoughts had been very similar after meeting Kat. She wasn't at all what he expected his friend's wife to be like, but he completely understood Tryst's attraction to her. If they weren't already married, Cole may have considered pursuing her himself.

Cole expected Jay to begin his campaign to lure him to KSI, but Jay focused only on their workout and nothing else. Before long, Cole was also lost in the satisfaction gained from pushing his limits and testing his strength. The gym equipment was state-of-the-art and everything the two men needed to put themselves through the paces. Sweat poured from Cole's body. After about an hour, he knew he'd feel the burn of the workout before the day's end.

"Jay!" The voice carried across the gym floor, effectively drawing Cole and Jay's attention.

Cole blinked as he watched Tryst, dressed in workout shorts and tight-fitting t-shirt, jog over to them. As his old friend drew closer, Cole started noticing little things about Tryst's appearance that messed with his senses. Were Tryst's golden locks longer than they were the last time he was in his friend's office? Was his build stockier than Cole remembered? Why had he never noticed his friend's easy-going grin was a bit crooked?

"Hey, Travis," Jay greeted the man as he drew closer. "I was wondering if we were going to see you."

Cole stared at Tristin's brother, stunned his old friend had a twin he never knew existed. The features, build and carriage were identical to the point Cole wondered if they were pranking him.

"You probably wouldn't have seen me except I need a huge favor, man. I called Tristin, and he told me you were already here."

Jay's eyes narrowed, his expression unreadable. "Don't tell me," he said more as a warning than a statement.

Travis' smile was meant to charm as his eyes pleaded with Jay. "I'm shorthanded. I've got a class starting now, and Isobel just called. She got in a fender bender on the way here and can't make it. I'd handle it alone, but we had some last-minute sign-ups that makes this one of the larger classes we've had. I need an assistant. You've got to help me out."

Jay cut his eyes to Cole with a dramatic eye roll before he explained.

"Travis offers a free self-defense class once a month for women in the community. Sometimes he talks Tryst into assigning one of us to help out, sort of a trade for letting us use the gym to train. But I had my turn last month." He raised his voice on the last statement as he shot Travis a pointed glare.

Travis raised his hands in front of him, palms facing out, in a defensive gesture. "Hey, I get it, but the class is starting now. It'll take too long for one of the other guys to come in, and I don't want to have to cancel. Some college students from Madison State enrolled after a rape was reported on campus a couple of weeks ago. Don't make me turn them away, man."

Cole could see Jay caving into Travis' persuasion, but before Jay could acquiesce, he stepped in to extend a hand to Travis.

"Hey, Travis. I'm Cole Atwood. Your brother is an old friend of mine from BUD/S."

Travis shook his hand, flashing a bright smile. "Good to meet you, Cole. You must be one of Tristin's new hires over at KSI."

"Not yet," Jay spoke up. "Working on it."

"You know, I can help out with the class if that's okay," Cole offered. "If I can help those girls feel safe and know how to protect themselves, it would be worth donating some time. Then Jay wouldn't have to take a second turn."

"Forget it," Jay grumbled. "If I take a pass, Tryst will never let me hear the end of it."

"I could use both of you, if you're willing. Like I said, it's a big class."

"Give us a minute to grab some water, and we'll be right there," Jay gave in.

"Great. I'll get it started and buy you some time. Thanks, guys."

Travis jogged away. Jay used a towel to wipe the sweat from his face before motioning for Cole to follow him to the juice bar. In no time, both men were chugging bottles of water. Cole studied the other man as he drank.

"You were going to help all along, weren't you?"

Jay smirked. "Of course. I mean, it's not the greatest assignment. There's always a woman or two who signs up just to hit on us, so that gets old. But it's still cool to know you taught someone how to protect themselves from being attacked. I just like to mess with Travis about it. He knows the right button to push, though, to talk me into it."

"What do you mean?"

Jay met his gaze directly. "My baby sister was a rape victim. It's a long story."

Cole's jaw stiffened. "They put the SOB away for what he did to her?"

Jay turned away, but not before Cole saw the hatred brewing in the depths of his eyes. "Nope. Come on. We'd better get moving."

Cole let the matter drop though his curiosity burned to know more behind that story. He felt a kinship to Jay after hearing his motivation for helping with the self-defense class. He had no siblings and only a mother to speak of, but he often tried to teach his mother ways to protect herself from the abusive husbands and boyfriends she managed to collect. She refused to admit her problem of falling for the wrong kind of men, and Cole knew nothing but frustration every time she refused his offer of help.

He followed Jay back toward the front of the gym and down a hallway lined with classrooms. Because of the large-pane windows, people could see the classes being held in all of the rooms, except for one room at the end. Easily the largest of all the rooms, it was closed off for privacy.

"Just follow my lead," Jay murmured as they stepped into the private room.

Travis was in the midst of discussing ways to identify and avoid potentially dangerous situations, so Jay and Cole quietly took positions behind the gym owner. The discussion turned to techniques they could use to escape an assailant. The room was packed with women of all ages and body types, who listened raptly to Travis' instructions.

"You may have noticed my assistants behind me. Ladies, this is Cole and Jay. We're going to demonstrate the techniques I've just described to you, so you can see first-hand how they work. Then I'm going to ask you to pair up to practice. We'll walk through the room to observe and offer suggestions on how you can improve your technique to be more effective. Then those of you feeling brave enough can try out what you've learned with one of us. If at any time you have questions, just speak up."

The women nodded their understanding, some of them voicing their agreement. Once Travis was satisfied everyone was up to speed, he looked over his shoulder.

"Jay, come on up."

Jay wore a scowl meant only for Travis.

"I'm guessing you want to play the attacker," Travis joked once Jay was by his side.

"You would guess right."

Cole had to grin at their antics, suddenly reminded of the camaraderie of his former SEAL team. They considered themselves brothers as much as soldiers. The pranking and good-natured ribbing was commonplace, and he believed it made them work better as a team. Could he find that same friendship with the Alpha Team? The sudden thought had him wondering if he'd been hasty with his rejection of the job.

As Travis and Jay went through the drills with practiced ease, Cole allowed his eyes to survey the crowd. When his scan rested on one woman toward the front, he realized she watched him more than the demonstration. Petite, busty, with hair a color so pale it could only come from a bottle, she flashed him a seductive smile and a quick wink. Cole kept his expression neutral as he continued his scan. The last thing he wanted was for her to misinterpret his resting gaze for interest.

Then he saw *her*.

He almost looked past her but quickly jerked his eyes back. He felt the air being sucked from the room, and his jaw slacked. Dressed in black yoga pants and oversized T-shirt with a cutesy faded logo on the front, she looked different, but he would have recognized her anywhere. Her innocent beauty was seared into his brain.

Her russet hair was secured in a braid, her creamy skin void of any makeup. He could see each freckle that dotted her cheeks and nose. Her expression spoke of nervousness even as she soaked in every word Travis spoke like a sponge. The last time he saw her, she was dressed to perfection with not a hair out of place. Now she looked more natural, earthy, and he couldn't decide which version he found sexier.

A memory of their kiss – that brief, passionate kiss – replayed like a high-definition movie in his brain. His heart raced as a zing of excitement shot straight to his groin. What were the odds that the one woman he'd been unable to forget would wind up in the one place he'd never planned to be?

As if some force shifted around her, alerting her to his presence, she raised brilliant sapphire eyes to meet his. Fascinated, he watched her emotions play across her face – first confusion, then uncertainty, and finally recognition.

A slow smile twisted his lips. He never questioned fate when life threw him a curve ball. He'd learned over the years to just roll with the punches. And in this case, he wasn't about to let this opportunity pass without action.

No way was he letting her walk away from him a second time.

Chapter Six

"My friends and I are heading out to Torch for drinks later. You should join us."

"I appreciate that, but I have plans," Cole returned smoothly, withdrawing his arm from the gym bunny's tight grasp.

Cole's eyes narrowed as he watched the redhead talking intently with Jay. The self-defense class had wrapped up, and most of the women then dispersed after giving the three instructors compliments for conducting a successful class. A handful hung back, vying for their attention.

Cole saw his opportunity to approach the redhead once Travis finished. During the class, he'd never found a moment to get close to her, much less talk to her. The desire to know her name, to ask to get to know her better, burned within him. Just as he moved to approach her, the gym bunny blocked his path.

"Come on. All work and no play makes Cole a dull boy," the gym bunny purred, running a bony finger down his bicep.

"That's me. Dull and boring."

"Now why don't I believe that?" The other woman's flirtations were wearing on Cole's nerves.

"Whether you believe me or not doesn't change the fact that I can't meet you and your friends for a drink. Since this was my first time helping out, if you have any questions about the class, you should probably ask Travis. Excuse me."

He could see the mask of fury that dropped over her face. Travis probably wouldn't ask him back to help considering he was just rude to one of the students, but Cole couldn't care less. He had to get to the redhead. He brushed passed the gym bunny with purposeful strides.

"Is he stalking you?" he heard Jay ask her once he drew close.

Cole's plan to get to know her took a backseat to the concern that tightened his chest. Before he could stop himself, his hand lightly grasped her elbow. She turned startled eyes toward him.

"Is that guy still bothering you?"

Shock radiated in her expression. He should have released her elbow and stepped back. He'd obviously caught her off-guard and probably freaked her out with his probing question. But the feel of her skin beneath his fingertips felt too good for him to let go. He felt calmer and more in control just by touching her. Jay's puzzled gaze regarded him, but Cole was focused only on her. If that man she ran from at the hotel was harassing her, he would personally see to ripping the jerk's arms from his torso.

"Stand down, Panther. The lady and I were having a private conversation," Jay warned.

Her eyes flickered between the two men. Cole could feel the tension start to leave her body.

"It's all right," she told Jay first before addressing Cole. "I thought I recognized you. You're the guy who helped me Friday night, right? It was kind of dark in the garden, so I wasn't entirely sure that was you. I mean, what are the odds that you would be teaching my first self-defense class?"

"It's me. You didn't answer my question. Is Jay right? Is that guy stalking you?"

She turned away, dropping her eyes to her feet. "Um, no. No one is stalking me."

Jay shifted his eyes between the two of them. "She was just asking me about protecting herself against someone who's harassed her for a while. Cole, why don't you give her some pointers? I'm going to help Travis wrap up, so we can get out of here."

Cole nodded and waited for Jay to wander off. "I'm sorry if I startled you. I guess I have a way of doing that around you." The pretty flush to her cheeks told him she remembered their interaction on Friday night as vividly as he did.

"It's all right. I just saw you talking to that other woman and didn't want to bother you."

"Will you tell me what you and Jay were discussing?"

She took a step back, and he released her arm. "It's no big deal. I was just curious about something. I should be going."

Not yet, Cole said to himself before speaking calmly to her. "We never had the chance to formally meet. I'm Cole, by the way."

She lifted her gaze, and Cole wanted to shout in triumph. "I know."

"Right," he returned with a grin. "I'm glad to run into you. I've thought about you. I wondered if you were all right after what happened at the hotel Friday night. Not just with that guy, but with…"

"The kiss." Her voice had dropped to just above a whisper. Indecision crossed her lovely face. "I'm fine. Thank you for your concern and for your help that night."

Cole's heart constricted. He could sense her pulling away, and he wasn't ready to see her leave – not before he discovered who she was.

"I'd like to offer my help to you anytime you need it."

Her smile was slight, but it was enough to give Cole hope. "Thank you, but you don't owe me anything. You don't even know me."

"Tell me your name, and then we'll know each other." He almost cringed at the cheesy line. Her smile widened, and he tried to think of something witty to say to keep the smile on her face.

"Sydney. Do you help with the class often? I wasn't sure what to expect since this was my first one, but I'm planning to come back. Maybe I'll see you again."

Cole chuckled. "This was my first time helping, but I don't think Travis will ask me back. I sort of pissed off one of the students."

Amusement flashed in her eyes, turning the blue color even brighter. "Bleached blonde with the big boobs? I heard one of the other ladies say she comes every week no matter how many times Travis and his assistants shoot her down. They say she could teach the class because she comes so often. I don't think she actually learns anything because she's too preoccupied with landing a bodybuilder husband."

Cole threw his head back with a hearty laugh. "I sort of figured her story went something like that. Hey, would you want to grab some coffee or something?"

"I can't. I have to get to work and then meet my best friend for a girls' night. Thank you though."

"Sure. Where do you work?"

"From home. I do freelance work in cyber security for some companies in town. Since Chloe — my friend — and I will probably be up late tonight, I want to get some work in before she comes over."

"Makes sense. You two don't party too much." He didn't want to let on how much the idea of her partying at a bar — probably drawing the leers of every pervert there — made him uncomfortable.

She released an unladylike snort that he found adorable. "That will not be a problem, unless you consider gorging on tacos until we fall into a food coma partying too much."

"Sounds like a fun time to me."

Her cheeks flushed, and she dropped her eyes shyly. He wondered what was going through her mind to cause that blush.

"It is usually, even if it's not very exciting. Most people prefer the club scene or something like that, but I've never enjoyed that kind of thing. I keep to myself mostly, unless I'm hanging out with Chloe."

"Nothing wrong with that. I'm sort of a loner myself. Maybe we can hang out sometime if Chloe isn't free. We can get a coffee or eat tacos or go over self-defense techniques – whatever you want. I can give you my cell number, and you can call me anytime."

Cole wondered if he sounded desperate. Hell, he was. Everything in him screamed not to let her leave until he had a way to get in touch with her again.

Her face scrunched up in a cute scowl. "You're trying awfully hard to get me to hang out with you."

He grinned. "True. Which is why you should take pity on me and give me your number."

She laughed, the sound melodic and pleasing. He wanted to hear it again and hoped she was about to give him an opportunity to do so.

She held out her hand, palm up. "Your phone."

He gladly unlocked the touch screen and surrendered the cell phone to her. As she programmed her number, he studied her. Her skin was so light and smooth. He imagined it felt like silk to touch. Her lips were full, and he recalled how sweet they tasted when he'd kissed them in the garden. He wondered how old she was. Her pixie face, covered with freckles, made her seem young and innocent. She was probably too sweet to be with him, but he would be damned if he let her slip away.

"Here," she said as she held his phone out to him. "Next time you're in the mood for coffee or tacos, shoot me a text. And if I need help remembering how to kick some guy in the groin, I'll call you."

"Sounds like a plan. Enjoy your girls' night, Sydney."

"Thanks. Good to see you again, Cole."

He watched her walk away, her hips swaying gently. He had to admit while she would have looked good in the sports bra and lycra shorts that most of the women in the gym wore, he liked that she chose a more modest outfit. She looked pretty but didn't attract the unwanted attention of others in the gym. He probably would have picked a fight with anyone who made a move on her. He wasn't sure when – probably when he kissed her or when he actually saw her big blue eyes for the first time — but he had started to think of her as his. Until he was able to get her out of his system, he did not want her entertaining the advances of any other man.

Once she was out of sight, he lifted his hand, which still clutched his phone. He quickly scrolled through his contacts until he found the coveted number he searched for. Sydney Reede. Her name was there, tempting him to text her. She'd only just left, and he oddly missed the contact with her already. As much as he wanted to reach out to her, he needed to move slowly. The last thing he wanted was to drive her away before he could convince her to go on a date with him.

He tucked his phone in the pocket of his shorts and searched the room for Jay. The man stood in the corner, talking earnestly on his own cell. After the tough workout followed by the exertion of the self-defense class, he needed a shower. Hell, after seeing Sydney again, he needed a cold shower. He threw his arm up to get Jay's attention, pointing in the direction of the locker room. Jay nodded his understanding without pausing his phone conversation.

"Hey, Cole, thanks for helping out. You and Jay really got me out of a jam," Travis told him as he walked by.

"No problem. I enjoyed it."

"I could tell. I saw you talking to the new girl."

"New girl?"

"Yeah, she was one of the last-minute sign-ups. Dana in the front office pointed her out to me when she signed in at the registration desk. She called right before closing Saturday, saying she found our website when she'd Googled classes in her area. When Dana told her about today, she'd practically squealed at the chance to sign up. She even offered to pay a late fee for registering at the last minute. She was thrilled to find out the class was free."

Cole was quiet as he processed the information. He stared at the door through which she'd disappeared, wondering just what her story was. He finally shot a glance at Travis, who watched him expectantly.

"I think she's being harassed, or possibly stalked."

"Well, if you end up getting close to her, you might want to talk her into meeting Tristin. He's taken on stalking cases pro bono before. He would probably help her," Travis suggested.

"Tristin volunteers with your classes, and he takes on stalking cases for free. I never knew he had such a soft spot."

"You know, if you'd agree to work for him, you might figure out you have it in you, too. Feel free to come back anytime, even if you don't join KSI. See you around, Cole."

Cole had a sinking suspicion Travis was an active participant in Tristin's crusade to get him to join the Alpha Team. Travis' odd comment about joining KSI seemed too convenient to be anything but a ploy sanctioned by his old SEAL buddy. The irony was, he was reconsidering joining the Alpha Team.

First things first, though. He needed that shower. Then he owed a phone call to his old SEAL buddy.

"I'm telling you, he's still in the picture," Jay hissed into the phone. "We need to bring her in now."

"It's too soon, Jay. She's going to think we're no better than he is when we ambush her this way," Tristin said.

"You convince Cole to come on board, and he'll convince her. I'm telling you, there's something going on with those two."

"Tell me."

"Did you know she was going to be here?"

"Kat told me. She was entered into the gym's system when she signed up for the class. Kat was alerted almost instantly. That's why I had Isobel working the class today. I figured Miss Reede was more likely reach out to a woman before she would you or the other guys. I didn't have a backup when Isobel called about the accident, so I told Travis to recruit you. I wasn't expecting Cole to stay, but I'm glad he did. You really think he can help us get closer to her?"

"You should have seen them. Cole came up to her all possessive and concerned she was being stalked. It's like I wasn't even there. She only had eyes for him. When I approached her, she seemed a little afraid of me, even though she knew I was a friendly. She wasn't like that with him. I think after Cole protected her Friday night, he earned her trust. We can use that to bring her ex down. That asshole has her skittish and afraid of her own shadow. She hung on every word and practiced every move over and over until we called time. She wouldn't spar with any of us, but she watched liked she was trying to commit every move to memory. It's like she's preparing for something. I say the time is right for us to reach out to her."

"I agree she's our key to bringing him down. And if you think Cole is the right person to convince her, then I need to persuade him to join the team."

"He's thinking about it. I thought after hanging out with him this morning, I could change his mind, but no such luck. I think the ball's back in your court."

"Cole hasn't been an easy sell, but he's restless for some action. I'll kick it up a notch. Once he's on board, he can help convince Sydney Reede to join our team."

"She's the key to bringing Emmett Carter down. I can feel it, Tristin. I'm tired of that SOB being one step ahead of us."

"I know. This is personal for you, but I want Carter stopped too. We all do."

Jay paused. He ran a hand through his hair as he battled his inner turmoil. "I want this to be over. Whatever I have to do, I will."

"For now, there's nothing you can do. Let me handle it. If we make the wrong move, we could blow our chance. I'll get Kat to help me figure it out. I just need you and the team ready to act when all the pieces fall into place."

"You got it. I'll touch base with you later. Good luck."

Jay ended the call. Time for a shower, and then he could get back to work. He was fine with leaving the fate of Cole Atwood and Sydney Reede to rest on his boss' shoulders.

Chapter Seven

Tony's Taco Shack occupied a simple wooden building with an unlined gravel parking lot that barely accommodated the restaurant's clientele on a busy night. And tonight was one of those nights.

After seeing the near-full parking lot, Sydney was glad she had the forethought to call in her girls' night order. She squeezed her compact car between two SUVs and made her way inside, not surprised to see the line of customers waiting to order reaching the door.

On the outside, the mom-and-pop restaurant looked like it should be condemned. The inside wasn't much better. The limited space was overfilled with small round tables, each with a set of four uncomfortable, mismatched chairs. The wood flooring was dingy and scuffed. A dim light bathed the dining area, and ceiling fans provided some relief from the unseasonal heat generated from bodies crammed into the restaurant.

Rich aromas reminded Sydney of how much time had passed since she'd last eaten. The line for picking up call-in orders was a bit shorter, but she still waited behind three other customers before she could get her food.

She smiled when the restaurant's owner, Antonio Sanchez, greeted her at the counter. "Good to see you, Sydney. We need just a couple of minutes to finish your order.

"No problem. Chloe got tied up at work and is running late, so I'm not in a hurry."

"I figured you two were having a girls' night. Let me see if I can hurry your order along."

"Thanks." Sydney moved over to the side as she waited.

The smell of taco seasoning and tomatoes teased her taste buds as she scanned the faces in the restaurant. She was always amazed at how crowded the small establishment was each time she came. It was Grayson Cove's best kept secret, in her opinion, and she had Chloe to thank for cluing her in on its existence.

A month after she met Chloe, she'd started feeling more comfortable around her wedding planner enough to relax when they were together. Emmett had insisted they hold their planning sessions at their apartment, but one particular afternoon, Chloe breezed through the door announcing she'd skipped lunch and needed tacos. Before Sydney could feel a moment of panic at Emmett's reaction to her going to a restaurant with their wedding planner, she was whisked away to Tony's Taco Shack. It was the first of many shared meals between the friends. It was while they indulged in Tony's famous quesadillas that Sydney finally confessed Emmett's abuse.

As the memory sailed through her mind, her eyes rested on the table by the front window where they were sitting when she revealed the secret. She had kept staring out the window into the parking lot as she told the details of her relationship – how she'd resisted Emmett at first only to be charmed into a relationship, how she chose him over her family because she was convinced they were meant to be, how cowardly she felt at falling victim to his cunning.

She moved closer to the table, her smile faint as she pictured the scene as clearly as if it had occurred yesterday. Tears had streamed down her face, her hands clasped so tightly together her knuckles were white. Chloe had reached across the table to cover her hands, surprising Sydney into looking at her friend's face. She'd been shocked to see Chloe's own tears and expected to see pity in her eyes. Instead, she'd seen the fierce determination her friend carried like a shield.

"None of this is your fault, Sydney. And you are not alone. Not anymore. You have me now, and we will find a way for you to escape him. I promise you that."

The couple now occupying the table stood and disposed of their trash before leaving. Sydney paused beside the table and ran her fingers across the knotty wooden surface. That afternoon had been a turning point for Sydney – both in her friendship with Chloe, and in taking her life back.

"Your order's up, Sydney."

She swallowed the emotion that welled up with the memory. Whirling around with a brilliant smile, she took the bag from Antonio's hands and wished him well. She pushed her melancholy down and allowed herself to be excited for the girls' night as she moved through the door. The gravel crunched under her shoes as she crossed the parking lot to her car. On an impulse, she pulled out her phone to call Chloe and hurry her along so their fun could begin.

"Hello, Sydney."

Her finger hovering over Chloe's name in her contacts, her head whipped up, her jaw dropping. She stumbled to a stop just a few feet shy of her car. Emmett, dressed in a dove gray suit that hugged his shoulders and made his eyes appear a deeper blue, lounged against her car. His legs were crossed at the ankles, his arms across his chest. His smile dripped charisma, and Sydney's stomach churned.

"What are you doing here?" Her eyes darted around them. With all the cars in the lot, she didn't see a single person. She didn't think Emmett would hurt her when they could be discovered so easily by patrons leaving or arriving, but she couldn't be sure. She tapped her phone screen, connecting the call to Chloe. Her friend would recognize Emmett's voice and make a beeline to the restaurant to back her up. For now, she was on her own.

"We need to talk."

Anyone overhearing them would think the encounter was between two acquaintances who happened to bump into each other. But Emmett's casual tone and abrupt answer chilled her. His most violent outbursts were preceded by a deceptive calm. She braced herself for what was to come.

"I don't have a thing to say to you, so you can just leave. Right now." Sydney hated the tremble underlying her voice, robbing the heat from her words.

"I have plenty to say. And you'll listen." There it was, the hardness that showed his tenuous grip on his control.

"I stopped having to listen to you when I left, Emmett. I thought you accepted that."

He straightened to loom before her, and she gripped her bag of food in front of her, as if it provided a barrier between her and what was to come.

"I *let* you go because you'd no longer served my purpose, but you'll never be free of me. Not as long as there is a use for you."

"I was never any use for you except for being a punching bag. And I'm through with that." She was proud of her bravado, even if her insides shook. This was her moment to challenge his control.

He chuckled, and the fine hairs on her arms and neck stood on end. "That one self-defense class really has you believing you can fight me. You always were naïve and stupid."

Sydney took a step back, her eyes widening. "How…how did you…"

"I know your every move, Sydney. Do you really think it was an accident that we were both at the fundraiser that night?"

"You were out of the country. We checked. You couldn't have known I would be there."

He smiled and took a step closer to her. "I was out of the country. But I did know you would be there. It's cute that you hid from me, as if that would keep me away. You can't escape me, Sydney. I always know where you are and what you're doing."

She swallowed the lump that suddenly clogged her throat. "Why do you care? I was nothing to you. We haven't been together in months. Why now?"

His jaw tightened, his stature stiffened. His hands balled into fists at his side. His eyes regarded her with an icy glare. She fought the urge to retreat, instead holding her ground.

"Who do you think you are to question me? I don't explain myself to you. You should be falling at my feet, thankful that I still have a purpose for you. You're worthless otherwise."

"The only worthless thing I see here was our so-called relationship. And the only stupid thing is you thinking you still have any say or any hold on my life. You should leave."

She had no idea where the words came from, but as soon as she said them, out loud, to Emmett's face, she felt the weight of years of abuse lift off her shoulders. She widened her stance and braced herself. Hot anger flared in his eyes. He wouldn't let her get away with standing up to him. But she was ready.

When he lashed out this time, she would fight back with all that was within her.

Chapter Eight

"Cole. We're so glad you could come tonight. Come on in."

Kat Walsh opened the door to her home wide, and Cole stepped inside, trying not to look as uncomfortable as he felt. As soon as he saw Tristin's fortress, dusk shrouding it in a formidable glow, he started to wonder what he was signing up for. The Tristin he remembered from their military time wasn't the indulgent kind, but the palatial house with its state-of-the-art security was definitely over the top.

"Tristin is in the kitchen putting the finishing touches on dinner. It's right through there."

"Tryst is cooking?"

Kat giggled, and Cole was struck by just how pretty she was. Her dark eyes tilted up at the corners, and her nose wrinkled with her smile, pushing her glasses higher against her face. Her ponytail curled where the shiny strands hit her back. Her black top and dark wash jeans molded to her figure, the look classy and comfortable.

"Oh, hell no. Tristin doesn't cook. He just helps me when I do. No need to worry. Dinner should be better than edible."

He chuckled, feeling some of his tension start to ease. "After living on fast food and frozen dinners, anything sounds good right about now."

She winked. "I think you can raise your standards a little. Steaks are on the menu for tonight. I don't want to brag, but I grill a mean steak."

"Sounds good. Lead the way."

Kat showed him to the kitchen where he and Tristin exchanged a quick greeting and bro-hug. They settled down to the meal, and the conversation stayed light. No mention was made of Cole joining KSI or of Sydney. Cole was surprised at how much he enjoyed their easy banter.

Tristin kept the teasing and stories from their BUD/S days flowing, but Cole was more impressed with Kat's sharp wit and sarcastic sense of humor. She had a way of verbally sparring with her husband that was both charming and entertaining.

Watching them interact so lovingly with each other embarrassed Cole. He felt like an intruder as he watched them share heated glances and intimate touches. He debated whether or not to cut the evening short, despite the fact he still had to discuss the job offer with Tryst.

"You boys want dessert first or to talk business first?" Kat rose to clear the table.

Cole started to help her when Tristin raised a hand to stop him. "Business first. We'll eat dessert to celebrate."

Cole settled back in his seat, his eyebrow cocked. "You sound very sure of what I'm going to say."

Tristin grinned as his wife left them alone. "You already turned me down. Then out of nowhere, you call. You agree to come to dinner. And you look like a man on a mission. It's not hard to figure out you've had a change of heart."

Cole relaxed against his chair. "I have conditions."

"I'm guessing Sydney is one of them."

"I want in on the case to bring her ex down. But I don't want her involved. In any way."

"That's a tall ask. Without her help, we don't have a case. We need her to make the takedown possible."

"She's been through enough because of him. She's starting over, and getting involved with him again will only hold her back. I want him out of her life. Completely."

The two men held each other's stares, challenging each other. Neither wanted to back down. The silence weighed on them, the tension burning the air.

"Oh my God. Give it up, you two. No one has time for your macho, Navy SEAL stare-down."

Both men whipped their heads around to look at Kat as if an alien had just interrupted them instead of Tristin's wife. Her fists rested on her hips, her dark eyes gleaming with laughter. She moved to stand behind the dining room chair she'd vacated and rested her hands on the back. She gave each of them a long glare before finally addressing Cole.

"It's like this. Sydney is a gifted computer hacker, and her skills would be very useful at KSI whether she helps us close the Carter case or not. So I plan to offer her a job, and you'll just have to get over it. I also think that considering what that asshole put her through, you're doing her a disservice by not allowing her to help. The choice should be hers, not yours. By taking the decision out of her hands, you've treated her like a possession, and you're no better than Carter."

Cole rested his hands on the table top, their clenching the only outward indication of the battle he waged with his anger. He didn't want to be irritated with Kat when he'd just started to like her, but comparing him to Sydney's abusive ex was an insult he couldn't ignore.

"I am not—"

His cell phone trilled in his pocket, startling him. He almost ignored the persistent ringing, but no one had called him since he'd moved to Grayson Cove, other than Tristin, so he anticipated the worst. The idea that his mom was calling to tell him she was in trouble had him reaching for the phone. His anger dissipated when he saw Sydney's name flash on the screen.

"Sydney, I—"

"I don't have a thing to say to you, so you can just leave. Right now."

Cole faltered, something in her tone setting his nerves on edge. He already guessed she wasn't talking to him, but the fact that she called for him to listen to her conversation had his gut churning.

"I have plenty to say. And you'll listen." Cole could barely make out the words, but he could distinctly identify a male voice. Even before she spoke again, he guessed the identity of the other speaker.

"I stopped having to listen to you when I left, Emmett. I thought you'd accepted that."

He was on his feet in a flash. Tristin and Kat tensed, watching to see what had their dinner guest on alert.

"It's Sydney. Her ex is with her. I need to get to her."

"I'll drive you. Where is she?" Tristin was already moving to grab his wallet and his keys when Cole responded.

"I don't know."

"Give me your phone." Kat snatched it from his hand before he could react. She reached for hers, where it rested on the kitchen counter.

"What the hell are you doing?"

"Give me a sec."

"Let her work, Panther."

He glared at Tristin, but as frustrated as he was, he let Kat use his cell phone for whatever she had in mind. In less than a minute, she handed his phone back. When he glanced at the screen, he saw a map with a red dot pointing to a location only a few miles from the Walshes' home.

"She's there. I programmed a shortcut for you. Just do what the GPS says, and you can be there in less than ten minutes."

He didn't have time to be impressed with Kat's skills. He nodded to her and Tristin and ran out the door to his truck. The lack of traffic allowed him to roar down the road and make it to Tony's in record time. His fury brewed as he listened to the conversation with Sydney and Emmett. His hands slammed against the steering wheel when he heard Emmett insult her.

The tires slung gravel as he navigated the crowded parking lot until he found them. Slamming on the brakes, he threw the gear shift into park and jumped from his truck. A red haze clouded his mind when he saw Emmett reach for Sydney's arm and jerk her closer to him.

"Hey!" He shouted at them a couple of times before Emmett seemed to hear him.

Though the scum turned to face him, he didn't release Sydney. Cole saw her eyes widen when she realized he was there, and his hands clenched at the fear in their depths. Cole grabbed Emmett's shoulder, squeezed until his grip loosened on Sydney's upper arm, and shoved Emmett against the car next to Sydney's. To his credit, Emmett didn't fight back. He regarded Cole with a cool, detached glare.

"Stay the hell away from her." The steel underlying Cole's tone left no room for argument.

Emmett's mouth slowly stretched wide in a sinister grin. He held his hands up in a sign of surrender and moved away. He pierced Sydney with his icy blue gaze.

"I'll be seeing you, Sydney."

"Like hell you will. You need to leave. *Now!*" Cole took a menacing step closer, but Emmett turned and retreated to his car. Cole followed the vehicle's hasty exit from the parking lot and down the road before turning to Sydney.

"Are you all right?" He didn't like the shivers coursing through her body nor the lack of color in her face.

"Why are you here? How did you know?"

He blinked at the awe in her voice. "What? Sydney, you called me. Did he hurt you? I can take you to the hospital to get checked out."

She shook her head. "I'm fine. Emmett was mostly talk. This time. What do you mean, I called you? I've had Chloe on the line listening…" Her voice trailed off as she lifted her phone and saw whose name was actually on the screen.

"Oh, God." She closed her eyes as she rubbed her fingertips against her forehead. "I'm so sorry. You and Chloe are right next to each other in my contacts. I never meant to bother you. You came to my rescue. Again."

"As soon as I heard you say his name, I sped over here. You can call me anytime. For any reason."

"Thank you. But how did you know where I was?"

Cole didn't have a good answer for that, so he evaded it altogether. "Did he hurt you?"

"I'll have a bruise on my arm from where he grabbed me, but he's done worse. You got here before he could do much more than yell at me."

Cole instantly regretted not beating the shit out of Emmett Carter when he had the chance. While Sydney seemed all right, she was shaken. Her pupils were dilated, and the pulse at her throat throbbed. He had to focus on her before shock settled any further into her system.

"Why don't I take you home?"

She pointed her thumb over her shoulder. "It's okay. I have my car. I just came to get some food because Chloe and I are having a girls' night."

"You sure you're feeling okay enough to drive home?"

She inhaled deeply and released the breath slowly. "Yes. I'm fine. I promise."

"Then let me follow you home. Just for my peace of mind."

"That's not necessary. Emmett doesn't know where I live, and my building has very good security."

"I'm glad, but I just want to make sure. Once you make it home, I'll leave you to your girls' night."

Finally, she nodded, and he relaxed. "Great. I'm in that truck over there. Just pull out of your spot, and I'll come around behind your car."

Soon they were on the road, traveling a short distance from Tony's Taco Shack. Cole was pleased to see Sydney pull her car into a parking garage. She hadn't been joking about living in a high-security apartment building. After she disappeared inside, his phone buzzed with a text from her giving him the garage access code. He immediately texted back for her to wait in her car for him. His ever-watchful eyes scoped out the perimeter, searching for the high-end sports car he'd seen Emmett driving. The block seemed clear of the jackass' presence, but Cole remained on edge.

When he stepped into Sydney's line of sight, he could see the tension leave her body. He opened the door, and she stepped from the car with a sweet smile just for him.

"If it's all right with you, I'd like to check out your apartment before I leave you alone," he told her as he placed a hand at the small of her back to guide her through the garage.

"There's no way for Emmett to get in, Cole. That's why I chose to live here," she said, pulling away. Her face flushed as she clutched the bag of food.

"Humor me," he coaxed. "I promise once I've looked around and made sure no one is lurking nearby, then I'll leave you to your girls' night."

She sighed as she lifted beautiful blue eyes to his face. "Girls' night got canceled. Chloe called me just a moment ago to tell me she had to work later than she thought."

Cole narrowed his eyes. "Really? She's not going to come by? You're going to be alone tonight, then?"

She sighed again. "Yes. I, uh, I didn't tell her about running into Emmett. She can be very protective, and I didn't want to take her away from her work. She would have dropped everything to be there for me, but I didn't see a need since you chased Emmett off. It's really fine. I'll fill her in on everything tomorrow, and tonight, I'll just chill in front of the TV with my obscene amount of Mexican food."

"Are you sure? I don't like the idea of you being alone after the scare you had."

"I'm sure, Cole. Please don't worry about me. I'll be perfectly fine. I promise."

He couldn't stop the smile curving his lips. Despite her scare, Sydney was tough. Probably more than people gave her credit for, he guessed.

"All right. Come on then. Let's get you safely inside before all of this food gets cold."

Despite what she'd told him, Cole scanned their surroundings repeatedly as they rode the elevator to her apartment. Though the security of the building was solid, he had learned never to underestimate people when they wanted something. If Emmett wanted to get to Sydney, and he obviously did, security codes wouldn't stop him.

They were quiet on the ride up, giving Cole a chance to study Sydney. She wore faded jeans with holes ripped in the knees and a nondescript t-shirt. Her shiny hair weaved into a long braid that fell over one shoulder to rest against her breast. Her beautiful face was again makeup free, and Cole realized he preferred her natural look.

"You know," Sydney suddenly spoke. "I ordered way more food than I could ever eat by myself. You're welcome to join me for dinner, if you haven't eaten already."

Though he had a delicious meal at Tryst's, he didn't hesitate to accept her invitation. He didn't relish the idea of leaving her alone, but more than that, he was eager to spend an evening with her.

"Sounds good. Thanks."

She led the way out of the elevator to her apartment, digging one-handed into her purse for the keys. He took them from her and, once he unlocked the door, motioned for her to wait in the doorway while he did a walk-through. Satisfied no one lurked in any of the rooms, he pulled her inside and secured the door behind her.

"Don't you think that was a little unnecessary?" A teasing glint shined in her eyes.

"Just being cautious. I don't like to leave anything to chance." He took the sack of food from her hands. "Where should I set this?"

"Are you good with eating in front of the TV?" she asked.

"Sure. Whatever you want works for me."

"Okay. Let's put everything in the living room, and we'll spread everything out on the coffee table to eat. I'll get some plates and napkins. Just make yourself comfortable."

Only a few minutes passed before they settled down with plates of Mexican food. They sat opposite each other, he in an armchair and she on the couch. He grinned at the large bite of a taco she took. Her eyes rolled back in her head in pure pleasure.

"OMG!" she moaned. "Tony's never disappoints."

Cole shifted uncomfortably in his chair. The sound of her moan shot straight to his cock, but fortunately she didn't seem to notice. If Sydney ever realized how sexy she was, he'd be in serious trouble.

"Do you have a preference of what we watch?" She grabbed the remote.

"I was hoping we could talk." He tried not to cringe at how much he sounded like a girlfriend wanting to hear the latest gossip. He dove into his food to avoid the awkwardness.

She slowly returned the remote to the table. "You want to know about Emmett."

Just hearing the name left a bad taste in Cole's mouth. He forcibly swallowed the bite and watched her closely. Sydney voiced her words more as a statement than a question, so Cole didn't feel the need to respond. Finishing off one taco, she chewed thoughtfully. Cole ate silently, letting her begin in her own time.

"It's hard for me to talk about. I always feel like I have to explain why I was with him or why I stayed with him."

"You don't have to explain or talk about anything you don't want to. I would never pressure you."

"Thank you. People always say that, but they can't always control how they feel. But you...I believe you." She held his gaze for a heartbeat before she exhaled a long sigh. "I was supposed to marry Emmett. I left him six months ago, after spending two years with him. You've already guessed that he was very abusive and mean." She placed her plate on the table, her appetite gone.

"How did you meet him?"

"I had just gotten a job in the IT department at his investment company. I had worked there four months before I ever met Emmett. I was on a coffee run for the folks in my department, and Emmett rode the elevator with me when I returned. We barely said two words to each other. I never thought about him again until the next day. He specifically asked my supervisor to have me to check out a computer problem he was having with his laptop. I'm not sure how he knew my name. He was an executive in the company, and whenever the top dogs had a problem, my supervisor would handle it. I hadn't been there long enough to cross paths with most of the executives, but there I was, in Emmett's office at his request. Turns out, there wasn't anything wrong with his computer. He just wanted to be on his turf when he asked me out.

"People at work told me I should have been flattered that Emmett went to so much trouble just to get a date with me, but I wasn't interested. He seemed too arrogant and bossy for my tastes. Plus, I worried that I would lose my job if the date went bad. He had a lot of power within the company. So, I said no and went on my way. I've wondered if I had said yes to him in the beginning, if he would have lost interest and left me alone. Instead he pursued me."

Cole remained quiet as Sydney took a long sip of her water before continuing. "I'm ashamed to say he charmed me. He made me feel special. Every date was unique, and he spoiled me with gifts for no reason. I fell for it. By the time he started to show his true personality, I was already in love with him.

"One minute, he would do or say something to make me feel horrible. Then he'd apologize and do something to make me feel like a princess. It's such textbook behavior for an abuser that I should have known better. I'm still not quite sure how I let it happen, but I trusted him over everyone else in my life. I had people, including my parents, warn me about him, but I refused to admit just how wrong he was for me. I foolishly thought I could change him if I just loved him enough.

"After Emmett and I became engaged, he convinced me to quit my job. He said it was a conflict of interest for both of us to work for the same company, and since he was an executive and I had a wedding to plan, it made sense for me to quit."

Tears brewed in her eyes, but she blinked them away. Cole had stopped eating, but he still held his plate because it gave his hands something to do. Otherwise, he would give in to the temptation to finish what he started with Emmett in the parking lot at Tony's.

"Because I was unemployed, I moved in with him to save on expenses. He started hitting me soon after. I know this is hard to understand. Believe me, I've asked myself over and over why I stayed with him as long as I did. Pride was part of it, as much as it pains me to admit it, and shame was the rest. I didn't want anyone to know what a mess I'd made of everything. Emmett and I were together for two years, and for more than a year of that, he hurt me and made me feel worthless. I severed any relationships I had, so when I started to fear him and what he would do to me, I had nowhere to go and no one to turn to."

"What happened to your family?"

"It was just my parents. They died in a car accident after I was engaged to Emmett. My dad never liked Emmett, and he tried to warn me that Emmett was the wrong guy for me. I was close to my parents, although I wasn't what they had envisioned for a daughter either. I was rebellious. I always wanted to push the envelope. When they tried to talk to me about Emmett, I shut them down. Emmett convinced me they were being controlling. I cut off all contact with them. I reached out to them when I left because at the time, I didn't know what happened. No one called me about the accident. I never got to say goodbye."

"I'm sorry, Sydney. I'm sorry he robbed you of that."

"Me, too."

"What made you finally leave him?"

She smiled, and his heart clenched. "I met Chloe. She had quickly made a name for herself as an event planner, and someone convinced Emmett to hire her to help with the wedding. Chloe is a force of nature. Strong and fierce. Our first meeting was so fun. She reminded me of all the things I had given up being with Emmett.

Emmett wasn't around when Chloe and I met, so he couldn't stop us from becoming friends. She helped me leave him. He threatened to destroy her career, but she was already sought after to the point that he couldn't touch her.

"He let me go without much of a fight. Then I saw him at the hotel, and it's like I've traveled back in time. I don't know what he wants with me now, and I can't seem to stop being afraid of him. That's why I signed up for the self-defense class. I thought if I could learn how to protect myself, then I wouldn't have to be afraid anymore. It didn't seem to work though. I freaked out when I saw him tonight and had to call for help. I'm sorry you had to interrupt your evening to come to my rescue. You didn't have to do that, but I appreciate it all the same."

He rose, setting his plate on the coffee table. He moved to sit beside her and took hold of her hand. "It's okay to ask for help, Sydney. No one deserves to be treated the way Emmett treated you. Did you ever report Emmett's abuse?"

"Emmett was careful to only hit me when we were alone, and it was never bad enough for me to seek medical treatment. It was my word against his. He also has a lot of influential connections, while I'm a big nobody. I told myself I didn't have to turn him in as long as he left me alone. I never thought he'd reinsert himself in my life."

"You are somebody, and you're not alone. He's not going to get to you again as long as I'm around. If you'll let me, I'll make sure you don't have to be afraid of him anymore."

She regarded him with wide blue eyes that captivated him. "Thank you. You'll never know how grateful I am to you for protecting me when you don't even know me. But if I'm going to break free of Emmett, I have to figure out how to do it myself. I want to do this myself."

Suddenly, she chuckled. Cole couldn't imagine what she found to be funny, but the sound was a pleasant change from the seriousness of the moment. "You know, I could steal his identity and bleed his accounts dry if I wanted to. By the time he'd realize what happened, he'd be broke."

"So why haven't you done that?"

She pursed her lips. "I don't know. I suppose I didn't want him to make me a criminal when he'd already made me a victim."

The tears reappeared, this time slipping from her eyes to trail down her cheeks.

A woman's tears always made Cole uncomfortable. Sydney's tears were his undoing. He cupped her face in his rough palms, dropping feather-like kisses to her cheeks to wipe away the tears. Then he pulled her close, cradling her head against his chest. No sobs came. The only way he knew she was still crying was the wetness he felt on the front of his t-shirt. He rested his head against her hair, breathing in a sweet scent that was like ambrosia to him.

"Cole?" Her voice was muffled by his shirtfront, but Cole heard her clearly.

"Yeah, sweetheart?"

"Can I ask you a question?"

"You just did," he teased. "What's on your mind, Syd?"

"Why were you working security at the charity benefit last Friday and then teaching my self-defense class today?"

He smirked at her change in topic but had no problem humoring her.

"Both times I was helping out an old friend. He owns the security firm that worked the benefit, and Travis is my friend's brother. The benefit was a test to see if I want a job at the firm full-time. The class was a fluke. Jay and I were working out at the gym when Travis asked for help."

"Are you quitting your job to work for your friend?"

"I don't have a job. I'm retired from the military. I was a Navy SEAL. I've been trying to figure out what to do now, and this job offer from my friend is a good one. His name is Tristin. He went through BUD/S training with me. That's basic training for SEALs," he explained, feeling her calm as he spoke.

"That's nice that the two of you are friends after all this time. You were a Navy SEAL? That's awesome. I've never met a SEAL before, but I've heard stories and seen movies. You guys are badass."

He grinned. "Well, it's not quite like the movies, but the bad-ass part sounds about right."

She pulled back to peer into his face with a grin. "Conceited much?"

He was pleased to see the light back in her eyes despite their redness and puffiness.

"It's not conceited when it's true," he returned, prompting her laugh. The sweet sound washed over him like a warm shower easing the stresses of his day away.

"So, you probably know how to kill a guy with your thumb, right? Here I am trying to have the guts to kick a guy in the nuts, and you're like a lethal weapon. If I wasn't intimidated before, I sure am now," she told him playfully.

"Why would you be intimidated at all?"

She pulled away, and though he was loath to break the contact, he figured she needed the distance.

"Because I'm awkward that way. I'm a computer geek, Cole. I'm better with ones and zeros than I am with people, especially hot looking Navy SEALs." Suddenly, her eyes widened even more if possible, her hand flying up to cover her mouth. "Oh, God," she mumbled into her palm. "I can't believe I just said that out loud."

Cole was well aware of his effect on women, but hearing Sydney considered him hot stroked his ego like nothing else.

"What is it about you that makes it so easy to talk to you?" She regarded him as if she could find the answer to the mystery in his expression. "Anytime I've ever met a guy I was remotely attracted to, I would be too tongue-tied to do anything about it. But I feel like I could talk to you all night and never run out of things to say."

"Maybe that means you're not attracted to me." He was shamelessly seeking affirmation from her, but the deep blush rising from her neck to her face made it hard to regret the question.

"That's not it. That kiss should have made you realize that." She dropped her gaze, and he didn't miss her cringe, indicating she revealed more than she meant to.

"I was hoping that kiss affected you as much as it did me." He watched to see how she handled his admission. He was pleased to see her mouth open on a silent exclamation.

"You did?" Her tone was breathless, and Cole felt its affect as keenly as if they'd kissed again.

Her cell phone rang before she could say more. She exhaled loudly and scurried off the couch. "Saved by the bell," she mumbled, causing his grin to stretch wider.

"Hello," she answered, avoiding looking at him.

He grabbed his beer and took a swig. If she thought the conversation was over, she was sadly mistaken. He was more than willing to patiently wait for her call to end to pick it back up.

If he hadn't been watching her, he would have missed her reaction. He lowered the beer bottle slowly. Sydney stiffened, her already pale skin losing what little color it possessed. When she swayed slightly on her feet, he rose instantly to wrap her in his arms. She sank into his frame.

"You need to leave me alone." Her voice quivered.

"Is that him?" Cole's tone was low. He didn't have to say

Emmett's name for her to know to whom he referred. She nodded woodenly, and Cole plucked the phone from her hand while supporting her limp frame with his other arm.

"How dare you spread your legs for that bastard! You're more of a whore than I gave you credit for."

Cole was thankful Sydney missed her ex's comment. His fury had him seeing red.

"You listen to me, you son of a bitch. You stay away from Sydney, or I will personally rip your heart out."

The line went dead. Pulling the cell back, he saw Emmett had hung up like the coward he was. He threw the phone on the counter and turned Sydney so he could envelop her in his embrace. His hands caressed her back.

"He knows you're here."

"What do you mean, sweetheart?"

"When I answered, he asked if I was enjoying my evening with my new boyfriend."

"He was taking a guess, Syd. There's no way he could have known I was here with you until I talked to him on the phone."

She shook her head. "He said he left a surprise for us and that we should check out your truck."

Cole's heart pounded in his chest. To get to Cole's truck, the little SOB had to have gotten into the secure parking garage, which meant Sydney wasn't as safe in her apartment as he'd hoped.

"Sweetheart, I need you to wait here. I'm going to check out the garage. Lock the door behind me. Don't let anyone in while I'm gone."

Panic flashed in her eyes as she stepped back to stare at him. "No, Cole. You can't go down there. If Emmett's there, he'll be waiting for one of us to check out what he said. He'll try to h-hurt you. Please, I don't want you to get hurt because of me."

His anger evaporated. "Syd, he can't hurt me. I promise. I've been in much more dangerous situations. Emmett has met his match. I just need you to secure the door behind me, so I know you're safe while I'm checking out the garage. Trust me, Syd."

She took two deep breaths before nodding. He waited in the hallway until he heard her flip the latch on the door. He opted for the stairwell versus the elevator, so he could make sure Emmett wasn't lying in wait. Considering the bastard had hung up as soon as Cole got on the phone, he figured Emmett didn't linger waiting to spar with him. But there was no way he was taking any chances.

He pulled his gun from his ankle holster. Instinct had him bring it even though he only planned to spend an evening with friends and not chasing abusive ex-fiancés. Reaching the bottom floor, he peered through the small square window in the door to assess what he could see of the garage. His truck and Sydney's car were out of his line of vision.

With silent movements, he stepped into the garage on full alert. A quick search revealed he was alone in the structure. Then he focused on his truck and Sydney's car, his anger boiling. His truck was busted up as if Emmett had taken a baseball bat to it. The windshield, headlights and taillights were smashed. Dents marred the body of the truck. Sydney's car was untouched except for the blood red paint on her windshield and the body of her car repetitively spelling the word "whore."

Cole pulled his cell phone out of the back pocket of his jeans. He made quick work of placing a call. "Tryst. It's me. I need your help. Oh, and I accept the job with KSI."

Chapter Nine

Sydney clasped her hands tightly, but the shaking wouldn't stop. She barely remembered how she ended up in the black SUV with Cole behind the wheel. She wasn't sure where they were going, and she wasn't sure she even cared. Her home was no longer safe. She couldn't stay there a moment longer knowing Emmett could get to her so easily.

She stole a glance at Cole's profile out of the corner of her eye. The cab of the SUV was cloaked in darkness. Very few streetlamps lined the road, so he was a shadowy outline to her eyes once they were accustomed to the night. His eyes were fixed to the road, his jaw tense. His hands clenched around the steering wheel. He was angry. Furious was probably a more apt description. She wanted to apologize for involving him and setting him in Emmett's sights, but he likely didn't want to hear that.

Even though he was angry, she was relieved that he was all right. When he left her in the apartment alone, she'd jumped to the worst-case scenario, imaging Emmett getting the jump on him and injuring him before coming to search for her. When Cole came back, she'd been so relieved to see him unharmed, she hadn't immediately registered his anger. He paced, ranting about how he was going to beat her ex to within an inch of his life, and ordered her to collect her things. She hadn't asked why — she just wanted to leave.

"Everything's going to be okay. I promise."

She started as his husky voice shattered the silence. Though he was angry, he spoke gently, reassuring her. Surprisingly, she believed him. She felt safe with him. She didn't feel the need to question him because she trusted him.

"I don't know why Emmett took all of this out on you. Or why he still wants to harass me. None of it makes sense. Not after he's left me alone all this time. I never wanted you to be caught in the middle."

"None of this is on you, Sydney. It's Carter, and we'll make sure he doesn't bother you anymore. Remember the friend I told you about? He's going to help you. Carter's not getting to you."

She couldn't think of anything to say, so she fell silent, trying once again to calm her shaking hands. She jumped in her seat when he placed a warm hand over hers, engulfing hers long enough to calm her and chase away the chill that settled in her bones.

"Thank you." Her tone was soft, but she knew he'd heard her when he squeezed her hands.

They stayed like that for several more minutes until Cole turned into a driveway and stopped in front of a tall wrought iron gate. Lowering the window, he tapped a button on an intercom box twice, and the gates swung open for them to drive up the long, winding driveway. Solar lights illuminated the path otherwise shadowed by elm trees lining the drive. Once they broke through the trees, she gasped at the home beautifully displayed in front of them.

The sprawling stone two-story home was lit up brilliantly with solar lights. Three wide steps led to a porch and wide, white columns lining the front. Dark shutters only enhanced the deep red door. The landscaping was brilliantly green with manicured shrubs placed strategically to give depth to the lawn. It was beautiful but formidable, and all Sydney could do was gape.

"This is my friend Tristin and his wife Kat's house. The security here is top-notch. They offered for you to stay with them for as long as you need. You'll be safe here."

Sydney felt tears well up in her eyes. The house was beyond what she could have imagined, and she was overwhelmed that Cole's friends would open their home to her.

"Why?" She was barely aware that she asked the question.

Cole lightly gripped her chin between his thumb and forefinger and tilted her head to face him. The front of the house was lit brightly enough to illuminate his face. She was shocked to realize his face had softened from the mask of anger he'd worn the entire ride. His eyes seemed to glow like fiery embers, pulling her out of her emotional state.

"Why what, sweetheart?"

She swallowed, wishing she'd kept her wondering to herself. "Why would they open their home to me like this? They don't know me or anything about me. They're offering to protect me, and it's… hard to believe."

"Come inside and meet them. I think you'll understand better then."

She nodded, but he didn't release her right away, not even when she started to shift toward the door. She stared at him with a question in her eyes, and he smiled.

"Do you trust me?"

"I shouldn't. We've just met. With my track record, I can't trust myself."

"Sydney, do you trust me?"

She swallowed the lump clogging her throat. "Yes."

"Then you can trust them. I wouldn't have brought you here if you couldn't. But we can sit here for as long as you need, until you're ready to go inside."

He allowed her to pull away from him this time, and she dropped her eyes to her hands, which had somehow stopped shaking without her realizing. It suddenly struck her how foolish she was behaving, letting Emmett scare her into questioning the motives of everyone trying to help her. She shook her head as she shoved her old, familiar uncertainties down. Without a word, she pushed open the door and stepped from the SUV. She waited for Cole to reach her side before she moved with him to the house.

The door was thrown open before either of them could press the doorbell or knock. Sydney stared at the pretty woman smiling warmly at her. Wide glasses sat on her pert nose, the dark rims complementing her olive skin and round face. Wisps of dark hair escaped her ponytail and brushed against her cheek. They stood eye-to-eye, studying each other, before the woman stepped forward to wrap an arm around Sydney's shoulders.

"Welcome to my home, Sydney. I'm Kat. I know you've been through a lot tonight, so I figured you would want time to yourself to deal. If you'll come with me to our guest room, we can draw you a warm bath so you can relax. If you need anything else – something to eat or drink or anything – you just say the word, and I'll take care of it."

"Thank you. It's nice to meet you."

"Kat, Tristin wants to talk—"

Kat threw up her other hand to silence Cole as she continued to propel Sydney toward the sprawling staircase. "I know, but Sydney needs time before she answers any questions. They can wait, Panther. Let me take care of your girl."

"I'm not his girl," Sydney protested woodenly. "What's Panther?"

Kat's smile widened as she hugged Sydney. "You don't know? I'll be happy to tell you the story while we get you settled." Her tone was lighthearted, easing Sydney's anxiety.

"Kat," Cole growled in warning, which only sparked their hostess' mirth.

Sydney couldn't stop the slight smile on her face from their antics. The room Kat led her to was beautiful, decorated in calming whites and grays with a pop of bright yellow in the curtains and throw pillows. She sank down on the queen bed as Kat bustled around her, setting out some pajamas for her to wear.

"Kat, why would you call me Cole's girl? He and I have only just met."

Kat smiled. "That's a conversation for another time. For now, you need to unwind in the bath and sleep. Just forget about everything for a little while. You're safe here. Cole and my husband and their friends will make sure of that, and they're good at what they do. Do you need anything?"

"Unless you have some advice on how to forget, I think I'm good for now."

Kat sat beside her on the bed. "That was a stupid thing for me to say. Of course, you can't forget. I have no idea what all you've been through."

"It's okay. I appreciate the sentiment. And I appreciate you allowing me to crash in your home. I don't know many people who would do that for a complete stranger."

Kat smiled. "I have a feeling we're not going to be strangers for long. I'll leave you to your bath. Call if you need anything."

Sydney watched her hostess leave, the door closing with a soft click. She didn't move right away, just sat in the stillness. She should probably call Chloe and fill her in. But for now, she felt fatigue weighing her down. Stretching out on the soft mattress, her head sinking onto the pillow, she told herself she would rest for only a few minutes. The bath sounded too heavenly to waste, but before she could form another thought, she drifted into a deep slumber.

Sydney woke slowly, keeping her eyes closed as her mind shook off the last remnants of sleep. Her body stiffened as she realized she wasn't in her own bed. This bed was larger with sheets that were a higher, more luxurious thread count than what she was accustomed to. She was still dressed in her clothes from the night before, though she wasn't wearing her shoes.

As her recall returned, her eyes flew open. Memories of the previous evening invaded her mind, setting her heart to racing. Sydney sat up in the comfortable bed, her eyes lighting on her cell phone resting on the nightstand. Reaching for it, she gasped to realize she'd missed two texts and a phone call from Chloe, all coming in before 8:30 a.m., more than an hour ago. Without hesitation, she called her best friend.

"Where the hell have you been, and are you all right?" Chloe shouted into the phone.

"I'm fine. I'm sorry I worried you."

"I went by your apartment. I freaked when you weren't there. I saw your car, Syd."

Sydney cringed. She never expected Chloe to use the access she'd given her friend to the parking garage and her apartment to check up on her. "I'm sorry. There's a lot I need to tell you. I just would rather tell you in person than over the phone. But I assure you I'm fine."

"Are you at home? I'm coming over."

"Aren't you at work? You have too much going on to leave this early. I can fill you in tonight. Please don't put things on hold for me."

"I worked late last night. Liam can hold down the fort for one day. I know you don't want me to, but I'm worried about you. I want to see for myself that you're all right. I'll be at your apartment in ten. And I'm bringing muffins and frappuccinos."

"I'm not at home. I'm at a—" Sydney hesitated, not sure how

to explain her relationship to Tristin and Kat or her relationship with Cole, for that matter. "I'm safe, Chloe. Just stay at work, and I'll let you know when I get home."

"Why are you being so shady?"

Sydney's lids slid over her eyes as she fell back against the pillows. She could never hide anything from Chloe, who knew her better than anyone in the world. And if Chloe was suspicious of what was going on, she wouldn't stop until she received an explanation. "It's a long story. I'm sort of hiding out from Emmett at the home of a friend of a friend."

"*Emmett?* Where are you, Sydney? I'm coming for you. *Now.*"

Sydney sighed. "I'm fine, Chloe. I promise. I had a run-in with Emmett yesterday, and he ended up vandalizing my car. But my friend helped me and brought me some place safe. Please don't be worried."

"Why didn't you call me? You know I would have dropped everything to help you."

"I did. Well, I thought I did. It's a long story. I promise I'll explain everything. I'll text you the address."

"I'm coming to get you, and we'll spend the day unwinding and brainstorming. I don't mean to steamroll over you. I remember how vulnerable you were when you were with him. I know you're not that person anymore. I see that, but you're my best friend. I can't stop being protective. I promise, though, I'll tone it down."

"Thank you. I love you," she said as a soft knock sounded on the bedroom door. "Listen, I'm going to let you go. I'll send you my location. Just text when you get here, and I'll meet you outside."

She ended the call as panic settled in. What if that knock meant Cole was coming to check on her, and here she was looking a fright—rumpled, tangled hair and splotchy skin, wrinkled clothes, and the worst – morning breath.

"Sydney? It's Kat. Can I come in?" A voice drifted through the closed door, and Sydney immediately relaxed.

"Come in," she called.

As the door opened, Sydney hastily pulled up her messages to send Chloe her location. The map pin successfully sent, she glanced up with a smile only to have it freeze on her face. Her insecurity about her appearance returned full force as Kat quietly closed the door behind her. She wanted to be grateful to see her hostess holding a cup of what she hoped was coffee, but instead, she wished she had at least brushed her hair before granting the flawless woman entrance.

"Good morning." Kat settled on the edge of the bed, handing the mug over to Sydney.

Sydney took a scalding sip to buy time to collect herself. Kat's thick hair fell softly around her face, her olive skin practically glowing even though she wore no makeup. Dressed in distressed jeans and a loose-fitting blouse, she smiled sweetly as her eyes regarded Sydney with sympathy. The look was familiar. Sydney had received many of them from acquaintances who heard about her split from Emmett. She was sick of it.

Placing the mug on the nightstand, she pasted a fake smile on her face. "Thank you for letting me stay here, but you won't have to put up with me much longer. My friend will be here to get me soon. I'm just going to shower and get dressed first, if you don't mind."

Kat lightly covered Sydney's hand with her slender one, halting her guest's attempt to rise from the bed. "There's no rush for you to leave. Stay as long as you need."

"I'm fine. Really. Like I said, my best friend is on her way to pick me up, so I'll only need a minute to get ready. Then your guest room will be empty once again," Sydney said in a terrible attempt at lightheartedness.

"I'll let our security guys know your friend is coming." Kat withdrew her cell phone from her jeans pocket. "What's her name? She's welcome to join us for breakfast."

"Security? You and Tristin have your own security?" She'd noticed the safety precautions when she arrived with Cole last night, but she hadn't seen anyone but Kat and Tristin in the house or on the grounds.

Kat regarded Sydney silently for several moments. She finally dialed a number, her dark eyes holding Sydney's as she spoke. "BB, it's Kat. Sydney has a guest coming by. Her name is—" She paused, her expression turning expectant. Sydney supplied the information. "Her name is Chloe Stephens. She's Sydney's best friend. Would you make sure the security guys let her up to the house when she arrives?"

Kat listened, nodded, and said, "Thanks."

Sydney regarded her suspiciously, her instincts screaming there was more going on with Cole's friends than meets the eye. "I don't mean to be rude, Kat, but I think it's time I got ready. Chloe won't take long to get here."

"I know you're freaking out. This can be very overwhelming. Believe me, I know firsthand. If you'll hear me out, I want to explain some things to you, so hopefully you'll know I only want to be your friend. Chloe can be there as we talk. I promise things aren't as scary as they seem."

"Are you in witness protection or something?" Sydney voiced the first thought that came to mind as she tried to make sense of the situation.

Kat chuckled. "No. It's nothing like that. Look, I have an idea. When Chloe gets here, the three of us can go to my favorite place for breakfast. I'll answer all of your questions, and hopefully you'll see we only want to help you. What do you say?"

Sydney studied Kat intently, but the other woman's expression was closed. She couldn't get a read on her hostess, and that was unsettling. Curiosity burned within her, and she did like the idea of Chloe—with her keen sense of discernment and her mistrust of just about everyone— joining her as she tried to figure out what was going on. Her good sense told her to leave and never look back, but something more ingrained in her had her relenting.

She could walk away from Kat. But walking away from Cole – that didn't feel so easy.

"Where's Cole?" The question burst forth from her before she could stop it.

"He's here. He and Tristin are meeting with some guys they work with. He wanted to come and say hello, but I convinced him you needed some time to yourself first. You'll see him before we leave, if you're up to joining me for breakfast."

"Why do I feel like you're about to turn my world upside down?" Sydney's voice held a small catch.

"Because you've had a lot of stuff thrown at you within the last few days, but I'm hoping you'll see that turning your world upside down is not my intention at all."

There was a time in her life that Sydney didn't trust her instincts where other people were concerned. Yet, looking into Kat's eyes, Sydney was shocked to realize she trusted what her hostess was saying.

"I'll text Chloe to tell her you're coming with us. Just to warn you, she's freaking out about not knowing what happened last night. She worries."

Kat grinned. "I'd expect nothing less."

Kat stood and moved to the door. With one last smile in Sydney's direction, she stepped out, leaving Sydney alone with her tumultuous thoughts.

Tired of analyzing her situation, Sydney rose to shower and change. She made quick work of drying her hair and taming the flaming locks in her signature braid. She debated the need for makeup, taking in her pale complexion that only enhanced the freckles dotting her cheeks and nose. Even knowing Chloe would tease her about it, she opted for foundation, lip gloss and a touch of mascara. It was a natural look but was more makeup than she usually wore. Her simple gray t-shirt and black jeans were her usual casual style, though she wished she had something more Chloe's style to wear for seeing Cole again.

Sydney took the stairs slowly, her slender hand gliding down the smooth, wooden banister. Voices drifted up to her the closer she drew to the first floor, and she paused two-thirds of the way down to listen.

"Why didn't you tell me any of this before?"

If she didn't already recognize his voice, Sydney would have known Cole was the one who spoke simply by the tingle that traveled her spine. His deep vibrato washed over her, and she shivered.

"I needed you on board before I could share any details of the case we're working on. I had no idea you knew her until Jay gave me a heads up. You didn't make up your mind to work for me until last night. I couldn't read you in until you were part of the team."

Sydney wasn't sure whom the other voice belonged to, but she suspected they were talking about her. How could she be a part of a case they worked?

"You didn't think to fill me in last night when we showed up on your doorstep?" Cole raged, confirming the other voice was Tristin's. "You didn't think I needed to know there was more going on—"

The conversation abruptly halted. A sinking feeling settled in her stomach. Though she'd made no noise, she realized she'd just been caught spying on them. She finished her descent and turned a corner into a dining room. In one quick scan, her eyes noted Tristin and Kat along with three muscular men who overpowered the enormous room with their very presence.

She recognized Jay from the gym, but she studied him with the same sweeping glance as the other men. Jay and the other two guys varied in looks, but each one was just as hot as the next. Dressed in jeans and nondescript t-shirts, they exuded power and a sense of mystery that were both magnetic and frightening. Her eyes finally landed on Cole, and her heart raced. With all the testosterone in the room, Cole seemed to be the only one to set her blood on fire.

Cole's body was tense, his jaw rigid. His dark eyes, though, regarded her with a mixture of emotions – concern, warmth and something she couldn't identify. After a heartbeat where they held the other's gaze, he crossed the room to her. Her breath caught, thinking he may embrace her or kiss her. Instead, he simply rested his palms on her upper arms.

"Good morning," he said only for her ears. "How are you?"

"I'm fine. I slept like a baby, considering what happened. I haven't had any more messages from Emmett, either."

"You won't. Thanks to Kat." His eyes left her face long enough to send a glance Kat's way.

Sydney's brow furrowed. Slowly, she turned away from him, causing his hands to drop, and stared quizzically at her hostess. Kat smiled sheepishly and gave a slight shrug.

"I blocked his number from your phone."

"Thank you. But I've done that before, and he has a knack for finding a way around it."

"That's why we're equipping you with a secure cell phone, one he can't hack or access. If you find yourself in trouble, all you have to do is hit a specific button on your phone and it sends an alert to my system. We have a tracker on the phone, so we can pinpoint your location. And if Emmett attempts to access your phone from a number we've associated with him, I'll receive an alert and intercept the communication. I already have a nasty little virus ready and waiting that I can send back to him to mess with his device."

Sydney's eyes widened. She wasn't sure if she should be moved by the efforts made to protect her, freaked to have someone she hardly knew intercepting private messages and tracking her whereabouts, or angry that Kat had done all of this without consulting her first.

"Kat is an IT genius, in case you haven't realized that yet," Tristin spoke up in a jovial tone. "Guys like Emmett thrive on terrorizing other people, and my team specializes in bringing guys like Emmett down."

"What do you mean bring him down? You have a team? What, exactly, is going on?" Sydney's eyes swept the room.

A loud buzzing interrupted the moment. Tristin walked over to a small white intercom fixed to a wall. Depressing a button, he said, "What's up, BB?"

A deep voice came over the speaker. "Chloe Stephens is here for Sydney. Sam's bringing her up."

"Sam? Why is Sam here?"

"I invited him," Kat said with a satisfied smile. Husband and wife exchanged a look that spoke volumes, but only the two of them understood the silent communication.

Tristin turned back to the intercom. "Thanks, BB. Has your backup arrived?"

"Yeah. I just finished briefing him."

"Come on up then. We have a lot to do."

"Copy that."

"Sydney, Chloe and I are going to brunch and then for mani-pedis while you men do your thing," Kat announced as she exchanged another look with her husband.

"You won't be going by yourselves," Tristin said smoothly, with steel lacing his tone. "I'll have one of the guys go along."

"I've taken care of it already. Why do you think Sam is here?"

Sydney had the distinct impression everyone in the room knew more than she did, and they were all conspiring to keep the information from her. The familiar panic bubbled up within her, but before it could consume her, she heard her best friend's welcomed voice.

"If I find out you guys are holding Sydney prisoner here, so help me I'll kick all your asses. Believe me, you do not want to mess with me. I don't care how big you are," Chloe ranted at the top of her lungs, and Sydney instantly felt sorry for whomever she spoke to.

Kat grinned as she caught Sydney's eye. "I think I like her already."

"Oh, she's definitely a force to be reckoned with," Sydney mumbled.

When she moved into the other room, she saw Chloe squaring off with another man, not as tall or as muscled as the others Sydney had seen that morning, but he was nonetheless intimidating. Handsome in an understated way, he scowled at Chloe, his dark eyes a stormy gray. His lips set in a firm line, his arms crossed his chest. His white-blond hair stood in wild spikes on the top of his head, oddly giving him a boyish quality that belied his badass demeanor.

"Look, I already told you we don't hold anyone prisoner. If your friend is here, she's here voluntarily. And from what I understand, she's probably safer here than anywhere else. So instead of being pissed off, you should be thankful she's with us."

Chloe's eyes flashed fire as her arms straightened rigidly at her side. Sydney decided it was time to intervene.

"Chlo, I'm right here. And I'm fine." She stepped up to her

friend's side. Her slender hand rested on her friend's arm to calm her down.

Chloe soundly turned a cold shoulder to the man and wrapped Sydney in a hug. "You're lucky I'm so glad to see you, or I'd be kicking your ass too. Don't you ever disappear on me like that again."

"Sorry. The last thing I wanted was to worry you again."

"We're family, Syd. Worry comes with it. You know that."

Sydney pulled away, smiling warmly at her friend. "I know. I had Cole looking out for me, though. I wish you could have seen how he put Emmett in his place."

"I don't know who Cole is, but if he got the better of your scumbag ex, I love him already."

Chuckles rippled through the room at Chloe's words, and Sydney flushed to think of how odd the situation was from her friend's viewpoint. To hide her awkwardness, she grasped Cole's hand and pulled him to stand beside her.

"This is Cole. Cole, this is my best friend, Chloe. Cole has rescued me from Emmett more than once."

Sydney watched the two of them size each other up as they shook hands. She released a pent-up breath when she saw quiet acceptance in their eyes.

"So, you're the one," Chloe drawled. "I can see why my best friend is so taken with you. Thank you for watching out for her."

"You're welcome."

Sydney rushed to continue introductions to hide her embarrassment at Chloe's words. It was true she was taken with Cole, but she wasn't ready for him to know that.

"And this is Kat and her husband Tristin. This is their house, and they were kind enough to let me hide out here last night."

"You had to hide out? Let me guess. From Emmett?" Chloe's

tone was dangerously calm. "I swear I'm going to hurt him. I don't know how, but I will."

"I'll have a go at him when you're done," Cole drawled, earning a smirk from Chloe.

"Honey, if I get a hold of that prick, there won't be anything left for you to hurt. Trust me on that." Chloe swept the room with her gaze before resting it on her friend.

"Who are the rest of the guys? Rejects from the wrestling league?"

Sydney bit back a laugh. "I haven't been introduced to them yet."

Tristin stepped forward with the showmanship of a used car salesman. "Allow me to take care of that. All of these gentlemen work for my security firm—"

"Knight Security," Chloe interrupted. "I thought you looked familiar. You came by Horizons Marketing to meet with Liam about the security for our charity event."

"Good memory. Yes, my company handled the security, and these guys worked the event. Well, all of them except Sam, who you came in with. By the way, his name is Sam Montgomery. This is Jay Colter, Wings Tyler, Zane Wilder, and—" He pointed to the man who just walked into the room behind him. "This is Brennan Beckett, but everyone calls him BB."

"Nice to meet you all. Now tell me, why are you all here, and why are you holding my best friend prisoner?"

Kat laughed. She stepped forward to drape arms around Sydney and Chloe's shoulders. "Sydney is not a prisoner. In fact, I was just telling everyone when you came in that the three of us are going out for a girls' day courtesy of my husband. I'll be able to explain everything over lattes and mani-pedis."

"On me?" Tristin quirked an eyebrow that indicated he had no idea he was footing the bill for the women's pampering.

"Yes, dear. On you. Sydney and Chloe, come with me. Sam, you'll follow behind us. I texted you our itinerary, so you'll know where we're heading." Kat led her stunned guests to the door.

"Wait," Chloe stopped her. "If this is a girls' day, why is the Neanderthal coming?"

"Neanderthal? Really?" Sam grumbled.

"Sam is coming to keep a watch for the scumbag Carter, so we can enjoy our day without worry."

"So why not take one of the other guys? No offense," she threw at Sam before continuing to question Kat. "But these other guys look way scarier than the Neanderthal."

The other men snickered as Sam uttered "hey" in protest. Kat held up a hand to silence everyone. "Sam is just who we need. He'll blend in whenever we go, and he's as mean as a pitbull when he needs to be. Trust me."

Chloe shrugged carelessly, but Sydney could see the disgruntled gleam in her friend's eyes. Until Chloe knew more about what was going on, she wasn't going to let her guard down to trust any of them, even if Sydney vouched for them.

"Let's go, ladies," Kat said breezily. "We'll leave the gentlemen to do their business. Come along, Sam." With a quick kiss to her husband's lips, Kat led her small entourage out the door.

Chapter Ten

Cole studied each man seated around him at the kitchen table in the Knight home. They were the ones he was trusting to protect Sydney. He knew next to nothing about them – except for Tristin, but after going years without contact, he had to admit he didn't really know his old friend at all.

When he'd realized how close Carter had gotten to Sydney, he'd reacted without thought, bringing her to Tristin's fortress of a house. He knew her ex wouldn't know to find her there, and the security measures made the house the safest place for her. He didn't regret the decision, but he had reservations about putting her in the hands of the Alpha Team. If he was wrong about trusting them, it could mean Sydney's life. He wasn't sure he could take that gamble.

Everyone's body language indicated they were all business. He wanted to hit something because, for him, this was personal. If Carter had only come for him, he could have easily handled it. But he'd come for Sydney, and Cole was concerned with how far her ex would go to get back at her.

Cole rested his stare on his friend, who sat at the head of the table.

"I'm not going to beat around the bush. We don't have time for that. Emmett Carter is not a stranger to us, Panther. The Alpha Team has been investigating him for a while. We've come close to taking him down, but just when we catch a break, he slips away, or our evidence disappears."

Cole's eyes narrowed. "Why are you investigating Carter?"

"Human trafficking."

The words hung heavy in the air, echoing in the ensuring silence until the two words rang in Cole's ears. "What the... Sydney never said anything about human trafficking."

"As far as we can tell she doesn't know."

"Why are you investigating and not the feds?"

They sat in silence once again, the men's eyes dropping. Cole sensed a shift in the air, but he couldn't pinpoint what was going on. Finally, he slammed his fists on top of the table to grab their attention.

"Answer me!"

"Because there's not enough evidence to link him to his criminal activities, so the feds can't waste the resources to investigate," Jay explained. "We're not letting this go until we bring him down."

Cole leveled a glare at Jay and then Tristin as the truth dawned on him. "If you think for one minute that I'm going to let you use Syd to get to Carter, then you're crazy. He beat her and now he's harassing her. You can't expect her to become involved."

"We need her, Panther. She could be the link to put Carter away and stop him from hurting any more women. Before you get angry and threaten to beat the shit out of us, just listen. Once you hear us out, I think you'll want in on this."

Cole glared at Tristin for several seconds before motioning for him to continue.

"We've been tracking him for years, but he's adept at keeping his criminal activities secure while maintaining a public image of someone with power and influence. At one time, we had a witness connecting him to the kidnapping of young women to sell to the highest bidder. She was one of his victims who managed to escape, but somehow he got to her while she was in witness protection and threatened her and her family. She committed suicide to be free of him."

The fact that the entire group sobered at that bit of intel didn't escape Cole's notice. Cole's eyes flashed and his body tensed. He kept quiet, wanting to hear it all, but his stomach churned.

Jay took over. "Our evidence couldn't stand up against Carter without our witness, so the case fell apart. But with the intel we had, we felt confident we could take the operation down from the inside. We sent in an undercover operative, Sam Montgomery, the man you saw just a moment ago."

"No offense, but he doesn't seem like the type Carter would trust," Cole returned.

"None taken. That's what made Sam perfect. They never saw him coming," Tristin said. "At that time, Carter was using a local gang to run his drug trafficking operation to keep his own hands clean. Sam started by getting in good with the gang, and the opportunity came for him to be present when the gang leaders met with Carter. It turns out Carter was also using the gang's connections to transport his kidnap victims to various locations. The gang offered up Sam as a possible transporter. His new role gave us what we needed to join the FBI and DEA in a planned raid during one of these transports. We figured we could turn those involved to implicate Carter and put him away."

"Before the raid," Jay continued, "somehow Sam's cover was blown. We're not sure how. His cover was deep, air-tight, but they found out about him and about the raid. We didn't realize it until we went to conduct the raid, and we were ambushed. A DEA agent lost his life, and others were injured. We took down some of the gang members, but Carter and his partners were nowhere to be found. And neither was Sam. We finally broke one of the gang members into confessing where they were keeping Sam. We infiltrated the drug den, but not before they beat Sam within an inch of his life."

"Shit!" Cole hissed.

"Sam's girlfriend, Monica, gave birth to their son, Aidan, at that time. That's when he decided to step back from the Alpha Team and move into investigations. It's his spot you're filling," Tristin explained. "We've put away many of the gang members, even some major players. But for some reason, they won't turn on him, and Carter got away again with no evidence to connect him to what went down. They're afraid of something, maybe him."

"We're closer than we've ever been, but we still need more to lock him up," Jay said fiercely.

Cole's blood ran cold. "And Sydney is your key. But how can she help if you're sure she wasn't involved?"

BB interjected. "From what we've been able to tell, she was part of Carter's cover. He kept her under his thumb and brought her out when he needed someone on his arm to keep up appearances. The guy's a master when it comes to living two different lives. As far as his society contacts are concerned, he's a shrewd businessman. No one suspects that he's selling women off to the highest bidder, or that he even abused Sydney. He has everyone believing he dumped her because she was after his money."

"That still doesn't explain how she can help."

"Before we get into that, I want the team brought up to speed on what happened last night," Tristin suggested.

Cole fought the urge to demand more information. If he wanted to be a part of this team, he needed to follow the boss' lead and let this briefing play out as Tristin intended.

"You probably already know most of it," Cole began. "After knowing exactly why Sydney was running from Carter at the hotel, when I saw her again at the gym, I made sure she had a way to contact me. I wanted her to know she had someone to call on if Carter decided to harass her. Anyway, Sydney was at this taco place getting food for a girls' night with her friend who was just here, and

Carter ambushed her in the parking lot. She dialed her phone so her friend could hear what was going on and call for help, but instead of Chloe, she dialed me by mistake. I was here with Kat and Tryst and headed straight over there when I realized what was going on. I sort of gave Carter the impression Syd and I were together, so he'd know he couldn't mess with her without going through me. I followed Sydney home to make sure Carter wasn't lying in wait for her. Since Chloe ended up canceling their plans, Syd invited me to stay for dinner. That's how I was there when she got a call from Carter. He somehow managed to get through the security at Sydney's apartment building and gain access to the parking garage. He vandalized my truck and Sydney's car and then called to harass her and threaten me. I brought her here to keep him from getting to her until I could figure out how he managed to get in."

"He didn't hurt her last night?" Zane asked, his voice rough and deep from lack of use.

"No. I'm guessing he didn't try because he knew I was there," Cole explained. "I'm sure he didn't like seeing me come to Sydney's rescue, so the vandalism was retaliation. What I don't get, is why he's harassing her now. Syd said she left him months ago, and he's left her alone until recently."

"We can't answer that either," Jay returned. "We knew about his relationship with Sydney, but after she left him, Carter moved on to other pursuits, so we never approached her about helping us. We've been tracking Carter after getting wind of another auction he's involved in. KSI was already lined up to provide security at the charity event, but when we found out Carter had decided to crash the party, the team went in instead of our typical security team to get close to him."

"What do you mean, crash the party? I thought you said this was the sort of social circle Carter ran in."

"Yes, but he wasn't on the guest list for that night. Horizons Marketing shared the list with us so we'd know what to expect in terms of security. Sydney was on the list, so I figure her friend made sure Carter wasn't," Tristin explained.

"Do you think Carter knew she'd be there?"

"Maybe," Jay replied. "We don't know for sure. We forced Carter out of the ballroom, but he managed to slip away from us before we could take advantage of the situation. After what happened, though, we started looking at Sydney again as a resource for intel on Carter. Seeing her at the gym was a surprise, but realizing you knew her gave us a way to reach out to her."

Cole's desire to protect Sydney rocketed through him. "I told you I won't let you use Sydney – or me – to get to Carter. It's not happening."

"Stand down, Panther," Tristin growled. "It's not like that. Kat did some research on Sydney some time ago, and we learned she excelled as a computer programmer. When we decided to reach out to her for help with the case, Kat suggested we hire her to work at KSI. Her employment is not contingent on her help. We want her to work for us even if she decides not to get involved. We will also protect her regardless of what she decides about the job and the case."

"I don't just want Sydney protected," Cole said quietly as rage burned within him. "I want her to feel safe from Carter. I want this guy taken down."

"That's the plan," Zane said, surprising everyone. The most he customarily contributed to conversation were nods of affirmation or grunts of dissent, and he'd already spoken more than usual in this one meeting.

"What, exactly, is the plan?" Cole grumbled.

"First, let's fill you in on what we've done to protect Sydney," Tristin said. He nodded to BB to continue.

"Kat tapped into Sydney's phone records, and we were able to track the number Emmett called her from. We've blocked it from Sydney's phone, which will only work for a little while as Sydney said. I have a burner phone set up with a tracker implanted. There's no way it can be hacked, so the only way Carter can get her number is if someone gives it to him. If Sydney runs into trouble, there's a special button she can press. An alert is instantly sent to the KSI network, and we have immediate access to track her phone and pinpoint her location. I've also gained access to the security feed at Sydney's apartment building. It confirms what Jay found out about how Carter gained access to the parking garage."

BB pulled out a laptop and booted it up before motioning for the team to gather around him. He cued the video footage to play. Cole shook his head in disbelief as he watched Emmett charm a female security guard into allowing him access to the parking garage.

"I questioned the guard this morning," Jay added. "She's brand new to the job. Carter told her he was leaving a surprise for his girlfriend. He never mentioned Sydney by name, so she had no idea who he was. He even had a dozen roses to sell his story. He tried to gain access to the building, but she knew that could cost her job even if his story was legit. She's been placed on probation in light of what happened."

"Kat and I have a call in to a friend of ours who owns a high-security building. He's checking into what vacancies he had, and we should know by the end of the day when we can move Sydney into a new place. We've vetted the security there, so we know she's safe from Carter getting to her. In the meantime, she's free to stay here," Tristin offered.

Cole's mind felt ready to burst with all of the intel the team threw at him. One looming question still remained unanswered. "How do you plan to take him down?"

"First, we need Sydney to accept my job offer. If I know my wife, she's convincing Syd to do that as we speak."

"She doesn't need a job."

"I get that Sydney has her own private clients, but she has a great reputation in cyber security. I see no reason why she can't keep her clients and still work for KSI. We could use her. We're hoping she can use what she knows of Carter to gain access to the SOB's movements, his known associates, his accounts, everything we need to catch him but might have missed. But she would also be an asset to our special ops teams when they're on missions."

"And by involving her in your investigation on Carter, you've increased the danger she's in. You just said her ignorance of his activities is what kept her alive. If this guy is as good as you say, he'll figure out she's involved once she goes to work for KSI."

"He won't hurt her again," Zane spoke up, his expression as hard as if carved in granite.

"Sydney has the protection of Alpha Team now, Panther," Jay said. "We'll protect her with our lives, if that's what it takes."

"That's not enough, I'm afraid," Tristin said gravely.

Cole shot his friend a look that would have cowered a weaker man. "What do you mean?"

"Look, Panther, we're going to do everything in our power to protect Sydney and Chloe—"

"Chloe?" Cole interrupted.

"Carter is not above attacking a loved one if he feels threatened by someone or wants to blackmail someone," Tristin explained. "We know from our research that Chloe is as close to family as Sydney has. We can't risk the chance that Carter will use Chloe to lure Sydney away from us. He has resources everywhere, even in law enforcement. In fact, we should make sure Sydney can protect herself even if we're not around, just in case."

"She wants that too, apparently," Jay returned. "She signed up for Travis' self-defense class. I think she'd be open to one-on-one lessons."

"I'll teach her," Cole growled.

"That's not a good idea," Tristin disagreed, not cowering under the death glare his friend sent his way. "You're too emotionally involved in this now. Plus, we could use you more in tracking Carter."

"I'll do it," Zane offered.

Though they were his teammates now, the idea of one of them spending that much time with their hands-on Sydney was enough to make Cole see red. "Like hell, you will!"

"Actually, that's a good idea," Jay intervened. "Zane, you'll take over Sydney's training. We'll put Sam and Isobel on Chloe's protection detail. The rest of us will focus on closing in on Carter."

"If anyone is going to train Sydney, it will be me," Cole protested, his tone dangerously low.

"Relax, Panther," Tristin spoke good-naturedly but firmly. "You don't have to worry about us making a move on your girl. I'm happily married, and we all live by the bro code. I told you. Sydney is one of us, so we'll do whatever it takes to protect her and equip her to protect herself."

Cole rose from the table and angrily paced the dining room. Finally, he pierced Zane with his eyes, attempting to read the man's expression. The guy's face was like granite, giving nothing away. Zane had a story, one that Cole didn't think his old friend Tristin would share with him. Some stories were for the man and no one else to tell, and Cole sensed Zane's situation fell into that category.

One thing Cole did know was Zane was a pro. Tryst wouldn't trust him to train Sydney or be a part of the Alpha Team if he wasn't. Cole never imagined relying on another team the way he did his old SEAL team, but here he was with the opportunity to do just that. And it started with him placing Sydney's protection into Zane's hands.

"Train her. I don't want her to be afraid of that scum anymore."

Zane gave a single nod, and the deal was made. Tryst's eyes gleamed with approval. He nodded to Jay to continue the meeting.

"Now that we have Sydney taken care of, we need to set our next move. BB, have you had any luck tracking down our leak?"

"Leak?" Cole latched on to the word as a scowl darkened his face. "You have a leak in the company?"

"We don't think so," Tristin explained. "We think it's someone among our DEA contacts or a confidential informant of the DEA's who tried to play both sides. First, an undercover DEA agent was killed. Then Sam's cover was blown. If the leak was someone at KSI, the cartel would have known Sam was working with us and was not another undercover DEA agent. The intel was faulty, so it has to be someone familiar with the investigation but not close enough to it to know of our involvement."

"I've been going through our surveillance of Sam's movements, his wire-taps, and any other intel we had on the cartel. Kat and I have dug into any known associates of the cartel and Carter. Nothing panned out. So, I started scoping out the DEA's known informants. A couple have dealings with the cartel, but no red flags turned up," BB reported dismally.

"In other words, we got nothing," Wings returned dryly.

"Kat is doing some more digging, but Carter's good. He leaves no footprint, makes no mistakes. My guess is whoever is tipping him off is someone who follows his example. He's going to be hard to find," BB explained.

"If he's that good, how did he ever wind up on the DEA's radar in the first place?" Cole asked.

An eerie silence fell over the room. The team's eyes, including

Tristin's, rested on Jay. The team leader showed no signs of losing his cool other than the subtle stiffening of his jaw. The fine hairs on the back of Cole's neck tingled. He waited, watchful of each man. No one seemed in a hurry to answer his question. Just when he thought he was being soundly ignored, Jay spoke while his eyes focused unseeingly on a spot in front of him.

"Three years ago, a girl was kidnapped while shopping here in town. There were no leads to her whereabouts until a year later. The girl escaped and found her way to the police, who called in the FBI who called in the DEA. She was a pretty girl, so they kidnapped her to sell her in an online auction on the dark web."

Jay's voice was deadpan, but Cole felt the emotional charge of his words. He stayed quiet, letting the story unfold while wondering at the rest of the team's silence.

"Before she could be sold, she caught Carter's eye. He decided instead of selling her, he would keep her as his own toy. He had the cartel keep her prisoner until he was able to break her. He starved her, abused her and raped her. She convinced him she was under his spell because she knew it was her only hope of survival. When he was certain he'd broken her, he moved her to his home. That's when she escaped. She found her way to the police and told them everything, including who her captor was. Carter was arrested and set to go to trial."

"So, what happened?" Cole asked quietly when Jay's story faltered. "Did he stand trial?"

"The prosecution's case rested on the girl's testimony. Before the trial date, he got to her somehow. He told her garbage about how she belonged to him, and he would find a way to get to her, even if he had to kill her family and her protectors to do it. She was convinced he would haunt her forever. She committed suicide."

Tristin walked up behind Jay and placed a hand on the man's

massive shoulder, effectively stemming the flow of words. Cole's eyes met the tortured gaze of his old friend.

"The girl was Jay's baby sister, Addison," Tristin explained, taking Cole's breath away with the pronouncement. "She was in town visiting Jay and was spending the day shopping while Jay was at work when she was kidnapped. We never stopped searching, but we never knew to watch out for Carter until Addison escaped and told us and the authorities everything. If we went by our intel and investigations alone, we wouldn't even consider Carter a suspect. His record is that squeaky clean. But we now know better. And we'll take him down. The evidence against him before now has been weak and circumstantial. We hope Sydney can help us build a more concrete case."

Cole folded his arms across his chest as the silence stretched between them. He realized they all waited for him to make the next move.

"It's up to Sydney, if she wants to be involved. Either way, I'm in. This guy needs to be stopped."

"Then let's regroup in the war room at KSI. We'll get Panther's perspective on this case and strategize our next move. The next auction can't be too far down the road, and I want him stopped before we lose any more women."

As the group moved into action, Cole couldn't stop himself from walking up to Jay and extending his hand. The team leader stared at the palm for a moment before accepting the handshake. Cole caught the other man's gaze.

"We are going to take him down," Cole vowed, his voice low so only Jay could hear his words. "For Sydney and for Addison."

The team leader simply nodded as he returned Cole's firm grip. The next instant they dropped the handshake and joined the others in going to work.

Chapter Eleven

Sydney couldn't recall the last time she had laughed so hard. Kat and Chloe seemed to click right off the bat. Both shared a dry sense of humor that fed their easy banter. Sydney had tears in her eyes and a stitch in her side from the laughter. She had actually forgotten they were being followed by their very own bodyguard, and so far, they had managed to talk about everything but her problems with Emmett and what was going on with Cole, Tristan and the others. Curiosity still burned within her to know what was happening, but she couldn't escape the doubt that made her question having involved so many people in her problems.

Sydney wondered how much longer Chloe would allow the lighthearted fun to continue before she demanded an explanation. She hid it well, but Chloe was hurt.

Brunch brought the three ladies to a small but intimate bistro Sydney never knew existed. Bistro on the Corner provided them with a booth where they had privacy but were visible to their bodyguard, who sat nearby but not within hearing distance. Their light-hearted conversation and laughter continued until their waitress brought mimosas and an assortment of omelets, fruits, and muffins. That's when Kat steered the conversation to more serious subjects.

"There's a lot we need to talk about. Please know, both of you, that what we say here now stays between us."

Sydney nodded, but Chloe merely pierced her with a reserved stare. Sydney shifted uncomfortably in her seat next to Kat.

"What happened last night?" Chloe demanded.

Holding her friend's gaze, Sydney described running into Emmett, how Cole came to her aid when she mistakenly contacted him, and how Emmett retaliated by vandalizing her car and Cole's truck. Once she concluded her story, silence stretched between them. Chloe's expression never wavered, giving Sydney no indication of what she was thinking.

"I wasn't there for you," Chloe finally said.

Sydney placed her hand on Chloe's forearm. "You're always there for me. But mistakenly calling Cole made me realize how much I need to stand up to Emmett on my own, without relying on others. I can't expect you to drop everything to come to my aid whenever I call."

"You don't think it's weird that Cole dropped everything to come to your aid, without you even asking?" Chloe said.

"No need to ask Cole or any of the boys," Kat answered. "They just act out of instinct."

"What do you mean?" Sydney asked.

"Everyone at KSI has a protective instinct a mile wide. Most of it is a result of their military service, but it's also because they're good people. They're not perfect, but if you ever need anyone to have your back, you can't go wrong with any of them. Trust me on this. Even if Cole had never met Sydney before, if his gut told him she was in trouble, his instinct to protect her would overshadow everything else."

Sydney felt a stab in her chest. The idea of Cole wanting to be with her only out of an ingrained protective instinct bothered her.

Wake up, Syd. This is the proof you needed that you're reading too much in his interest in you, and you're allowing your emotions to rule over your better judgment.

"Too bad their instinct isn't to beat Emmett into a coma so he'll leave Syd alone," Chloe muttered.

"He'll leave me alone. Eventually," Sydney said softly. "He did it before. The only reason I'm back on his radar is because he was mad to see me mingling with his society friends."

"I hate to say this, but I don't think it will be that easy. There's a lot you don't know about Emmett Carter," Kat said cryptically.

Two pairs of eyes rounded on Kat, staring at her as if she'd grown multiple heads in the time they sat at the bistro. The woman smiled slightly before allowing her attention to be caught by something over Chloe's shoulder. Chloe never removed her gaze, but Sydney followed Kat's line of sight to where Sam sat some distance away, talking on his cell phone. Kat waited until Sam hung up, giving her a slight nod. She then returned her attention to the pair of friends.

"What do you know about Emmett that we don't?" Chloe demanded.

"Nothing good," Kat admitted. "Look, I'll tell you everything, but for you to understand, you'll need to hear me out without interruption. I'll answer all of your questions, but it's better if you wait to ask me until I've finished."

"Then start talking," Chloe ordered, even as Sydney sat by quietly. Dread filled her, and she almost stopped Kat from talking. She wasn't sure she could handle knowing more terrible things about her ex.

"I have spent a lot of time digging into Emmett's life. That's part of my job at Knight Security and Investigations. He's been on our radar for a long time, for a lot of reasons. It hasn't been easy. He's very good at keeping his personal life and his criminal activities separate and private."

"Criminal activit....You mean, the abuse?" Sydney's voice broke on the word "abuse," a shudder passing through her body.

"You don't think Sydney hasn't checked out the SOB? What

could you possibly know that she doesn't?" Chloe interrupted.

"This is why I asked you to listen until I finish," Kat gently admonished. "No, Sydney, I'm not just talking about the abuse. There's more. The reason I know this is because we had access to intel that you didn't – information from another one of his victims."

Sydney dropped her gaze to her mimosa. She hated that word – "*victim.*" It felt like too apt of a description for how helpless she felt when she was with Emmett.

"Was she a girlfriend?" Chloe again failed to hold her question until Kat finished.

"Not by choice."

Sydney's head snapped up. "What do you mean?"

"This isn't easy to say. The witness was someone he kidnapped. Or had kidnapped by some friends of his. Major players in the international drug trade."

"Drugs?" Sydney interjected before she could stop herself. "Kidnapping?"

"No way in hell!" Chloe exploded. "Emmett is a little chicken shit. No way does he have the smarts or the balls to sell drugs or kidnap someone."

"I would have known. He couldn't be involved in something like that without me knowing." Sydney felt her body grow cold.

"Emmett didn't want you to know. He's very good at covering his tracks. Believe me. It's very true. Sam can attest to that," Kat told them, prompting both Sydney and Chloe to send curious stares at their bodyguard. He merely nodded in their direction before continuing his surveillance of their surroundings. "Sam went undercover with a drug cartel almost a year ago – a drug cartel that worked very closely with your ex. He was tortured because of how close he came to uncovering Emmett."

Tears pricked at Sydney's eyes. "Emmett tortured Sam?"

"He ordered it, but he was very careful not to reveal himself to Sam once he suspected Sam of being a DEA agent," Kat elaborated.

"He's a DEA agent?" Chloe interrupted. "I thought he worked for KSI with you."

"He does. Maybe I should start again," Kat suggested. "It's a long story. Our witness who helped us connect Emmett with kidnapping was also able to tell us about his drug cartel connection and his involvement with human trafficking."

"Did you say human trafficking?" Sydney felt the color drain from her face.

"This is unbelievable," Chloe muttered.

"I know this is hard to take in, but our witness was very reliable and trustworthy. She was the reason we know as much as we do about him. But before Emmett could stand trial, the witness died, and the case fell apart. The DEA sent someone in undercover to get close to him, but he was killed when his cover was blown. That's when the DEA came to us for help. This case is very personal for us. Sam was sent in undercover with the drug cartel with the hope that would open the door to Emmett. He got very close, but then his cover was blown. They never suspected our involvement. They thought it was the DEA trying to get to them again."

"You expect us to believe the DEA would hire you to close one of their cases. That doesn't make any sense." Chloe crossed her arms over her chest to emphasize her disbelief.

"There's more to KSI that just simple surveillance and investigations into cheating spouses. This is where I'm going to have to ask for your discretion. There's a reason only particular people know this about the company, so I have to ask you that no matter what happens today, you'll not tell anyone about this. There's a division of KSI that deals with cases government or law enforcement agencies can't close for various reasons. Usually there are government sanctions that prevent them from gaining the intel they need to close the cases. They come to KSI because we are under no such sanctions."

"I can't believe this. It sounds like a bad action-adventure movie," Sydney muttered.

"It's hard to wrap your mind around, I know. And it's a lot of information all at once, but I think you need to know everything. We can take a break if you want though. We can order a second round of mimosas."

"I might as well hear it all." Sydney nodded for Kat to continue.

"What Sam went through was…horrific. He was a member of the same special ops team that Cole has now joined, the Alpha Team. After what he went through, he stepped down to work the security and investigations side of the house. His girlfriend, Monica, had just had their baby, a sweet boy named Aidan. With all that happened, he and Monica decided his role as a dad was more important than his role on the team.

"Only a select few knew of our involvement, and still Sam's cover was blown. All this time, we've come so close to getting evidence on Emmett's criminal activities, but he's managed to stay one step ahead of us. The DEA suspects they have a mole within their agency who's working with the cartel and Emmett. They decided to back down and let us take over the investigation. We chose to take a different route. And we're hoping you can help us."

Sydney blinked, her mouth flying open in a surprised oval. "Me? I already told you I didn't know Emmett was involved in any of this."

"And we believe that. During our investigation, we found out about your relationship with Emmett, and we knew he kept you in the dark about everything. We never considered involving you in this at all. Especially since you ended things with him. But when he came after you at the hotel, we wondered if you might hold the key to this whole thing."

"Wait." Chloe leaned forward, bracing her arms on top of the table. "Was the reason you guys took the security job for the charity benefit was to get to Sydney?"

"Your company came to us first. But who we put on the job had something to do with Sydney. Our regular security team was lined up to work the event, but we got word that Emmett was in town and planning to crash the event. So, we sent the Alpha Team to work it just in case. It also gave Cole a chance to work with the team and consider joining."

"Did you know he was going to come after me?" Sydney started wringing her hands. Just when she thought she had her act together, she realized people were working to control events in her life without her knowledge. The thought was unsettling.

"No, of course not. We knew you were on the guest list, but just like you, we thought he'd moved on once you left him. We never expected him to harass you or even threaten you like he has."

"So why didn't you arrest him at the party? Instead he shows up at Sydney's apartment building and destroyed her car." Chloe's eyes narrowed. "I think I've heard enough. Let's go, Syd. We'll call an Uber."

"Please, wait. You said you would hear me out. I want to finish." Kat's eyes pleaded with them to give her a chance, and it was Sydney who nodded her agreement, forcing Chloe to begrudgingly agree to listen.

"Our plan was to detain him for questioning. We hoped he'd give us a clue as to what his next target is, but he slipped away before our guys could get to him. And we weren't expecting him to go after Sydney like he has. They've been over for months, and he's never approached her or contacted her at all during that time. His behavior now doesn't make sense."

"He needs me for something." Emmett's words returned to her in a rush. He had a purpose for her, and knowing what he was involved in, she felt her stomach churn at what that might be.

"What?" Chloe demanded.

Sydney met her friend's probing gaze. "He told me. When he confronted me at Tony's. He said he let me leave because he didn't have a use for me, but now he does. And that's why I can't escape him."

"What could he want?" Kat reached out to place a hand on Sydney's forearm where it rested on the table.

Sydney shrugged. "I don't know, and I really don't want to know. I don't want anything to do with him or anything he's involved in."

"I understand. But if we can figure out what he wants from you, we can figure out what he's up to. It could be our key to bringing him down." Kat's earnest gaze belied the gentleness of her tone.

"You're not using my best friend as a pawn in whatever this is." Chloe's eyes flashed.

"Not a pawn. As a resource. With Sydney's computer skills and inside knowledge of Emmett, she could help us," Kat explained. "But even if she didn't help us, we still want her a part of KSI. As part of our technical support team."

Kat nudged Sydney's shoulder so the redhead would look at her. "I'm offering you a job, Sydney. At KSI. And not because of your connection to Emmett. But I do think you are the key to helping us bring him down. And I think he believes that too. That's why he's so intent on intimidating and scaring you."

"What can I do that none of you have been able to do after all of this time?" Sydney countered. "I'm not the one to help you. I have to worry more about helping myself. If Emmett isn't going away, I have to learn how to fight him."

"Our guys can help you with that. And our guys can protect you and Chloe, too."

"Me?" Chloe interjected. "Why do I need protection? He's not after me."

"Emmett would not be above hurting someone Sydney loves if he thinks it will get him what he wants," Kat said gently. "Truth be told, Sydney, after I discovered your relationship with Emmett during my research, I wanted to bring you on board then. As an employee of KSI. You're an amazing hacker, and even if you don't work on Emmett's case with us, you would be an asset to the company. Tristin agrees. Even if you choose not to help us, even if you and Cole are no longer friends or whatever you are, we would still like for you to work for us."

"I can't believe you're offering me a job in the middle of all of this."

"I know it's an unorthodox way to do it, but yes, I am. I know you have your own clients. You're welcome to keep them, but you'll be working with them under the KSI umbrella. They will remain your clients. You will be the only tech working with them, and if you leave KSI, your clients go with you. We hope you'll help, but we hope you'll also find you like working for us. And the protection is there until Emmett is no longer a threat. Tristin can put it all in writing for you, so you know we're legitimate."

Sydney caught Chloe's eye, the two communicating with that one look. Kat's story was tough to swallow. As cruel as Emmett had been to her, she had a hard time believing he was involved in such heinous crimes without her even suspecting. How close had she come to being kidnapped and sold herself? What would have happened to her if she hadn't left him when she did?

"I'm sorry to have thrown this all at you, especially since I've had a great time getting to know both of you. I'm going to leave you alone. You two need to talk without strangers listening. Finish your brunch, and let Sam take you to the salon for those mani-pedis. Then you can have him take you back to my place, where you're welcome to stay until we find you a safer place to live. Please know, as crazy as all of this seems, we're on your side, Sydney." Kat placed a gentle hand on Sydney's shoulder before she walked over to Sam, probably to fill him in on the change in plans.

The best friends sat silently for several minutes. When the waitress came over to check on them, Chloe ordered another round of mimosas. Chloe sipped her fresh mimosa before she finally spoke.

"Wow."

The one word was enough to break the tension of the moment. Sydney smirked as an inappropriate bubble of laughter threatened to burst forth. Chloe's eyes gleamed. Then as if someone flipped a switch, both started to chuckle, which grew into a giggle which expanded into full-fledge belly laughs. They drew attention, including a curious look from Sam, but they didn't care. The absurdity of the brunch and the crazy turn Sydney's life had just taken hit them full force. It was a matter of laughing uncontrollably or crying their eyes out over the circumstances. Sydney and Chloe always chose laughter over tears.

"Leave it to me to be engaged to a criminal and never know it," Sydney managed to say as she struggled to control her amusement. "Could I be any more of a loser?"

"You're not the loser. Emmett is. I've just never dreamed Emmett had it in him," Chloe drawled. "Who would have thought he had the cunning to live a double life? I mean he's a manipulator for sure, but to operate two separate lives like that without anyone suspecting, that takes some serious intellect that I never gave him credit for."

Sydney managed to calm down and sobered. "I don't know what to do."

"Do you trust them? Or at the very least, do you trust this Cole person?"

"It's crazy, and it scares me. But yeah, I trust him. He helped me hide from Emmett at the hotel, and then he came all the way to Tony's to help me without me even asking him. He stayed with me last night, so I wouldn't have to be alone. And then the minute Emmett threatened me, he took me somewhere safe. I don't know him very well, but I do trust him. And if he trusts the others, then so do I."

"How can you be sure you can trust him? Or any of them, for that matter?" Chloe insisted. "All of this seems to be a huge coincidence. They could have been tracking you, looking for an opportunity to gain your trust so you would help them."

Sydney sighed again. "I know. I thought of that. If they orchestrated anything, it was without Cole's knowledge. I'm sure of it."

"What are you going to do?"

"What do you think I should do?"

"It's not for me to say. This is your choice. I'm just here to back you up no matter what."

Sydney shot her friend a disbelieving look. "Come on, Chloe, I know you too well. You have an opinion. So, spill it."

Chloe regarded her friend over the rim of her glass as she took another swig of her mimosa. "I think you should take the job but keep your distance from Cole."

"Why?"

"Why should you take the job, or why should you keep your distance from Cole?"

"Both."

"Well, first of all, you don't know anything about Cole. I appreciate he was there for you and protected you when you needed it, but all of this is too much of a coincidence. Your life is complicated enough right now without him adding to that. As far as the job, before we contracted with KSI to provide security, I screened them closely. They're the best. Their reputation is solid. Plus, I like Kat. I think she was giving it to you straight. I think taking the job will be good for you. And it could be a way for you to stick it to Emmett. Can you imagine his reaction when he finds out you were instrumental in having him arrested? I hope I'm there to see it."

"I work in cyber security, not crime fighting. I think they're overestimating my abilities. Plus, I like setting my own hours and not answering to a boss," Sydney argued. "I'm not sure taking the job makes sense."

"If anything, you're underestimating yourself. Do what you want, but I think this would be a great opportunity. The whole cyber security thing was to get you on your feet after leaving Emmett. This…this could give you a purpose that you've been looking for."

"That's true," Sydney said thoughtfully. "Okay. I'll at least talk to them more about the job. I'm not saying I'll take it. I need more details first."

"And Cole?"

"I don't know. I felt a connection with him I've never felt with anyone before, and it's scary how fast it happened. I should be careful because I don't know if he even feels the same. But I'm not afraid of what I'm feeling. It's crazy to say, but it's the truth. Staying away from him won't be easy."

"And if you don't, he could easily shatter your heart. I just want you to be careful."

Sydney smiled at her friend's candor. "Could you at least talk to him first before you peg him as a heartbreaker?"

Chloe shrugged. "Fine. Until he gives me a reason not to, I'll give him the benefit of the doubt that he's a good guy. You just have to give yourself some distance. Don't put yourself in a situation to be dependent on him."

"How do you suggest I do that? Especially since he and his team of super soldiers are my 24/7 bodyguards."

Chloe grinned. "I have to admit. That is the one thing about this situation that doesn't bother me. I mean, come on, if all the guys at that house this morning are on your protection detail, man, oh, man! I would have a hard time choosing one. They are all hooooottttt."

Sydney laughed. "Very true. Maybe we can find you a boyfriend among them."

Chloe sipped her mimosa before shaking her head. "I wouldn't mind hooking up with one or two of them, but a boyfriend? I can do without that. Boyfriends are too high maintenance."

"Maybe you're right. I could do without some high maintenance in my life. I just want things to be normal, but that's not in the cards for me, is it?"

"No," Chloe returned candidly. "There is nothing about you that's normal, Sydney, and nothing about your life has ever been normal. But that's okay. This is just one more challenge in your abnormal life, and believe me when I say, you will overcome this one as you have overcome them all. You're stronger than those challenges. Believe that."

Unexpected tears pooled in her eyes as she was reminded once again why Chloe was the truest friend she had ever known.

Chapter Twelve

Cole strode through the door to Tristin's office but paused when he saw his old friend on the phone. Tristin motioned for him to sit while he continued the conversation. It didn't take long for Cole to realize whom Tristin was on his cell phone with. The grin on his friend's face piqued his curiosity.

"Wow, Sam. Sounds like you need to watch your back while you're watching theirs," Tristin teased with a chuckle. He paused, listening to Sam's reply. "And Sydney never mentioned anything about the job or Carter?" Another pause. "Okay. Keep me posted."

Cole stayed silent as Tristin ended the call and tossed his cell onto his desk.

"Your girlfriend and her friend are giving Sam a run for his money, but they're good. He said there's been no sign of Carter. That could mean one of two things—either he hasn't found out where Sydney escaped to, or he's laying low trying to decide how to get to her."

"It's hard to guess, but I don't believe he's given up on her."

Tristin studied him. "She could be the key to drawing him out, getting him to make a move."

Cole returned his friend's regard. "I won't let you use her as bait. We take him down without her."

Tristin released a breath, his expression grave. "We've been trying, but he's one step ahead of us. I want to bury him."

Cole growled. "We'll get him. I swear we'll get him. We don't need to use Sydney to do it."

"How? You got any leads? Because right now, Sydney is our only one."

"I will keep Sydney safe, and that means keeping her away from Emmett Carter. I meant it when I said you will not use her. I will find something to bring him down. I want to bury him worse than you."

Tristin's eyes narrowed. "Not alone. No cowboy stuff. You're part of Alpha Team now. They're the best. Trust them, Panther. Carter is not someone to take on by yourself. He's managed to give the best agents in the world the slip. If we don't use Sydney as a resource, then I don't know how long it will take for us to get him."

Cole's eyes narrowed, his scowl furrowing his brows. Tristin held up a hand to silence his friend's next words.

"I'm not talking about using her as bait. I'm talking about making her part of the investigation behind the scenes. She may know more than she realizes. We need all the leads we can get. Jay and his family and the families of his other victims deserve to see him rot in jail."

Cole fell silent. He brought one leg on top of the other, resting the ankle of the right on the thigh of the left. His elbow rested on the arm of his chair, and his hand cupped his chin as he considered his friend – and now his boss. Tristin's words rang true, but the truth didn't sit well with Cole. After what Sydney went through at Carter's hands, Cole wanted her as far away from her ex as he could get her.

"I won't let you bully her," he finally said. "You involve her only as much as she wants to be involved. If she's had enough, you back off. Catching this SOB is not on her shoulders. It's on ours."

"I want to help."

The sound of Sydney's delicate voice was like a jolt to Cole's system. He unfolded his legs so he could twist in his chair to see her. His eyes drank in the sight of her. Her fiery hair hung over her shoulders, the strands curling softly to frame her face. Her cheeks flushed as she met his stare.

Tristin stood with a warm smile for his guests. "Hello, ladies. Enjoy your trip to the salon? How did the pedicure turn out, Sam?"

"Shut up, Tryst," Sam growled.

"Tryst?" Chloe piped up, her gaze moving between the two men.

"Short for Tristin," Sydney explained, earning a snort of derision from Sam, who muttered "among other things" under his breath as he sat in one of the chairs close to Tristin's desk.

"We appreciate the pampering, Tristin, but I asked Sam to bring us here so I could talk to you about the job offer Kat told me about. And to ask how I can help you get the evidence you need against Emmett."

Cole rose in one fluid motion and stood in front of her before she could blink. His hands encircled her biceps, his grip light, and he lowered his head until he was eye-to-eye with her. Her eyes were wide, the blue irises darkening. A silent gasp left her full lips slightly parted. This close to her, the urge to kiss her welled up within him, but he forced it away to focus on the task at hand.

"You don't have to do this. Take the job if you want, but there's no need to put yourself back in Carter's sights. We'll protect you either way. You've been through enough with him."

"I never knew there were other women he abused. And to sell women to the highest bidder…I can't believe I never knew just how much of a monster he is. I don't know how I can help, but I can't live with myself if I don't try."

His gut churned. He resisted his instinct to order her to stay away from the case. As much as he wanted her to hide away until they took Carter down, he couldn't smother her act of bravery. If anything, she managed to endear herself to him even more.

"Promise me something?"

"What is that?"

"The minute things get too dangerous for you, you'll let me take you to a safe house to wait it out. Your safety is too important for us to compromise for the sake of a case."

Her smile was soft, her eyes darkening with warmth. "I promise not to do anything to compromise my safety."

She didn't exactly agree to his demand, but he would accept it for now. He dropped his hands and stepped away as Tristin moved to join them.

"Kat is down at the command center. Why don't we go there and get the details worked out about the job? Then we'll call everyone together and start working the case. Thank you, Sydney, for being willing to help us."

"I don't know how much help I'll be."

"Considering our case has been nothing but dead ends for a while now, anything you do would be a plus," Tristin said. "But it's only a bonus. What you bring to the company is so much more, and the last thing I want is for Carter to be threatening one of our own. And you are one of us now, Sydney."

The smile lighting Sydney's face lifted Cole's mood. He realized he'd give anything to keep that smile on her face and to be the reason it stayed there.

"Just follow me. Panther, you and Sam just hang out here," Tristin continued.

The trill of a cell phone abruptly interrupted him. Chloe scowled as she looked at her phone. "It's work. I've got to take this."

The woman left the room without waiting for anyone to comment.

"Since she's on the phone, can I talk to you a second, Tryst, before you guys head down to the command center?" Sam interjected.

"Yeah, okay. Excuse us," Tristin said more to Sydney than Cole.

The two men stepped out of the room as well, and Cole was finally alone with Sydney. He studied her, though she kept her eyes lowered. He still stood close enough to her to detect a hint of the scent he now associated with her – fresh with a hint of sweetness.

"We haven't had a chance to talk, not since last night. How are you?"

"Fine."

His lips curved slightly, his hand lightly grasping her chin to lift her face. When her incredible blue eyes met his, he broadened his smile.

"One thing I've learned over the years, when a woman says she's fine, she's far from it," he teased, coaxing a slight smile from her. "You can talk to me. You've had an overwhelming couple of days."

She snorted derisively, and he marveled at how cute the sound was. "You can say that again," she replied sarcastically. Then she sighed loudly and pulled her chin from his grasp. "It's just a little overwhelming. First, Emmett's back in my life. Then I find out he's more horrible than I gave him credit for. And now the new job. And everyone expecting me to help with the case. I'm not sure I can handle it all."

"You can handle it."

Her smile was slight. "I don't know about that, but thank you. I just feel so stupid. I never suspected what Emmett was up to. I don't understand how he could have fooled me so completely."

His brows furrowed. "You are not stupid. And I'm glad you weren't aware or involved in Carter's illegal activities. If you knew more, you would be in more danger. Right now, he only wants to intimidate you. If he thought you were a threat to his operations, based on what I've heard about him, he wouldn't stop until he eliminated the threat."

She shuddered. "Why did I ever fall for him in the first place? I mean, I always thought I was naïve before for believing his act. Now that I know what he's into, I feel downright gullible. How could I not have at least suspected the kind of person Emmett really is? Even Chloe hated his guts from the get-go. Me? I agreed to marry him."

"You have to stop beating yourself up about him. He's a master manipulator. But now you know the truth. That, alone, means you've broken whatever hold Carter had on you."

"Then why am I still afraid of him?"

He cradled her cheek with his palm. "Fear is not something to be ashamed of. It means you'll be careful. You'll be watching. Everyone gets afraid. The fact that you're helping to take Carter down even though you're afraid means you're stronger than you're given yourself credit for."

She gazed at him in awe, her expression soft. Cole's heart pounded hard enough for him to wonder if she heard it. He had no idea where the words of wisdom originated from. He was never one to wax poetic or know the right thing to say at the right moment. With Sydney, he only spoke the truth. Somehow, they seemed to be the words she needed to hear.

Their surroundings faded from his consciousness. He only saw Sydney, with her unique brand of sexy innocence and magnetic pull. The silence of the office shrouded them. Her breathing suddenly hitched, an indication she felt the chemistry as acutely as he did.

As if an invisible string pulled him to her, he leaned forward to close the distance between them. His breath warmed her skin as he tilted his head to capture her lips. The kiss burned hot, sweeping them both up into a tidal wave of need. His arms drew her body close enough for her heat to seep into his bones. He felt her fingers grip the fabric of his shirt. Their tongues danced. All thought flew from his mind. His senses were overwhelmed with the taste, the scent, and the feel of her.

Her hands unfolded, and her palms gently pushed against his chest. The touch was so light, his muddled senses almost didn't register the move. He forced himself to pull away. His chest rose and fell with his heavy breaths, but he kept his arms around her. He needed a moment before he could bring himself to release her.

The last thing he expected was the giggle that escaped her lips. Her smile prompted his own lips to curl with one of his own. "You really know how to make a girl feel better about herself."

"So, you're feeling better?"

"Yes. I'm not sure how, but for the first time in a long time, I feel like it's all going to work out. Thank you. For protecting me and for going up against Emmett. I don't know why you would do that for someone you've just met, but no one has done that for me since I first met Chloe."

"For the record, that kiss had very little to do with making you feel better and more about what I felt in the moment."

"It's hard for me to let myself go like that. I didn't exactly have the best track record in judging people's character, even before I met Emmett. I just…I need time. To figure things out."

"I get it. We'll just take it one step at a time. If you're good with that."

Her slight smile was breathtaking, a warm light twinkling in her eyes. "I'm good with that. I can't promise I won't have doubts, but I want to get to know you."

His rough palm caressed her soft cheek. "Let's start tonight. We could grab some dinner."

Her smile was shy but sweet. "I'd like that if you're sure it's a good idea. We may run into Emmett again."

"You let me worry about that. You just focus on having a good time."

The light shining in her eyes was enough for him to want to make good on his promise. His mind already started to formulate plans for the evening as Tristin and Chloe returned to the office.

Chapter Thirteen

Sydney sat on the unfamiliar but comfortable couch. Her hands rested under her thighs as her feet bounced against the floor as she stared through the window across from her at the view. The sky was streaked rosy with dusk's lovely fingers. The skyline was beautiful, definitely a more welcoming sight than the one from her other apartment. She wasn't sure how she would manage to pay Tristin and Kat Knight back for all they'd done for her, but at the moment, she allowed herself to appreciate the new space without dwelling on the debt she owed.

Once she'd signed the paperwork to begin her new job at Knight Security and Investigations, she'd been pleasantly surprised when Tristin announced he'd secured her a new apartment, one Emmett knew nothing about. The apartment building certainly made the high security of her old building look like a joke. Retinal scanners, 24-hour security guards, key card access, and panic rooms that came custom with each apartment. Access to the parking garage required a voice recognition scan as well as a four-digit code unique to her.

The apartment was minimalistic in its design. Wide open with a high ceiling, the living space flowed into a dining space that fed into a kitchen. A set of four steps led from the living room to a semi-private loft that served as the one bedroom in the apartment. Large enough for a king-size bed with matching dresser and nightstand and walk-in closet, the space promised to be her sanctuary. She could easily picture herself curled up in the bed, surrounded by pillows, watching an old movie on the large screen TV with a pint of chocolate chip ice cream. The bathroom wasn't as spacious, but it was more than large enough for her.

Two of the team who worked with Tristin and Cole had escorted Kat to her old place to gather enough of Sydney's belongings to cover her needs for a while. She half expected them to return with tales of Emmett ransacking her apartment, but evidently all had been as she left it the night her ex-fiancé had vandalized her car and Cole's truck.

They'd brought her to the apartment earlier that afternoon and then left her alone. Well, sort of. A bodyguard from KSI was stationed in the building somewhere to keep an eye on her. According to Kat, several KSI employees lived in the building because of its convenience to the office and its tight security. They were tasked with looking after her and watching for signs of Emmett. She was given a new cell phone programmed with all her contacts and info.

She wasn't entirely convinced Emmett wouldn't find a way to get to her, but for the moment, she felt safe. She shifted her thoughts from her ex-fiancé to Cole and their date. Closing her eyes, she could picture her protector as vividly as if he stood before her. His dark hair was so short it always fell in place, leaving her strong, rugged features prominent. His eyes glowed golden fire that warmed her from her head to her toes. One look or one word from him could send a shiver down her spine. He towered over her, strong and confident. She usually avoided contact with men of his size because they could so easily hurt her, but with Cole, she felt protected.

Just as she expected, being alone with her thoughts also opened the door to her doubts. Was she right in trusting her instincts about Cole, or was she being naïve and foolish? After all, she'd once thought of Emmett as someone who would take care of her and love her forever. Was she being duped a second time?

She didn't think so, and Chloe didn't think so. Chloe was more concerned with him being a player than a manipulator. The idea made Sydney more than a bit nervous about their date tonight. Her experience with men was limited. Growing up, she was too shy and too preoccupied with the ones and zeros of her computer programming to care about dating. Chloe said that why's Sydney fell so easily for Emmett—he'd managed to charm her in ways most men had never taken the time to. Now, she was taken with Cole's protectiveness. She cautioned herself not to lose her head and her heart until she got to know the man himself. Emmett's shadow over her life had so far made that difficult.

Tonight could change that.

Sydney decided to get ready early, taking her mind off her nervousness. She started with a long, scented bubble bath. She shaved, plucked, exfoliated and moisturized until she felt as smooth as silk. She almost expected to slide right off her chair when she sat to figure out her hair.

Her thick auburn locks were always a source of frustration for her. Unruly and unmanageable, she found it easier to tame by braiding it or at the very least, securing it in a simple ponytail. But she wanted it to look special for her date, so she painstakingly wound the thick strands around the barrel of a curling iron, allowing the heat to set a loose wave. The effect was pleasing even if it did take an exorbitant amount of time. The curls bounced about her shoulders, framing her pixie face. Once she was done, she set about applying the makeup she rarely wore. She couldn't bring herself to wear as much as Chloe often encouraged. She always felt it too unnatural, more like paint than something to accentuate her features.

Unfortunately, unless she just caked on the foundation, there was no hope to hide the freckles she'd been cursed with her whole life. They made her appear childlike, and she wanted Cole to see her as a woman. There wasn't anything she could do about them, except loathe them.

Her greatest challenge came in choosing an outfit. She lived in jeans and oversized shirts, which weren't exactly date clothes. Cole didn't tell her what they would be doing, so she wasn't sure what the appropriate attire would be. Even though Chloe was putting out fires at her firm, Sydney placed a 911 call to her best friend for advice. Over video chat, they dissected Sydney's entire closet until she found the right dress in the very back. It had been a gift from Chloe, and she'd never had a reason to wear it until now. The black dress had spaghetti straps and a neckline that dipped into a modest V. The bodice molded to her slender form before flaring into a fun, circle skirt that stopped just above her knees. She opted for simple ballet flats so she wouldn't worry about maneuvering in heels, and she topped the dress with a turquoise cardigan so she would feel more comfortable.

Once she finished primping for her night out, she realized she still had some time before Cole arrived. So, she sat on her couch in her unfamiliar apartment, her thoughts, anxieties and nerves all running rampant. Her view offered some solace, but her overactive imagination refused to allow her comfort for long.

What would they talk about? Would the mood be strained since the threat of Emmett still lingered between them? Would he realize how awkward she was and lose all interest in her? Could she handle the blow to her ego if he did?

The knock on her door caused her to jump several inches from the couch cushion. She instantly checked her wristwatch, amazed she had lost track of time. Cole was punctual. Though she was dressed for her date, she was far from ready. She nervously stood, wiping her sweaty palms on the sides of her dress. She couldn't bring herself to move to the door until she heard his brisk knock a second time. Her footsteps were slow, and butterflies danced a samba in her stomach.

Peering through the peephole, she saw Cole leaning casually against the wall, waiting for her. He took her breath away. Gray slacks hung low on his lean hips. The button-up black shirt was open at the collar, exposing the tanned skin of his throat. His amber eyes seemed darker than she remembered. The rugged planes of his face were relaxed, his full mouth turned up slightly. Exhaling a deep breath, she unlocked the door and opened it.

"Hi." Her gaze fixed on the top button of his shirt.

"Wow," he drawled, sending a shiver down her spine. "You look great."

He withdrew a bouquet of roses from behind his back with a flourish. The deep red color and rich aroma brought a smile to her lips. She accepted the flowers and immediately brought them up to her nose, breathing deeply.

"Thank you," she said, her tone breathy. "No one's given me flowers before."

He moved from his relaxed position to lean closer to her. His warm fingers cupped her chin and gently raised her head until her eyes met his. "You're welcome, sweetheart. I hope they're the first of many."

Sydney could feel heat flooding her cheeks. She took a nervous step back to put distance between them.

"Come in. I'll put these in water, and then we can go."

He closed the door behind him. His eyes swept the space as she pulled a glass from the cabinet. She watched him from the corner of her eyes as he took in her new apartment. As she took care of the bouquet, she realized she would pay good money to know what he was thinking.

"How are you liking the new place?"

"It'll take some getting used to, but I think I'll love it. I still can't get over how much Tristin and Kat have done for me, how much you've done for me. I'll never be able to repay you all."

He closed the distance between them. He didn't touch her, but she felt the heat from his powerful body seeping into her skin. The warmth calmed her even as her heart leapt in her chest.

"We don't expect repayment, sweetheart. Your safety is all we want. Are you ready?"

She smiled serenely. "Yes. I'll grab my purse on our way out."

Cole took her keys from her hand, securing the door before returning them to her. She stared at the keyring as a thought occurred to her.

"How did you get in the building?" Kat had explained to her that the security guard downstairs had to buzz her to give permission for a visitor to be allowed into the building. The guard used a code to activate the elevator before the visitor could come up to her apartment.

"Wings was getting a SitRep from the security guard on duty when I walked up. He buzzed me in." His palm rested on the small of her back as they walked to the elevator.

"SitRep?"

He depressed the down button for the elevator. "Situation report. Wings has an apartment in the building, so he has the evening watch. He wanted to get an idea of what the security guards had seen while he was at work. Don't worry. It's all good."

"And Wings is?" she prompted as she stepped into the elevator.

"Griffin Tyler. He's the pilot for our team. I'm not sure if you've met him yet, but he was at Tryst's house this morning. If he's still in the lobby, I'll introduce you."

"Do you like being a part of the team?"

"It'll take some getting used to. I haven't been a part of a team since my SEAL days. It's not something you step into overnight, but they're a good bunch."

"You miss it. Being a part of a team. Why did you leave the SEALs?"

He was saved from answering as the elevator opened, and they crossed the lobby. With no Griffin in sight, they exited to a truck parked in the front. It didn't escape her notice that he avoided her question, but she decided to let it slide.

"Nice truck," she said, once they were heading down the road.

"Thanks. Tristin got me a rental while mine is being repaired. He's arranging for someone to take you to work in the morning. He said your car should be ready tomorrow afternoon, and they'll bring it to you at KSI."

"I'll check with him about who I pay for the paint job."

"No need," Cole said as he eased into traffic. "Tryst called in a favor."

Sydney fell silent, the weight of all the things her new friends had done for her clouding her thoughts. She owed everyone so much with no way to pay them back. Suddenly, she felt her left hand engulfed in a warm, callused palm. She raised her eyes to find Cole shifting his gaze from the road to her and back again.

"Talk to me, Sydney."

Any other time, she would have insisted she was fine. Somehow, she sensed Cole wouldn't let her get away with that.

"I appreciate everything people have done for me. It's just overwhelming. How easily people have taken control of my life, taken care of things, and I haven't done a thing. I'll never be able to repay them for all they've done. I realize that they aren't expecting me to repay them, but I feel like such a…a…a moocher. And I don't like that feeling at all." She released a frustrated sigh.

Cole squeezed her hand. "I understand. You'll have your chance. For now, just let us help until you have a chance to return the favor very soon."

Tears pricked her eyes, and Sydney rapidly blinked them away. She swallowed the lump that suddenly clogged her throat.

"How did you know just what I needed to hear?"

He grinned. "It's part of my charm. And to answer your earlier question. I was injured, so the Navy granted me a medical discharge."

"Are you fine now?"

"I'm fine now. Are you curious about where we're heading?"

She smiled, unaware of how much the gesture lit up her entire face. "Yes, I am."

"Do you like Italian?" At her nod, he continued. "I know this place. It's a little mom and pop restaurant that's been around for years. It's called Mama Bella's."

She shifted in her seat to face him. "It's owned by Franco and Bella Maretti. They've been married fifty years, and the restaurant was where they met. Did you know Franco's parents started the restaurant, and Franco was the one who hired Bella to be a waitress? She had no idea what she was doing, but he fell in love with her the minute he saw her. He was afraid if he didn't give her a job, he would never have an opportunity to get to know her. And now they run the restaurant. It used to be called Italiano, but when Franco took over the business, he decided to name it for his wife. It's such a sweet story."

"How do you know all of that?"

"They hired me to design their website. I was still in college. They couldn't afford to have a professional web developer work on it, so they called the school to see if there was a promising student they could hire to do it for them. My professor recommended me. I bartered with them. If they supplied me in all the meals I could eat, I would design and maintain their website. The arrangement has worked out really well. Franco's lasagna is the best thing

I've ever eaten in my life."

Cole laughed, and Sydney felt the sound all the way to her toes. "Here I thought I was treating you to something special, and you already know all about it. You're just full of surprises."

"Not really. And just because I know the Marettis doesn't mean this isn't special."

His eyes glowed as he regarded her. They fell silent for the remainder of the ride to the restaurant. He kept a loose grip on her hand, much to her delight. The more she was with him, the less awkward she felt. It was as if she'd known him for years.

Mama Bella's was a small establishment on a back street, just off of Main Street. Easily overlooked, the restaurant was truly a well-kept secret. Locals and tourists who did their research knew it existed. Sydney considered the restaurant romantic, with its Tuscan décor and candlelit table settings. When she found out Franco and Bella's story, she fell in love with the restaurant even more. She once tried to get Emmett to come with her on their anniversary, but because the restaurant wasn't considered an upscale, ritzy eatery, he always declined, saying he wanted to do something more special to celebrate. She later figured out "doing something more special" meant going somewhere where the societal elite could see them.

Getting to experience the romance of Mama Bella's with Cole was so much better. It touched her heart for him to bring her here for their first date even if he had no idea how special it was to her when he made the choice. When they pulled into the gravel parking lot lit by streetlamps and lanterns lining the exterior of the building, Sydney was puzzled to see the parking lot empty. Even on a slow night, the Italian restaurant would have at least a few cars in the parking lot. Tonight it was deserted save for Cole's truck.

"I didn't realize they were closed," she spoke, disappointment slicing through her. "I hope nothing's wrong. I've never known

Franco and Bella to close for any reason."

Cole smiled as he squeezed her hand once more. "They're not closed."

Before she could question his cryptic remark, he got out of the truck and crossed the front to her side to open the door for her. She started to step down, but he placed his hands on either side of her waist. With little effort, he lifted her from the seat to gently set her on her feet in front of him. She was close enough to him to feel his breath caress her cheek. Her breath caught in her throat as he lowered his head. His lips captured hers, the kiss soft but nonetheless potent. His hands rose to cup her face, tilting her head to gain better access to her mouth. Her tongue met his in a passionate dance that both stole her breath and set her heart to pounding. He ended the kiss by lifting his head, but he continued to hold her. She worked to catch her breath, but he seemed hardly affected by their kiss.

"Have I told you how beautiful you look tonight?" His voice held an unusually gravelly tone that brought goosebumps to her skin.

"You may have mentioned it." Her words were a mere whisper, and she was surprised she had the presence of mind to speak at all.

He smiled. "I'm very glad you agreed to come out with me tonight. I like you, Sydney Reede. I like you a lot. I hope you understand that I want this to be the first of many dates for us."

She wondered if she would ever be able to catch her breath again. "I-I like you t-too."

His smile grew wider, and he reached down to grasp her hand. "Come on. I don't know about you, but I'm starving."

No matter what happened for the remainder of the evening, Sydney knew without a doubt this evening was the best of her life.

Chapter Fourteen

The night had gone just as he'd planned.

Soon after asking Sydney on a date, he had called Franco to rent out Mama Bella's. The restaurant was out of the way, but he wanted her all to himself without the concern of her ex showing up. Franco was only too happy to oblige when he didn't know Sydney was the one he planned to bring, but when the restaurateur recognized her as they walked in, Franco and Bella rolled out the red carpet. They welcomed her as if she were family, and her face beamed enough to steal his breath.

Their table was in one corner of the restaurant, just as Cole requested. It was intimate but allowed him a view of the dining area, the entrances and the exits of the restaurant. Even with Mama Bella's being closed to the public, he didn't want to take any chances with Sydney's safety.

They both settled on a delicious meal of lasagna and garlic bread with the wine recommended by Franco. He studied her after they were left alone, noting how she fidgeted under his gaze. Reaching across the table, he covered her hands with one of his, effectively pulling her gaze to him.

"Ready to start work at KSI?"

Her smile was slight, but the gleam in her eyes told him he'd chosen the right subject to take her mind off her nervousness.

"Yes. I was uncertain at first. I know they said my connection with Emmett wasn't the reason they offered me the job, but I couldn't be sure. I talked to Kat more about it, and the job is perfect for me. I can keep all of my current clients, which is great because most of them can't afford anything more than what I charge doing freelance IT work. Between the new job, the new apartment and... well, it's all too good to be true."

The sudden flush to her cheeks made him curious about what she was thinking but didn't say out loud.

"From what I've been told of your skills, KSI is lucky to have you on board. How did you get started in the tech world?"

"I took a computer class in high school as an elective. I had a break in my schedule for that hour, and it was the only elective that wasn't full during that time. I figured I could at least learn how to build my own website and start a blog or something. But the more I learned, the more I loved it. After I finished the class, I started learning code on my own. When I graduated, it was an easy decision to major in computer systems and cyber security."

"I knew some guys in the Navy who did that kind of thing. I never understood it. Of course, I never really took much time to try and learn more about it. I was focused on becoming a SEAL."

"Did you always know you wanted to be a Navy SEAL?"

He released her hands and leaned back. "No. I only went into the Navy to get away from home. My mom's guy of the moment didn't like me very much, and the feeling was mutual. I had a training officer who encouraged me to check out the SEALS, so I decided to give it a shot."

"Sounds like you don't have a close relationship with your mom," she said tentatively.

He shrugged. "I did before the divorce. She changed after Dad left us. He broke her, I think. She didn't know how to be alone, so once she got over the initial heartbreak, she started pursuing any man she thought would take care of her and her handful of a son. None of them ever worked out. Some of them never treated her very well."

"That's how you knew I needed help, isn't it? My reaction triggered something you're familiar with from your own experience with your mom. I've thought about that night a lot. If it wasn't for Emmett coming after me, I never would have met you, or Kat and Tristin. I never would have my new apartment or my new job. You changed my life."

"I don't know about that," he said, lowering his eyes to his plate.

Sydney smiled, amused that she actually made the big, tough Navy SEAL uncomfortable. "I do. And I'm sorry about what you've gone through with your parents."

Cole slid his fork into his mouth, chewing the gooey lasagna quickly. "Let's talk about something less unpleasant. Tell me more about you."

Now was her turn to drop her eyes, her cheeks blushing. "There's not much more to tell that you don't already know."

"I don't believe that," Cole returned smoothly. "I know about your best friend and your ex and your job. I want to know about you, who you are, what you like."

She placed her fork on her plate with a sigh. "My life is pretty boring compared to yours. I mean you've probably seen a lot as a Navy SEAL. I've always lived around here. My life has been pretty sheltered."

"Tell me something that makes you smile."

Her head whipped up, surprise lighting her eyes. "What?"

"Your smile is beautiful. Anything that keeps it on your pretty face is worth knowing about."

Her blush deepened. "Uh, I'm not sure what to say. Chloe can always make me smile, and laugh, for that matter. She's bold and outrageous and says just what is on her mind. She's the type of person I wish I could be. We have a lot in common, though. We love movies, especially the old black and white ones. I know they can be cheesy sometimes, and they don't have the special effects that movies today have, but there's something about them that I love."

Once Sydney opened up, their conversation flowed from one topic to another. He learned of her love for grilled cheese sandwiches, and she found out about his love of the outdoors. He learned about the first time she hacked a computer. She learned about the trouble he and Tristin got into during BUD/S.

Sometime through their meal, he realized just how much he touched her. He couldn't stop himself. He craved the connection. Touching her hand, caressing her cheek, tucking a lock of hair behind her ear, resting a hand on her bare knee, he was addicted to how she felt against his fingertips. The candlelight from their table danced in her cobalt eyes. She smiled, and his limbs tingled with electricity. She laughed, and warmth pooled in his belly. She made appreciative noises as she ate, and he felt the sensation all the way to his groin.

Sydney was enough of a distraction that it took him a while to realize their waitress was not who she seemed.

The woman was friendly and accommodating, as any good waitress would be. Her black hair was slicked back into a tight bun at the nape of her neck. Olive skin was devoid of makeup, and the crisp white shirt and black slacks did little to flatter her figure. But once Cole's brain registered how familiar the woman seemed, he realized just where he'd seen her before. Only then her hair had fallen in sleek strands to her shoulders. Her lovely face had worn enough makeup to emphasize her wide eyes and high cheekbones. The jeans and fitted tee she'd had on at the time showcased a trim, fit body that probably turned many heads.

Not wanting to ruin the relaxed nature of their date, he waited until there was a lull in the conversation to make his move. He smiled into Sydney's lovely face. "Sweetheart, will you give me a minute? I've got a call I need to make really quick."

He regretted his words the minute her face clouded over. "Is everything all right?"

His large palm covered her hand and squeezed reassuringly. "Yes. I just promised Tryst I would check in around now to let him know all was good. It won't take but a moment. In the meantime," he reached for the small menu in the middle of the table to hand to her, "look over our dessert options and choose something for us to share."

There it was. The happy light returned to her eyes. "I'm not sure I can hold much more food, but Bella's desserts are hard to resist."

He grinned as he slipped from the table. He withdrew his cell phone in case Sydney's eyes followed him. Once he was sure she wasn't looking, he moved into the kitchen and cornered the waitress. To her credit, she held her ground and faced him head-on.

"It's Isobel, right? Does Tryst know you're moonlighting as a waitress?"

She smirked as she crossed her arms over her chest. "Isobel Garcia. Welcome to KSI, Panther, though I have to say I'm disappointed. Tristin led me to believe you were the best. You never made me until the evening was almost over."

He shouldn't have been surprised that one of Tristin's investigators exuded such confidence, but he was annoyed that his buddy assigned him a babysitter. "Why are you here?"

"Relax. Jay assigned me to watch out for the target, so you could enjoy your date. Don't sweat it. I've got your six."

"How did Jay even know we were here?"

"Sydney told Kat, who told Tristin, who told Jay who told me. Jay overheard you making reservations, and it wasn't hard convincing Franco to let me fill in for the night. I'm keeping an eye on things in here, and Brick and Einstein are manning the parking lot."

He'd met Mason "Brick" Coffey briefly, but he had not as yet met the investigator's partner, James "Einstein" Albert. If they worked for Tristin, he was sure they were good at their jobs, but as a SEAL, he was more than capable of watching out for Sydney without the back-up.

"Wings is still watching over the apartment building," Isobel continued. "It's been an easy assignment so far. I've had a good time. Franco told me to look him up if I ever get tired of KSI. I'm one of the best waitresses he's ever had."

"You told Franco and Bella about Syd's situation with Carter?" Sydney would be embarrassed to have the couple she'd known for years aware of her trouble with her ex.

"No. They think I'm here protecting you. Believe me, Franco loved the thought that you – Mr. Big, Bad and Muscular – had a girl for a bodyguard." Her smirk widened into a full grin. "Einstein and Brick have been tailing you to make sure the target didn't ambush you. When it comes to Carter, we take nothing for granted. Relax, Panther. We got this. Sydney's obviously having a great time. Don't let the fact you have bodyguards assigned to you ruin that. Sydney is none the wiser. Besides, I can tell she really likes you."

Cole studied Isobel, trying to gauge just how much he could trust her. He had seen her around KSI but knew nothing about her. The fact it had taken him the entire evening to notice Isobel, and to never realize he had a tail on the way to the restaurant, was enough to tell him how good they were at what they did. Still, trust didn't come easy for him, especially when it came to someone he cared about.

And he would be a fool if he didn't realize that Sydney Reede was someone he was beginning to care for quite a bit.

"I appreciate you, Brick and Einstein giving up your evening to watch over Sydney," he said finally. "I don't imagine the investigators have many opportunities to work with the special ops teams, so we may not have a chance to work together again. I wish that could be different because I think I'd like to work with you when I'm not on the receiving end of your body-guarding skills."

"Actually, I work with the teams a lot. I'm a floater, sort of. I have a specific skill set, so Tryst has me working wherever I'm most needed, which means I work with all of the teams as well as the investigators. So, you'll get your chance to team up with me, Panther. But for now, your girl's in good hands. You should get back to your date."

He nodded. "Thanks, Isobel."

Cole made his way back to the table, pushing his curiosity about Isobel to the back of his mind. He had to admit, it was nice to have someone watch his back, so he could focus solely on Sydney. He just hoped their bodyguards weren't eavesdropping on his date too much. The growing intimacy between him and Sydney was for them alone.

His date flashed him a megawatt smile when he returned, and he felt his chest tighten. She was beautiful, way too beautiful for the likes of him.

"Did you choose?"

"Actually, Franco came out to check on things while you were gone. Since I couldn't make up my mind, he's preparing something special for us. Everything okay with Tristin?"

"Yes, everything's good. He told me not to keep you out late, so you wouldn't be too tired for your first day on the job tomorrow."

She giggled. "Thank you, Cole. In case I forget to tell you later, I'm having a great time."

"Here you go." Franco placed a plate on their table with a flourish. Isobel followed behind him with coffee to compliment the dessert sampler. "You have Bella's famous tiramisu, panna cotta, and cannoli. Enjoy."

"Thank you, Franco," she said. "This all looks amazing."

"Bella insisted the two of you have the best. She said you remind her of us."

Franco's words floated on the air, swirling around Cole and Sydney as they locked eyes. Electricity sparked between the two of them. He was hyper-aware of everything about her—the way she moved, the way she spoke, what made her smile, what made her laugh. The world around them fell away. He could detect the faint strains of music and idly wondered if the sound was actually in the restaurant or if he imagined it.

He was lost, no doubt about it. He was lost in her. In her beauty, in her intellect, in her strength, in her love for others. Oh, he felt the urge to protect her from threats, both known and unknown. But he was drawn to her in ways he'd never felt toward another woman before. He wanted all of her. He wanted her body, her heart, and her soul. The realization rocked him.

Then Sydney rescued him, oblivious to the direction of his thoughts. She picked up a dessert spoon and dipped it into the decadent tiramisu. She held it in front of her with a shy smile. He couldn't stop the devilish grin curving his lips. She bit her bottom lip as he closed his mouth over the spoon. Rich flavor danced on his tongue as desire exploded in his belly. The urge to kiss her was overwhelming.

"How is it?"

He leaned closer to her, his eyes darkening with passion. "Perfect."

He heard her breath catch in her throat. She placed the spoon on the plate and dropped her gaze. "I want us to go back to my apartment, but I feel rude leaving now, when Franco and Bella went to all of this trouble for us to have dessert."

Her words released a dam of emotion inside of him. He had cautioned himself to go slow with her, to give her time to understand he was nothing like her ex. But voicing her desire to be alone with him at her apartment obliterated his caution. He started to suggest they ask for a to-go box for the dessert, but if the evening progressed as he anticipated, once they reached her apartment, they would have better things to do than finish their dessert.

Instead he said, "Then I guess we should polish this off pretty quick."

They tore into the dessert, chuckling at nothing in particular. Once they finished, she used a napkin to wipe the remnants from his face before doing the same to her own. The innocent action only heightened the fire heating his blood. He needed to get her alone. Fast.

He threw up an arm to signal for the check. Isobel surprised him by appearing at their table almost instantly.

"Your meal has been taken care of. All of us here at Mama Bella's wish you a great night."

"Oh," Sydney exclaimed in surprise. "Please tell Franco and Bella thank you for me. Everything was just wonderful."

Isobel smiled and gave a brief nod. "You're very welcome."

The undercover investigator disappeared. Cole grasped Sydney's hand to help her from her seat. He kept the soft hand in his grip as they exited the restaurant. The lighthearted but charged mood followed them as they made their way to Cole's truck. He hoisted Sydney inside before lowering his head, not caring who witnessed the moment.

His lips captured hers, this kiss much different than any they'd shared thus far. His tongue pushed its way into her mouth to feast on her sweetness. His hand cradled her face, tilting her head to deepen the kiss. The taste of her drove all reason from his mind. Her own hands clutched the front of his shirt, and a moan escaped her throat. Heat fueled the blood roaring in his ears. Eventually, he forced himself to pull away. He reveled in her glazed eyes that told him she was just as affected by their kiss as he was.

"I need to get you home," he said, his voice gravelly.

"Please hurry," she whispered, the seductive smile curling her lips shattering the last of his resolve.

With a muttered curse, he secured her in the passenger seat and hurried over to the driver's side. Before he climbed inside, he threw up a hand at the Crown Vic parked in the shadows some feet away, alerting his tail that he knew they were there. He hoped they were prepared to keep up because he intended to employ all of his defensive driving skills to meet his girl's request to hurry.

He reached for her hand again, resting it on his thigh as he drove. He reminded himself that he transported precious cargo and tried to keep the accelerator to a speed that wouldn't scare her. He could feel her eyes on him, and he shifted in his seat as his cock strained against his zipper. Hell, he was so hard, he could pound nails.

"Sweetheart, if you don't stop looking at me, I'll never be able to concentrate on getting us back to your place in one piece." He briefly moved his gaze from the road to her. Instead of the passion he expected to see, he saw uncertainty and – fear?

"Talk to me, sweetheart."

"I don't do this. I mean I've never done this. You know, I, um, I'm not, um…"

"Sydney, we can slow this down. The last thing I want to do is rush you into something you don't want." He slowed his speed so he could control his truck and still talk to her.

"No," she hastened to tell him. "I want this. I want you."

Her words made his chest swell with male pride.

"It's just that I haven't had a lot of experience with men. Well, you know, except for Emmett, and that was bad. And even with him, I didn't feel like this, this fast. Or ever. You're different. This is different. And I want you. I want this, but I feel like I should warn you. I'm a, um, a little afraid. Of all of this. I don't want to mess it up." Her words tumbled from her mouth in a long stream that Cole struggled to follow while keeping the truck between the lines of his lane.

He wanted to hug her to him, to cuddle her until all of her fears abated. He settled for squeezing her hand. "It's a little scary for me too, sweetheart. I know it's fast, but it's right, Syd. I can't explain it, but it feels right. And we'll go as fast or as slow as what feels right to us. There are no rules for us, sweetheart. We make our own rules. It's about us, not our past. Okay?"

He looked her way to see the shaky smile, but it was a smile. He would take it.

"Okay. Thank you, Cole."

"Anytime, sweet—"

The SUV came out of nowhere. Black, nondescript, it sped through the intersection at just the right time and momentum to collide with Cole's truck. Striking the driver's side, the impact caused the truck to spin, run off the road, and smash into a power pole on the passenger's side. The airbags deployed against their faces as their seatbelts jerked them back against their seats. Windshield glass shattered around them. Cole attempted to shield Sydney from it all even as his own head exploded with pain.

"Sydney," he moaned as he slipped into darkness.

Chapter Fifteen

Cole woke quickly, his eyes popping open as he assessed what was going on around him. The distinct smell of antiseptic and the excruciating pain in his right shoulder brought his memories crashing back to his psyche. A persistent beep alerted him to the monitor he was hooked up to, and his body protested mightily to the thought of moving at all. His lids felt heavy, but he forced them open. The overhead lighting, albeit dim, blinded him. A moan escaped his lips as an ache pounded behind his eyes.

"He's awake. Zane, get the nurse."

Cole turned his head and instantly regretted the action when a wave of dizziness overwhelmed him. Once he was able to focus his vision, he saw his boss and old friend hovering at his bedside, his expression way too serious for the Tristin he knew.

"About time you woke up, lazy bastard." Tristin's lighthearted tone belied the concern in his expression.

Cole wanted to demand a play-by-play of what happened while he had been unconscious, but the only sound his dry throat could make was a croak that sounded like "Sydney."

"She's better than you. She's actually been waiting for you to wake up. Kat only just talked her into grabbing a cup of coffee and taking a break from sitting by your bedside. She should be back soon."

It didn't escape Cole's notice that Tristin failed to tell him about Sydney's injuries. The fact she wasn't in a hospital bed like him was a good sign, but he still wanted to know particulars for his own peace of mind.

"Hurt?" he managed to ask.

"Bruised ribs, a small abrasion on her cheek from the airbag, no concussion. She never lost consciousness. She's worried about you more than anything."

Before Cole could ask another question, a short, older gentleman with salt-and-pepper hair and a serious face came into the room followed by a petite nurse with her blonde hair in a ponytail. Both of them wore matching blue scrubs, though the older man had a white lab coat over his.

"Welcome back to the land of the living, Mr. Atwood," the doctor quipped as he stepped to Cole's bedside. Tristin moved out of the way so the nurse could stand at Cole's other side. She immediately started checking his vitals while the doctor peered at his pupils.

"What's wrong with me?" he croaked, only to start coughing from the effort. The spasm wracked his body, and he grimaced at the pain it caused.

"You were in a serious car accident," the doctor stated the obvious. "You have a head injury, most likely from impact against the driver's door window. The blow knocked you unconscious, but other than a concussion, you have no injury to your brain. The paramedics said the windshield shattered, which accounts for the multiple cuts and abrasions you have. Most are superficial, but there is a deeper cut on your arm. You have a few stitches to bind the wound. Your left ankle is deeply bruised and sprained. I understand that side of your truck is badly damaged and trapped your leg. Your shoulder sustained the most serious injury. You've had no broken bones, but your shoulder was dislocated. We popped it back into place and wrapped it to keep you from moving it as it heals. We should get another X-ray, and I've called in an orthopedic consultation. I'm thinking you're going to need surgery, but I would like to wait on that until your body has a chance to heal from the other injuries."

Cole processed all the doctor told him, and that information led him to one conclusion—he was in no shape to protect Sydney or to track down Carter. He closed his eyes against the frustration building within him. His gut told him Carter was responsible for the accident, which meant Sydney was still in danger from her ex.

"Are you in pain, Mr. Atwood? We can increase your pain medication. It would help you rest, and right now, rest is what you need," the doctor continued.

"No, I'm fine," Cole lied, his eyes flying open. He didn't want anything clouding his mind until he made sure Sydney was taken care of.

The doctor stared at him for a moment. "I don't believe you. I'll make you a deal. A few more minutes with your friends, you sip some water and then the nurse will kick everyone out and administer the meds to help you rest. No argument, Mr. Atwood," he silenced Cole as soon as he opened his mouth to protest. "I imagine you want to be well enough to leave this place as soon as possible, but to do that, you have to do as I say. No argument."

Cole stubbornly remained silent, wishing the doctor would just move on so he could talk with Tristin in private.

"I'll be back in later today to check on you," the doctor said before discreetly exiting the room. The nurse placed a pitcher of water on Cole's bedside table and held a full glass with a straw for him to sip. The cool water soothed his dry and irritated throat, and he felt marginally better.

Once the nurse left the room, Cole didn't have to wait long for Tristin to start the debrief.

"Do you remember anything?"

"SUV came out of nowhere. Hit my side head-on at top speed. Windows were tinted, so I couldn't see the driver. We spun, hit a pole on Sydney's side. I don't remember much after that."

"Seems like you remember quite a bit."

"It was Carter," Cole said vehemently. "I know it."

"He wasn't in the SUV, but I agree. He orchestrated it. Fortunately, Einstein and Brick were following close behind. From what they told me, there were no tire marks on the pavement, so the perps blew through the intersection intentionally. They were also prepared for the collision. They hit you head-on, but they both had on protective gear, so their injuries were probably minor. When Einstein and Brick rolled up, one was attempting to open Sydney's door. We think he was trying to kidnap her. The other, we think, was prepared to shoot you execution style, but they were both armed. I'm guessing they weren't expecting our guys to be there to stop them."

"You caught them?" Cole demanded.

"No. They retreated when they saw our guys roll up. We thought we had them when their SUV stalled, but they managed to get it going just as our guys reached them. Brick and Einstein shot at them and busted out the back windshield. Brick started to give chase, but your truck sparked a flame. You were wedged in there pretty good, so it took both Brick and Einstein to get you and Sydney out before they tried to extinguish the fire. Syd was pretty hysterical, worrying about you. She almost wouldn't let the paramedics examine her because she wanted them working on you."

"How did they know where we'd be? We were heading back to the apartment you arranged for Sydney. Do you think they know about it?" The expression on Tristin's face set Cole's teeth on edge. "Tell me."

Tristin sighed. "We don't know how they found you. Hell, we don't even know what they know or who they were exactly. Jay, BB and Wings are investigating as we speak, but so far, they don't have any leads. I'm sorry, man. We didn't see this coming."

"I want him. Dead or alive, I don't care." Cole's voice was dangerously calm, his fists clenching the covers at his side.

"Me, too, Panther. I'm done underestimating this guy. He's one step ahead of us all the time, and that stops now. I've put the brakes on some of our cases, so all of our special ops teams can be reassigned to this. Kat has been questioning Sydney while we've been waiting for you to wake up. Hopefully, she's been able to get some usable intel."

Cole closed his eyes and willed himself to calm down. "Sydney. He can't get to her, Tryst. I can't protect her. Not like this. He's getting desperate. That can't be good for her. He's managed to get too close."

"I'm on it. I called in a favor. Once you are discharged, you and Sydney are going into protective custody. Delta Team has already been assigned exclusively to you. For now, Jay is using them to assist your team with the investigation, but they're the most mobile and have the same caliber of training as Alpha Team. He's not getting at her again."

"I want to see her."

Tristin nodded. "I'll find her. Just rest, Cole. I need you back in top shape."

"Thanks, man."

Cole didn't share this with Tristin, but he knew he would not be able to rest until he saw for himself that Sydney was all right. Rage burned in the pit of his stomach that Carter had gotten one up on him again. He'd wanted tonight to be special for her. He wanted her to himself, to figure out how she managed to get under his skin when no other woman had ever accomplished that. The evening had been as close to perfect as he could plan, even with Tristin's appointed bodyguards watching over them. That slime Emmett Carter ruined it all.

"Cole?"

He raised his eyes to see Sydney standing hesitantly in the doorway. He could only imagine the stormy expression she had seen on his face for her to be almost fearful to come into his room. Hastily schooling his features, he used all of his strength to raise his hand and beckon her inside. His gaze drank her in as she moved to his bedside. A bandage covered a wound on her cheek, and she moved gingerly, a result of the bruised ribs she sustained. Her fiery hair hung limply about her shoulders, her dress rumpled, her makeup gone from her face. She captivated him.

"How are you feeling?" She wrung her hands as if she didn't know what to do with them.

He didn't have the strength to raise his arm again, so he lifted just his hand, wiggling his fingers to gain her attention. She stared at his hand for several seconds before grasping it between her two as if he was her lifeline.

"I won't lie, sweetheart. I hurt. A lot. What about you?"

She smiled at his honesty. "I hurt, but not as much as you."

"I'm glad you weren't injured worse. I couldn't have handled that."

Her eyes softened, glistening with unshed tears. She blinked them away, though her mouth trembled as she spoke. "I was just thinking the same thing about you. Just so you know, car accident notwithstanding, this was the best first date I've ever had."

He couldn't stop the grin lighting his face, and he kept it there though it pained him. "It was for me, too, sweetheart. We'll do it again real soon. I promise."

"All right, Mr. Atwood. Time for you to get some shut-eye," the nurse announced as she breezed into his room again. "I'm sorry, Miss Reede. He needs rest more than company. You're welcome to wait in the visitors' lounge down the hall."

"I'm not leaving," she told the nurse firmly. Cole bit back another grin. Her determined expression was adorable, and he was pleased to see her fire returning.

"She stays," Cole reiterated as he watched the nurse inject the painkiller into his IV.

The nurse disposed of the syringe. She looked from Cole to Sydney and back again. "She can stay. But I won't put up with a parade of visitors coming through here or your girlfriend distracting you. Your body can't heal if you don't rest."

Cole's eyes already grew heavy. He felt ridiculously happy hearing the nurse calling Sydney his girlfriend. He liked the sound of that. A lot. "Copy that," he said, his voice a bit slurred.

He saw the nurse's tough façade crack a bit. "Sleep, Mr. Atwood. We'll watch after your girl."

"Copy that," he repeated before falling into unconsciousness.

Chapter Sixteen

Sydney woke with a start. A creak reached her ears before she registered the fact that she was stretched out on a cot, covered with a thin hospital blanket. The last memory she had was of curling up in an uncomfortable hospital chair, watching Cole sleep. His thick lashes rested peacefully against his cheek, his hair shooting up in unruly spikes. With his features relaxed, he looked like a little boy without a care in the world.

"Sleep well?"

The gravelly voice startled her, and her gaze swung across the room. Zane Wilder occupied the chair she remembered sitting in before she slept. Her eyes narrowed. She'd only met him briefly when Tristin introduced him as her and Cole's bodyguard. He'd only nodded his head to acknowledge her but never spoke. Her mom would have described him as the strong, silent type. His build was muscular, but not as broad as Cole, and yet Sydney sensed he was just as strong and dangerous, should the occasion call for it. His brown hair was disheveled but didn't detract from his good looks. His icy blue eyes gave away nothing of what he was thinking or feeling.

"How did I get here?" she asked, indicating the cot with her hand.

"I moved you. Tryst had them bring you a cot."

Sydney wasn't sure how she felt about a strange man carrying her to the cot, but she decided not to dwell on it. Instead, she sat up and looked over at Cole's sleeping form.

"He's still out," Zane said unnecessarily.

"How long was I asleep?" She tried unsuccessfully not to wince at the pain at her ribcage.

"An hour, give or take."

Man of few words, she thought. She gingerly stood, careful in stretching the kinks from her body. She moved over to Cole's bedside, staring into his face. Her heart melted as she watched him sleep. She wasn't sure when it happened, but she knew without a doubt she was in love with Cole Atwood. Their date had been magical and romantic, but after the accident, when he was unconscious and hurt, she'd felt her heart stop. She'd given little heed to her own injuries because all she could focus on was making sure he received help. She had no doubt the men who'd caused the accident had aimed to kidnap her and kill Cole. She'd asked Tristin about it while they were waiting for Cole to regain consciousness, but he wouldn't talk about it. She knew, though. If it were not for Tristin's guys, neither she nor Cole would be alive.

"It's not your fault."

She whipped her head around to stare at Zane. "What?"

"None of it is your fault." His tone was direct, no-nonsense.

She'd only just met him. How could he possibly know the direction of her thoughts?

She was horrified to feel tears well up in her eyes. She needed him to leave. She wanted to be alone with Cole and her brewing emotions. No way could this guy, whose eyes remained unreadable, understand what she was feeling. But instead of telling him to mind his own business as she truly wanted to do, she studied him with tortured eyes.

"Cole wouldn't be here if he'd never met me. He wouldn't be a target if he'd never helped me in the first place." The tears leaked from her eyes to trail down her cheeks, and she didn't bother to wipe them away. Maybe Zane was a guy to be made uncomfortable by a woman's tears, and he would make a lame excuse to leave her with her misery.

"We've been pursuing your ex long before any of us knew you," Zane told her harshly. "Anyone working with KSI is destined to be Carter's target. Don't think for one minute you're special enough to your ex to be the reason he does anything he does."

Sydney gasped as if the bodyguard had punched her. Her sadness and guilt quickly morphed into anger – anger at Emmett, anger at her situation and anger at the sorry excuse of a human Tristin chose to watch over her and the man she loved.

"You shouldn't speak about what you don't understand," she raged, her tone even and deadly.

Sydney's anger typically registered in many ways – in emotional upset complete with tears, in full-on rage escalating into screaming and occasionally throwing objects, and in the scariest form – deceptive calm with a short fuse and sharp edge. The third was by far the form no one wanted to see. It was the form she always wished she could turn on Emmett because then he would never have targeted her. It was the kind her bodyguard now roused without much effort.

"Darlin', I understand plenty because I'm good at what I do." Arrogance dripped from his tone.

Sydney crossed around the hospital bed, her lethal gaze never leaving him. "I spent two years under Emmett's thumb. When I escaped him, I settled into a new life only to have him show up out of the blue and make my life a living hell. So, if I'm not 'special' to him, then according to your theory, he should have just forgotten about me. But now that I'm not in this by myself anymore, he's decided to target everyone who is in my life. When we were together, he made sure I had no one in my life. He alienated me from everyone I knew. I wasn't able to see my parents before they died.

So don't believe for one second that you understand anything about me, Emmett or my situation. You just do your job and leave me the hell alone."

His grin startled her, transforming his cold features into a devastatingly handsome face. *Damn.* Chloe would flip if she could see this guy right now.

"Don't you worry, darlin'. I'll do my job. But what I want you to do is direct that anger at the one who deserves it. Carter is a sadistic SOB. Don't make this about you. It's about him. Once you feel that way, you can help us take him down. Because we will."

His speech stunned her. All the fight left her in a rush. She collapsed back on the cot, her gaze dropping to her hands resting in her lap.

"How do I do that? How do I get him out of my head? I'm tired of looking over my shoulder. I'm tired of being afraid of him and what he'll do next. I'm tired of him targeting the people I care about. How do I change that? You seem to have an answer for everything. Do you have an answer for that?"

Zane contemplated her for a long time. "Tell me about him. Why did you become involved with him in the first place?"

She sighed. "I didn't want to in the beginning. He was so arrogant, I was turned off right away. I should have trusted my gut." She raised her eyes to stare at him. "That's what you guys do, right? Trust your gut?"

"It's saved my hide more than once."

"Well, no one ever taught me to trust mine. In fact, my parents always questioned my judgment. Emmett has a way of reading people, of knowing their weaknesses. He figured out I wanted to feel like I mattered. He knew by doing that, I would stay loyal to him. He played me."

"He's good," Zane said abruptly.

Sydney gave an unladylike snort. "My mother loved Emmett. She thought he was just the guy I needed to get my life on track. Basically, she saw him as her means of getting grandbabies. My dad hated him. He was always a good judge of character, but I wrote off his gut reaction as his trying to control me. Emmett convinced me that if Dad couldn't support our right to be together, then he didn't deserve to be a part of our life. I resisted at first, but I ended up having a big fight with my parents. My mom took my dad's side. They started to see how Emmett was controlling me, but I refused to listen. It was enough to convince me Emmett was right. So, I cut them off.

"I never knew until after I left Emmett that they had repeatedly tried to reconnect with me, but Emmett stopped their attempts. I just assumed they didn't want to have anything to do with me as long as I was with him. Once I realized what a mistake it was, I was too ashamed to reach out to them. I felt—" Her voice caught, and she swallowed the sudden lump in her throat. "I felt like I was being punished for my poor choices. They were right, but I wouldn't believe them. I thought I knew better, so the abuse was nothing I didn't deserve for my own selfishness."

"Something changed."

The fact he was pushing so hard for her to talk should have sent up red flags, but for some reason, she couldn't stop herself from obliging.

"Chloe, my friend. She never fell for Emmett's charm. She played him into believing all the wedding planning she helped with would only enhance his social image. It was the only reason he agreed to let us spend so much time together. She convinced me to leave him and helped me do it. Neither of us knew just how dangerous Emmett really was, or I never would have involved her."

"So, Carter retaliated against your friend when he realized she helped you leave him?"

"He—" She paused as a sudden realization threw her. "No, he didn't. He's never gone after Chloe. Not the way he's gone after me or Cole. He actually left me alone when I left. It wasn't until the charity benefit that he showed back up in my life."

Zane stayed quiet, but Sydney ignored the way he watched her. Her mind whirled. Talking to him actually helped her to sort through all that was going on and helped her life to not feel so out of her control.

"He told me that evening at Tony's that he needed something from me. But what?"

"You must know something that's a threat to him."

She shook her head. "Other than the abuse, I didn't know anything. I had no idea that he…" She gulped against the lump forming in her throat. "I didn't know he was kidnapping and selling people like they were possessions. I wouldn't have let him get away with that."

"But it was okay to let him get away with hitting you?"

Her head whipped up, and she pierced Zane with her gaze. "I tried to tell someone. There were times when Emmett dragged me out to a social occasion, so he'd have someone on his arm for appearances. I made a friend among one of the wives within his social circle. I confided in her about him, and she took his side. All of the donations to charity Emmett made and the way he charmed and treated the socialites with respect made him seem like someone he wasn't. She didn't believe me and ended up telling Emmett what I'd said. Emmett made sure I was…punished when we got home."

"You could have gone to the police," Zane insisted.

"You don't think Emmett had friends among the police? He has friends everywhere. That's probably how he's stayed off everyone's radar with his terrible crimes. Instead of badgering me, maybe you can answer some questions instead. How did Emmett find us? How did he know we would be at that intersection for his men to run into us?"

"We don't know yet."

"Why didn't he try to get to me at the restaurant?"

Zane shrugged. "My guess? He made the people who were guarding her at the restaurant. He figured his best shot was to wait until he could ambush you when it was just you and Cole. I think he expected his guys to get the job done before our guys caught up to you."

Sydney fell silent again.

"What does he want?" She voiced her question not really expecting a response. "What need could he possibly have to go to all this trouble to get to me so I can do whatever it is?"

"What reason did Carter ever have for you to do anything?" Zane countered.

"It suited him. He gained something from it. In the beginning, I was a challenge. He wanted to manipulate me. He controlled my actions and my contact with others. He only allowed my interaction with Chloe because it suited him. But now? How can kidnapping me possibly suit him now?"

Zane remained quiet, watching intently as she worked through the scenario. Sydney felt the answer hovering on the outer recesses of her brain, but she couldn't figure out what it was.

"He doesn't want me working for KSI or helping you with your case against him. But why? I don't know anything. Emmett never involved me in any of his business dealings. I went to social functions when he needed me to, but I never interacted with anyone without him there. It was all very superficial."

Zane leaned forward, his forearms resting on his thighs. "He could have said or done something in front of you without you realizing it was important."

She fell silent, her mind a jumbled mess as she tried to figure out if what Zane said was true. As she thought back to the last year of her relationship with Emmett, she vaguely recalled instances where he would take phone calls in front of her instead of using an excuse to take the call in the next room. On social occasions, he had stopped hovering at her side, concerned for what she might say to someone, when before he would monitor every word she said to his socialite friends. He let her go because he didn't hold enough regard for her to consider her a danger to him. Until now that she was associating with KSI.

When he said he had a purpose for her, was it just to find out what she might now and threaten her to stay quiet? Or was it something worse?

"I wish I had my laptop," she muttered, the urge to dig a little deeper into Emmett's life almost overwhelming. She had to figure out what he wanted with her before he hurt anyone else.

Zane straightened, a grin making a single dimple appear in his right cheek. *Man, he's even hotter when he smiles. I need to introduce him to Chloe, the sooner, the better,* she thought as she stared at him dazed.

"I can have your laptop here in half an hour." He withdrew his cell from the back pocket of his jeans.

She shook her head. "It's not a good idea for me to do any digging on an unsecured network. I can get it later."

"You should go to KSI."

The raspy tone reflected a parched mouth and throat, but she knew Cole's voice instantly. Her head whipped toward the bed, her heart thumping in her chest. She immediately rose to stand by his bedside, her hand reaching for his.

"You're awake," she said inanely, when she really wanted to tell him how sorry she was for dragging him into her mess. "How do you feel?"

"You should go to KSI. Work on the computers there. It's all secure, and I can tell something is stirring in that beautiful brain of yours." He avoided her question and attempted a slight smile.

"I don't want to leave you. I was scared I was going to lose you." Her voice dipped to a whisper, emotion making it quiver.

He squeezed her hand. "You're not losing me. It takes more than a car accident to take me out. You don't have to worry about me, sweetheart. Just do what you have to do."

"Kat and her team are working on it. I don't know if I will even be of any help."

"But something is nagging at you. That's why you want your laptop. Your gut is telling you something that only you can figure out. It's time to trust your gut, Sydney."

She chewed her lip, uncertainty making her pause. The idea of leaving him alone in the hospital left her cold inside.

"You can always come back, sweetheart. Go to KSI. Just for a little while. See what you can figure out. Come back and update me. By then I'll be more than ready to see your pretty face."

She smiled, her heart melting. "If I agree to go, will you answer my question? How are you?"

He grimaced. "I'm not going to lie. I'm sore, but they're giving me some effective painkillers. I'm already feeling sleepy again."

"OK. You rest, and I'll see you in a couple of hours. I, uh, I..." Her voice trailed off. She wasn't sure what she wanted to tell him, but the rush of emotion she felt urged to be expressed. Her cheeks flushed as she realized Zane watched their entire exchange. She dropped her gaze, but not before noting Cole's eyes burned with something she couldn't define.

"We'll talk later, sweetheart." He lightly squeezed her hand as he turned his eyes to Zane, their shade changing from gold to deep amber. "Keep her safe. If Carter gets to her, I'm going after him, and then I'm coming for you."

Zane grinned, obviously not concerned with Cole's threat. "Noted. Don't worry. He won't get to her. Brick's guarding your room. Your phone is by the bed. Hospital security is on alert."

"Don't transport her alone, Zane. Carter's slick. He almost got to her today. Call in back-up."

"I got this, Panther. No one's getting to her while she's with me."

Cole looked back to Sydney. "Promise me, you'll stick close to Zane. I don't want to lose you either," he told her softly.

She smiled. "I promise. Now rest."

As if all he needed was her permission, he closed his eyes, and his breath evened out. She watched his chest move up and down with each breath. Tears streamed down her cheeks. He was alive. She couldn't erase the hazy image of the men approaching the truck after the accident. One of them attempted to reach for her, but she was focused on the one who peered into the truck on the driver's side. She had screamed as he raised a gun and pointed it at Cole's head. If Tristin's team hadn't rolled up when they did, Cole would be dead. All because of her. She closed her eyes, willing her emotions under control.

"Sydney, give me a moment. Let me clear an exit for us, and then I'll get you to KSI." Zane left without waiting for a response, which was fine by her since she didn't think she could speak in that moment.

She sat back down, her eyes drinking in Cole's features as if committing them to memory. He told her to trust her gut. He believed she could help put an end to Emmett's criminal activity and his hold over her life. Since Cole was in the hospital because he'd helped her, she was determined not to let him down.

She just needed her laptop, and then Emmett Carter didn't stand a chance.

Chapter Seventeen

The yawn forced Sydney's mouth to widen until her jaw popped. She hastily raised a hand to cover the evidence of her fatigue, leaning back against her desk chair. She stretched her aching neck and back. One glance at the clock in the corner of the wide screen told her she'd been at her computer search for hours, and she was no closer to finding something on Emmett than she was when she left Cole at the hospital.

She knew her ex to be smart, manipulative, and conniving. She had no idea he was a criminal mastermind who could cover his tracks so well.

She'd spent three days tracking his movements, his patterns and his associates. She'd even run a deep background check on the hotdog vendor he visited at noon each Wednesday. All she'd manage to learn was Emmett must have an iron-coated stomach because the vendor's health rating should have ended his food truck business. If it wasn't for Jay's sister's eyewitness account of Emmett's criminal activities, she could almost believe KSI was tracking the wrong man.

Suddenly, a to-go cup of coffee appeared in front of her. She whipped her head around to see Zane leaning against the desk beside her, his own cup in his hand. His ever-present grin revealed his dimple, his icy blue eyes regarding her in amusement. She'd never heard him approach, but then she never did. To be as tall and well-muscled as he was, Zane moved with silent footsteps, seeming to materialize out of thin air when she never expected it.

"You realize Panther's going to kill me for letting you work so late," he drawled, earning an eye roll from her.

"He's the one who said he wanted me to pull out all the stops to nail Emmett. Plus, he said he didn't worry so much about Emmett getting to me while I was here."

She'd grown used to Zane's presence since he'd been assigned her personal bodyguard. He was a man of few words, which suited her just fine when she was lost in her work. But over the last few days they developed an easygoing rapport that made her start to regard him as the brother she never had.

"Yeah, but he took one look at those bags under your eyes and told me to make sure you got plenty of rest or he'd kick my ass." Zane's eyes gleamed, telling her he wasn't worried about Cole's threat.

Sydney's eyes narrowed. "Tell me again about the bags under my eyes, and I'll kick your ass."

Zane chuckled, lifting his chin toward her computer. "How's the hacking going today?"

She buried her face in her hands with an exasperated sigh. "It's going nowhere."

"That's what I thought. Grab your coffee and come with me."

Zane didn't give her a chance to respond, much less question him. He swaggered out of the command center with the expectation she would follow. One of these days, she would show him and not obey his abrupt orders. That guy needed to be brought down a peg or two, and she sorely wanted to be the one to do it. Unfortunately, since her curiosity got the best of her, today wasn't the day to do that.

Her coffee cup warming her palm, she trailed after Zane, barely registering the stillness of the office building. Most of the KSI employees had gone home for the day or were on assignments. Zane had remained true to his promise to Cole. He'd never left her side unless she was at KSI, and then he was within shouting distance of where she worked. She expected him to get bored and request Tristin assign someone else to watch her, but he never did. When she wasn't working, he drove her to the hospital, where she sat by Cole's bedside, chatting with him or talking to him if he slept. Neither expected him to be in the hospital for so long, but right before the doctor was set to discharge him, he'd started running a fever. The doctor wanted him under observation while the antibiotics fought off whatever infection had occurred. He'd called her a couple of hours ago with the news he was being discharged tomorrow.

Sydney wished she had good news for him. He'd showed such faith in her hacking abilities, and she wanted to show him it had not been misplaced. But she'd failed. Again and again. She, who knew Emmett the best of anyone at KSI, could produce nothing helpful. The idea of disappointing Cole drove her to keep trying, despite the long hours and little sleep. If it hadn't been for Zane's gentle reminders, she probably would have foregone eating in an effort to find a solid lead.

Even now, her annoyance had her scowling at his broad back. Zane took the stairs that led down to the basement floor of the KSI building, and Sydney began to question her sanity. Why follow him when all she wanted was to get back to work?

"Hey, where are you going?" Her voice echoed in the stairwell, but Zane ignored her, never pausing his purposeful stride.

He opened a heavy metal door and braced his back against it to hold it open. He gestured for her to enter ahead of him. She shot him a suspicious look before stepping into a small room that was probably a storage room at one point. Now, it was cleared out except for a punching bag hanging from the ceiling. She whirled around to face him when she heard the door close behind them with a resounding clang.

"Explain yourself, Houdini."

She'd given Zane the nickname after finding out that, unlike the other guys at KSI, he didn't have one. At first, she suspected he just didn't want to tell her, but after questioning the other Alpha Team members and realizing they didn't know either, she saw her chance to get under his skin by assigning him one. She thought it was appropriate, given his ability to appear out of nowhere as if by magic. The nickname didn't catch on with the others, but she insisted on using it anyway.

He strolled over to the punching bag. "You hear the guys talk about the steam room?"

"Sure," she said slowing, drawing out the single syllable. "In fact, I could use that about now after sitting in front of a computer all day. Why don't you take me there?"

"I did," he pronounced, opening his arms in a sweeping gesture. "This is the steam room."

"You've got to be kidding me."

"This is where we come to blow off steam. Sometimes, when you're working a case, you get tunnel vision. It keeps you from seeing the big picture. So, we come here, take our frustrations out on the bag."

He reached for a pair of boxing gloves resting on a chair against the wall. He extended them out to her. She looked at them and backed away as if he held out a handful of rattlesnakes.

"I don't know how to box. Believe me, if I did, Emmett would be on the receiving end of my punches instead of a stupid bag."

He stepped closer and secured the gloves to her hands. "You're angry, you're frustrated, you're scared, you're sad. Leave it all in this room, so when you walk out, you can bring your A game."

He moved behind the bag, using his hands and body to brace it. She stared at the gloves then at the bag and back again. "How do I do this?"

"Just punch."

So, she did, tentatively at first. Then gradually, she used more force until each punch vibrated up her arm. She grunted from the exertion as her mind focused all of her raging emotions into her attack on the punching bag. Years of living at Emmett's mercy, years of being unable to stand up for herself, unleashed from her. Her life played in her mind's eye like a reel-to-reel movie – the moment she'd given into Emmett's pursuit, the moment she'd walked away from her parents, the moment she realized she'd put Cole in danger, the moment she had admitted Emmett had outsmarted her again.

Sydney didn't realize she was crying until the strength suddenly leeched from her body. She collapsed to the floor, sobs wracking from head to toe. To his credit, Zane didn't attempt to stem the flow of tears. He stopped the punching bag from swinging before settling on the floor across from her. He waited out the emotional storm that tore the breath from her lungs. She had no idea how long they sat there. Eventually her sobs and her breathing evened. She hugged her knees tightly to her chest as the last of her tears subsided.

"How did you know?" She was a bit in awe that the big, bad bodyguard would know just what she needed – a good, cathartic cry.

Zane shrugged nonchalantly. "I have sisters."

"I love him, you know." She shocked herself by blurting out the declaration to Zane of all people, instead of to the one who held her heart, but once the words left her mouth, they felt right and good.

"Panther's a lucky man," Zane replied softly.

"I'm lucky. He's nothing like Emmett. Or any man I've ever known, including my father. Cole makes me feel special and important, like what I say and what I think matter. I haven't had that for a long time."

"Everyone deserves to feel that way." Zane's eyes were warm as he watched her.

Taking a deep breath, she swiped the remaining moisture from her face and stood. "I need to see him."

Zane also stood. "Are you going to tell him how you feel?"

Her eyes widened in horror. "No! Not now. Not yet. I have no idea how he feels, and I need some time to get used to what I'm feeling. And you'd better not tell him either, or I'll set up an embarrassing profile for you on every dating website known to man. Complete with digitally altered photos that should never see the light of day."

Zane chuckled. "Panther's my teammate, but one thing I've learned about you, Syd, is I never want to be on your bad side. Your secret's safe with me."

Her expression softened. "Thanks, Zane. You've been a great friend to me these last few days, and I appreciate it more than you know."

"All in a day's work, darlin'," he drawled with a wink. "Let's go. Panther is probably wanting to see you too."

As Zane drove her to the hospital, she marveled over her feelings for Cole – essentially a stranger to her, but someone she trusted. She had no doubt that he would never hurt her as Emmett had.

She had no idea what Cole was feeling, and since they'd only known each other a short time, she doubted he felt love for her. The fact he was still around after all her circumstances had put him through gave her hope. But once the threat of her ex was gone, would his interest in her still be there?

There was another scary realization that cast doubt over her. What did she have to offer Cole? Cole was amazing – handsome, powerful, sweet, caring. He was a Navy SEAL, so he thrived on adventure and excitement. She was average, mediocre, nothing to write home about.

She was in a new apartment with a new job and a new man, but all of it felt like it could be taken from her in a flash.

She chewed thoughtfully on her bottom lip before glancing over at her bodyguard, shocked to realize he was watching her. "What are you looking at?"

"You," he answered promptly. "What's going on in that big brain of yours?"

"It doesn't matter."

"Sydney—" he started, but she held up a hand to halt his speech.

"Leave it alone, Houdini. I just need time to figure it all out. On my own."

Silence stretched between them. Sydney held her breath, wishing she could read minds. Zane's poker face was too good to give away his thoughts, the darkness shrouding them notwithstanding.

"You don't have to do this alone."

His simple promise was all she needed to let her insecurities fall away. Now wasn't the time to question the direction her life was going. She had to focus on the positive now and rely on her friends – old and new – to face what was to come.

In a matter of minutes, they reached the hospital. She waited for Zane to survey the area before opening her door and escorting her inside. She wrung her hands nervously as they rode the elevator to Cole's room. Zane told her he'd wait outside with the investigator keeping watch over Cole – someone she had not yet met. She moved on tentative feet to stand in the doorway. The sight of him sleeping peacefully, illuminated by a faint light coming from the hallway, melted her heart.

Sydney moved closer to stand by his bedside, as close as she dared without waking him. In the dim lighting, Cole's skin appeared golden, his lashes dark where they rested against his cheeks. His head turned slightly to one side, his profile taking her breath away. Her fingers itched to stroke his firm jaw. Her heart swelled within her chest. She loved this man. When she was with Emmett, she'd yearned to experience the kind of love she now felt toward Cole. He had done nothing but protect her since they'd met, and she knew in her soul she would sacrifice her own life to protect him.

Cole stirred, his body gingerly shifting to face her. His amazing eyes fluttered open. At first, he squinted to focus on her face. Then he blinked a couple of times. "Syd?"

"Hey." Her smile lit her eyes.

"What time is it?" he spoke quietly, as if he felt the same as she did that their full voice would disrupt the stillness of the hospital at night.

"Late. You should go back to sleep."

"Where's Zane?"

"Close by. He's kept his promise to watch over me."

He reached a large hand to capture hers hovering over his bed. "You should go home. Get some rest yourself."

She swallowed before her tongue darted out to moisten her lips. His eyes narrowed as he caught the gesture.

"I wanted to see you."

"Ahhh," he breathed. "Sweetheart, it's good to see you. I can't wait to hold you without all of these monitors and IVs being in the way."

She hesitated, knowing to do what she desired would be a bold move, one completely unlike her reserved nature. But the moment felt right. She didn't want to let it pass.

"Let's not wait."

With great care, she nudged him to the side and gingerly stretched out on the small hospital bed beside him. They were cramped in the single bed, but she snuggled against his warmth. One arm laid under her body while the other lightly rested across his torso. His shoulder cushioned her head, his arm drawing her close. When his lips lightly touched her hair, she felt a tingle down to her toes.

"Just what I needed." The huskiness of his voice caused her stomach to flutter.

"Me, too."

"Too much time has passed since I last saw you."

"I'm sorry. I was trying to find a lead, but I kept hitting dead ends."

"Tell me." Though his voice was soft, his tone was commanding. She didn't want to burden him with work, not when he needed rest to heal, but she found herself unable to refuse him.

"I've wracked my brain and done everything I could think of to figure out what Emmett wants with me. They've all led nowhere. Kat and the other hackers have come up empty too. I failed you, Cole. I wanted Emmett to pay for hurting you, but—" Her voice caught on raw emotion clogging her throat, and she couldn't continue.

Lean fingers lightly cradled her chin, lifting her face to peer up at him. The angle was awkward, but Sydney was content to stare at him for hours. Even in the low light, his amber eyes glowed.

"You could never fail me, sweetheart. You are amazing." His gaze deepened in intensity. "You are strong and beautiful and sweet. You deserve someone so much better than me, but I'll be damned if I'm going to let anyone else have you."

His possessiveness sent a thrill up her spine. "Thank you."

"For what, baby? I just spoke the truth."

"You make me feel so special and safe. You've done so much for me. I don't know how I'll ever repay you."

He shifted a bit more. His face now dipped close to hers, his breath caressing her face. "If you truly want to repay me, there's only one thing I want."

Before she could draw her next breath, his lips lightly touched hers, the move so intimate she couldn't stop the gasp escaping. He teased and nipped at her full lips until she teetered on the verge of begging for more. A moan rose from her throat, providing just the green light he needed. His mouth fully captured hers, his tongue stroking the seam of her lips until she opened them to grant him access. Her hand cradled his cheek as the kiss deepened. Her skin felt feverish, and her lungs burned for more air. But she couldn't pull away and had no desire to. All she wanted was to be close to him, to allow his masterful kissing to drive away all frustration and fear. The world faded away, no longer existing outside of the two of them in this moment.

His hand grazed the hint of skin exposed between the hem of her shirt and the waistband of her jeans. Her mind shouted for him to slow down before they were caught by Zane or a nurse, but she silenced the internal voice. She didn't care if they were caught. She craved his touch like a drug. His hand glided up her side, crossing her rib cage until it rested just underneath her breast. The sensation was heady, his touch and his kiss vying for her response.

When Cole finally raised his head, she gulped much-needed air. He lowered his lips to kiss the sensitive spot on her neck just beneath her ear.

"Cole," she gasped, fully out of her mind with desire.

His hand cupped her breast, caressing the fullness through the satin material of her bra. His mouth kissed a path down her throat. How Cole's monitors weren't going crazy, she'd never know because she could hear his heart pounding a fierce staccato against his chest. *Wait, no.* That was her heart pounding in her ears. Sydney was ready to throw caution to the wind and rip his hospital gown from his toned body, but he stopped his assault on her senses. He pulled her close, tucking her head against his chest. Both fought to regain their breath and settle their desire. She could feel the evidence of his arousal against her, and knowing she caused this reaction filled her with satisfaction.

"Tomorrow," Cole finally gasped against her ear. "One more day, and we'll finish what we started."

"Yes," was all she could manage.

They held each other, the soft beeping of his monitor providing ambient noise. Soon, they both drifted to sleep, blissfully unaware that Zane watched them through the small crack of the partially open door to Cole's hospital room.

The bodyguard smiled at the sweet picture the couple presented, even as his eyes clouded with regret.

Chapter Eighteen

Cole rested his back against the wall, his legs crossed at the ankles, his arms crossed across his chest. A smirk curled his lips even as his eyes watched intently.

Sydney assumed her fighting stance, her lovely face a mask of concentration. Strands of her fiery hair slipped from the confines of her braid, but they didn't bother her. Her focus was on her bodyguard, who grinned at how seriously his pupil was taking his self-defense instruction. Zane talked her through the steps of the maneuver, confident that she wouldn't be able to hurt him.

One thing Cole saw that his girl obviously hadn't noticed was the warm haze to Zane's gaze and the flirtatious gleam that seemed to only surface when he thought no one was watching. He'd suspected for days that his teammate regarded Sydney as more than a client or a self-defense student. He battled indecision on what to do about it – ask Tristin to assign one of the other guys to Sydney's guard, confront Zane about what was going on, or just smash his fist into the other man's nose.

He did none of those, but since he'd realized what was going on, he did make a pest of himself. He never left the two of them alone if he could help it, which meant he attended all of Sydney's self-defense classes instead of using the time to hunt for her ex.

He began to realize Sydney had no idea her bodyguard was attracted to her. If anything, she treated him like a brother. She teased Zane mercilessly and insulted him good-naturedly. It was probably why the other man had not made a move on Sydney, but Cole still didn't trust the guy spending so much time with his girl.

His suspicious nature did have its perks. For instance, seeing Sydney dressed in fitted t-shirts and yoga pants that molded to her curves added something special to his day. Watching her learn how to kick ass made his chest swell with pride. An added bonus was that she was kicking the ass of the source of his jealousy.

Not that he could blame Zane for his infatuation. The more he was around Sydney, the harder he was falling for her. She was smoking hot with a sexy innocence that was hard to resist. There was also a softness to her that drew Cole in like a spider with its web. She was caring, putting others before herself. She had a way of making him feel invincible but could bring him to his knees with a gentle caress of her hand against his cheek.

But more than that, she was fierce with a laser focus that rivaled any SEAL he'd ever worked with. She analyzed every situation like it was a puzzle waiting to be solved. She bounced ideas off Cole and Zane, and oftentimes the conversations would spark a new idea. Sydney inspired was a sight to behold. She chattered non-stop, her graceful movements punctuating her words, her face animated and her eyes bright with fervor.

Her eyes... Thinking of them had his heart stuttering in his chest. He would be content to spend days staring into her eyes when they shone like that. He imagined they would sparkle the same way as he kissed her neck, making his way down her naked body, stroking her until she squirmed beneath him, moaning with desire.

He shook the thoughts from his head before his body betrayed his heightened libido. When he was released from the hospital, he had been determined to show Sydney just how much he wanted her. His mind was consumed with thoughts of her, and he was fairly certain she was just as attracted to him. Two problems stood in the way of his master plan. His injuries still caused him enough pain that any intimate interaction with Sydney proved a challenge.

Not to mention, with the threat of Emmett Carter still looming in their lives, they were never alone. Cole had two bodyguards from Delta Team – Wyatt "Rigger" Fancher and Lex Bishop. The two were easygoing and knew how to blend into their surroundings. Though Cole knew they were there at all times, he'd learned to ignore them. At first, Sydney's protection detail had alternated between Zane and Isobel. Lately, Zane had been solo in providing security for her, and it didn't take Cole long to understand why.

Since circumstances put their sexual relationship on hold, Cole and Sydney's rare moments alone were spent sharing about themselves when they weren't stealing a touch or a kiss. He never imagined the contentment that came from just spending time with another person, without sex being involved, but Sydney brought that to his life. It made finding and stopping Emmett Carter that much more imperative. Until Sydney was safe from her ex, she and Cole could never have the relationship they both wanted.

"Ugh!" Sydney's exclamation echoed in the empty gym. "I'm never going to get this!"

She sat on a mat, staring up at Zane in frustration. For the last few minutes, he had been trying to show her a particular self-defense move should someone grab her from behind. Instead of squirming out of his grasp and dropping Zane to the floor, Sydney had so far been the one to wind up on the floor with the bodyguard looming over her. Zane extended a hand to help her up. Cole was certain Zane was aware of his presence, but Sydney had yet to realize that he watched from across the room.

"You will," Zane told her. "It's not an easy move, especially against someone bigger than you."

"Maybe it's time to take a break," Cole pushed off from the wall and sauntered over to them, loving the happiness that sparked in Sydney's eyes when she saw him.

"Cole. What are you doing here? Is it time to go already?"

Sydney chose to practice her self-defense with Zane after she'd spent a day working in the KSI command center. It prevented her from working too long, and it helped her to unwind from the stresses of her day. Travis had secured space for them to use at Knight and Day Fitness Center, and Cole came by the gym to watch them until he was ready to take his girl home.

Home was actually a safe house Tristin had obtained for them. After the accident, they didn't want to take any chances in case Sydney's apartment location had been compromised. Tryst arranged for them both to move into the safe house to make protecting them easier on their security detail.

Cole planned to make that particular living situation permanent. He hadn't shared his intentions – or his feelings, for that matter – with Sydney yet. He wanted to wait until her attention wasn't split between him and the search for Carter. But there was no way he was ready to let her go.

Cole dropped a quick kiss to Sydney's cheek in response to her question. "It's time to go."

"But—" Her eyes darting between him and Zane. "I just—"

He squeezed her hand, his gaze tender. "Go ahead. Give it another try. This time, though, don't focus so much on doing it exactly right. Instead, relax into his hold. You can better identify his weak points and go in for your move."

She considered his words for a moment before nodding. "Okay. Just one more try, and then we can leave. I promise."

Cole stepped back, prepared to watch his girlfriend take out his teammate. He knew she would this time. The determined gleam in her eyes was the same one she got just before she conquered any challenge. It was a gleam he was becoming all too familiar with and loved seeing. Zane had no idea what was coming.

They took their positions, Cole on the edge of the mat, Sydney in the center with her back to Zane, and the bodyguard close behind her. He reached to grab her, his arm securing around her throat in a debilitating choke hold. Sydney coughed, her breath catching. But she followed Cole's advice to the letter. Rather than struggle against him, trying to attack whatever body part she could get to with her elbows or feet, she relaxed, her body limp. Zane started to drag her, but she suddenly twisted and dropped. Then with a sweep of her body, she knocked the bodyguard's legs, throwing him off balance before kicking him in the groin. Cole winced as if he had been dealt the blow. Zane had protective gear on, but he still moaned from the pressure to his sensitive area.

Sydney froze as she watched Zane roll to the side, retreating. Then in a flash, she was on her feet, jumping and shouting. She hurled herself into Cole's arms, wrapping her arms around his frame before planting a resounding kiss to his lips.

"I did it! I can't believe it! I did it! I finally did it!"

Cole grinned at her exuberance, pleased beyond measure by her excitement. The uninhibited hug and kiss sent a shock of electricity surging through his body. What he wanted was to drag her to their new place, undress her as quickly as he could, and then slowly worship her body until all conscious thought left her and the only word she could utter was his name. But his wants would have to wait.

As Zane gingerly stood to his feet, he offered congratulations to an excited Sydney, his eyes shuttered as he watched them.

"Thank you. Both of you. That felt amazing. I feel like I can take on the world. I wish we could celebrate. I've never done anything like this before."

Cole draped an arm across her shoulders, pulling her close to his side. "Actually, Tryst and Kat invited everyone over to their place tonight. Nothing special, just pizza, beer and blowing off steam."

"Great! Give me twenty minutes? Is that okay?" Sydney asked, her megawatt smile still lighting her face, beaming pure sunshine throughout his body.

"Perfect, sweetheart. I'll wait for you out here."

With a quick thanks to Zane for today's self-defense lesson, Sydney rushed off to the locker room adjacent to where they practiced. Access to the practice room and the locker room was restricted during Sydney's sessions with Zane. Travis had easily complied with the necessary safety measure once he knew of Sydney's situation.

With access to only one locker room, Zane waited with Cole in the practice room until Sydney finished cleaning up. Usually, Zane wandered off to talk with Travis, knowing Cole was watching over Sydney, but today, he stayed in the practice room.

Cole felt an undercurrent charged between them, like two jungle cats establishing their territory. He knew the time would come when he needed to confront his teammate about his feelings for Sydney. He just didn't expect that time to be now.

Tristin had assured him that Zane was one of the best on the team, but Cole couldn't allow himself to trust the guy. Not until they settled some things between them.

"She's yours, man. I get it," Zane broke the uncomfortable silence, using a towel to wipe the perspiration from his face.

Cole's jaw clenched, surprised Zane would so readily admit his feelings. "I should have you removed from her security detail. There are plenty of people here who can guard her and teach her self-defense."

"No need. I'm good at what I do, Panther. She's safe with me. On all counts. She loves you, man. There's no competing with that."

Cole couldn't stop himself from glancing over to the dressing room door. He and Sydney had not had a conversation about what they were feeling, but Cole knew he loved the woman and wanted her in his life always. He hoped she felt the same way. Hearing Zane say it out loud caused a strange fluttering in his chest. The desire to share with her his heart overwhelmed him, but the timing was wrong. He didn't want the threat of her ex hanging over them when he declared his love for her. He wanted the moment to be perfect because she deserved that.

"She's a hard one to resist," Cole said begrudgingly. "I appreciate you standing down."

Zane glanced at the door to the dressing room and then back at Cole. His expression turned dark in the blink of an eye. "Just so you know. If you hurt her, I'll be there to pick up the pieces. And to pound your ass."

"Won't happen," Cole returned, his tone just as fierce.

The two of them stared at each other until a silent understanding was reached. Cole couldn't say he trusted Zane, but if the man cared for Sydney as he said, then he would give his life to protect her. And if he couldn't be the one guarding Sydney, that's the kind of person he needed watching over her.

Finally, Zane nodded, flashing Cole a grin. "Think I'll go and talk to Travis. See you at Tryst's?"

Cole gave a curt nod and watched the other man swagger out of the practice room. He settled back against the wall he had vacated, the silence of the empty space swirling around him. The muscles in his shoulders throbbed. Though his injuries were healed for the most part, his shoulder still gave him fits and probably would until he had the surgery the doctors were insisting on. He really just wanted to go home instead of hanging out with his teammates, but he knew the relaxing evening was something Sydney needed to take her mind off everything.

He wanted that for her. He wanted to shoulder all of her worries, so she would know nothing but happiness. She consumed his thoughts more than any woman he'd ever known. She was vibrant, beautiful, and passionate. When she kissed him, she held nothing back, drawing him in until he drowned in her sweetness. He craved the taste of her. As much as he wanted her all to himself, he wanted her to let loose and enjoy the new friendships she was making.

Gentle steps echoed in the empty practice room. His eyes whipped up, his body froze. Sydney smiled tentatively as she stood in the doorway. Her fiery hair fell sleek and shiny over her shoulders, brushing lightly over her breasts. A loose-fitting green blouse sported a V neckline that gave a hint of cleavage, and black jeans molded to her long, shapely legs. The look was casual but devastating. Cole's mouth went dry.

"Hi," she said softly, her voice washing over him.

With deliberate movements, he crossed the room to meet her halfway. Their bodies didn't touch, but he could feel the heat from hers seeping into his skin. He devoured her with his gaze, his heart racing. Her breath hitched, so he knew she was as affected as he by the electricity surging between them. Lowering his head, he dropped a heated kiss to her lips.

"You look beautiful," he drawled as he released her lips.

She flashed him a stunning smile. "Thank you. Glad you like it. I borrowed it from Chloe. I thought it'd be a nice change from my usual t-shirts and braids."

He chuckled at her understatement. "Sweetheart, I like your t-shirts and braids, but this...I like it so well, I'm tempted to blow off our friends and steal you away to somewhere private."

She sighed, leaning forward enough to rest her forehead against his. "Oh, if only we could," she breathed, and his heart clenched.

"Soon, sweetheart. I promise."

"I can't wait."

Cole summoned all of his will power to step away from her. "Come on, sweetheart, before I change my mind."

He placed his palm at the small of her back and led her out the door where Rigger and Lex waited for them.

"I was wondering. Do you think Tristin would mind if we invited Chloe to join us? We haven't had much friend time together lately."

"Kat already has. Chloe's part of us now, whether she wants to be or not."

Sydney smiled. "She wouldn't tell anybody, but she loves your friends. I do, too."

He grasped her hand and held it as they followed their security to the parking lot. Cole tried not to be obvious in his perusal of their surroundings, but some habits he couldn't turn off. He could feel Sydney stiffen at his side, and he squeezed her hand as he allowed his gaze to rest on her profile. They climbed into the back of the SUV while Rigger and Lex occupied the front. As Rigger started the vehicle and exited the parking lot, Cole leaned over close to Sydney's ear.

"You're safe, Syd. Relax and enjoy the evening."

"I know. And I will. It's just hard not to have flashbacks of the accident whenever we're in a car together."

"It won't be that way forever, sweetheart. I promise."

She rested her head against his chest, and he raised an arm to drape over her shoulders, drawing her close to his side. She released a sigh, her brow furrowed. "I hope you're right. I'm beginning to think I'll never have a normal life again."

He wasn't sure what else he could say to reassure her, so he dropped a kiss to her hair and held her close. They finished the ride to the Knights' home in silence.

Chapter Nineteen

Sydney stared into the darkness, the gentle night sounds gradually easing the tension that knotted her shoulders. When she was a child, she'd hated the stillness of nighttime. Her imagination would run away from her with every foreign sound she heard. Many nights she'd find herself in her parents' room, hoping they'd allow her to crawl between them in the bed where she would feel protected. Inevitably, her father would walk her back to her room and assure her she was safe, that nothing would harm her.

She never considered her parents harsh for not indulging her. She knew they just wanted her to be brave. And she would eventually fall asleep, exhaustion winning out over the sounds that had frightened her.

She could remember exactly when she started finding solace in the tranquility of night. It was the second time Emmett hit her. The first time she explained away – he'd a bad day, and she'd pushed him too hard to talk about it, forcing him to lose his cool. He'd apologized immediately after, and the next day he brought her flowers and took her out for dinner and dancing to make up for it.

The second time had been different. He'd come home late, reeking of alcohol, and found her asleep on the couch, dressed in sweatpants and an oversized t-shirt. She never knew why he was so upset, but he woke her with a slap to her cheek followed by a body shake so hard her teeth clapped together.

He shouted about how she'd let herself go, that she should have stayed awake until he got home so she could have seen to his needs.

He threw her to the floor, and the punches kept coming. She tuned him out after that and rolled up into a ball to protect herself as much as she could. When he finished his tirade, he stumbled into their bedroom and passed out on the bed.

She wasn't sure how long she'd lain on the floor, her body aching like it never had before. Eventually she was able to get on her feet. Not wanting to wake Emmett and risk his ire once more, she shuffled out onto the balcony of their apartment and collapsed on the cool floor. She allowed the darkness to cloak her injuries and her tears. After she'd sobbed until she had no tears left, she sat with her knees pulled to her chest, her eyes closed, and let the night soothed her battered heart.

Looking back, she realized that night was a turning point for her. She should have gotten to a hospital, even if she'd had to call an ambulance to do it. She should have told someone what Emmett had done, used the opportunity to escape him. Instead, she'd allowed her shame to force her to hide and believed she was receiving payback for her poor decisions.

She hated to believe herself lucky to only have been Emmett's punching bag. Knowing the other things he could have done – doping her up, selling her to the highest bidder, forcing her to live as a sex slave to a pedophile, killing her – she was thankful she'd been able to walk away from him, even if it had taken her longer than it should have. If only she could find a way to save the others who had become unwilling victims…

"Hey."

Sydney started violently, whirling around with her arms raised in a defensive gesture.

"Whoa, stand down. It's just me."

The shadowy figure loomed large in front of her, but she relaxed when she recognized Cole's voice. She lowered her arms, thankful he couldn't see the sheepish flush staining her cheeks.

"Sorry. I was lost in thought and didn't hear you come outside."

The sound of raucous laughter drifted through the sliding glass door even though it was closed securely behind him. Sydney smiled at the sound.

"Everything all right?" Cole stepped closer to her, but he didn't touch her. "We can leave if you're not having a good time. I know you're disappointed that Chloe couldn't come, so if you'd rather not be here, I'm fine with that."

"Oh, no, it's not that. I haven't had this much fun in a long time. But I'm also not used to being around this many people in one evening. I just needed a minute to myself."

He stepped closer until there was only a breath between them. His hands rested lightly on her forearms. Gently, he pulled her forward until his legs bumped against a chaise. He released her long enough to settle his body on the lounger before reaching out a hand to draw her beside him. It was a tight fit, but it meant she had to nestle next to him, his arms wrapping around her and drawing her close. She rested her head against his chest and eventually the regular beating of his heart resounded in her ear.

"Talk to me, Sydney."

"What do you mean?" she whispered.

"You have a lot going on in your head. It helps you to talk it out. So talk."

She couldn't speak at first. His assessment was too accurate for her to know what to say. She hated how her body stiffened with his command. She wanted their intimate moment alone to last, and telling him the direction of her thoughts would shatter the moment.

"You can talk to me about anything. At any time. Whenever you're ready."

She closed her eyes against the rush of tears. She swallowed the emotion clogging her throat. She finally released a long-suffering sigh.

"I'm tired of talking about Emmett. We're not together, and he's been on my mind more now than he was then. I don't want to think about him anymore, but it's my job now. It's all messed up."

Cole tightened his embrace, but he remained quiet, letting her lead the conversation. She absently stroked his chest, lost in the intimacy of the moment. It was just the two of them, in their own world. When she finally filled the quiet, she spoke low, afraid to shatter the moment.

"I never wanted my life to revolve around a man. I wanted to be my own woman, to live life on my terms. That's why I butted heads with my parents so much. They had their own idea of how their daughter should be, and I rebelled against it. Yeah, I know, me being a rebel seems weird, but I actually was. I never felt I was good enough in their eyes, and it just made me act out more. I never had a close relationship with my parents, and I think that's how it was easy for Emmett to convince me to turn my back on them.

"Emmett wasn't always a monster to me either. I mean, he was definitely full of himself the first time we met, and that's why I refused to date him at first. But there were times when I felt he was almost human with me. I believed I got a glimpse into what made him tick."

"That's hard to imagine."

She tilted her head up to smile at him, though he couldn't see her. "I know, but it's true. I remember the first time he talked about living in a group home. He was orphaned when he was fourteen. His dad had died, and his mother abandoned him. He went to live in a group home. A bunch of other kids at the home bullied him. Once right before Christmas, it snowed, and the boys waited until their guardians went to bed. Then they took Emmett outside, beat him, stripped him naked and left him there. I remember crying as he told me, but he talked about it like he was talking about what he ate for lunch. It was like he'd detached himself from the memory."

"I don't want to feel sorry for him."

"I know. It was horrible, but he told me it worked out in the end. He met his foster brother, and everything changed."

"I thought you said he didn't have any family."

"I wouldn't call Danny family. Protector would be more accurate, I guess. The other kids knew not to mess with Danny. He was mean, but for some reason, he took Emmett under his wing."

"You ever meet him?"

She shivered. "Yes. Danny is…creepy. After the first time I met him, I asked Emmett to never leave us alone. He's intense, and the way he looked at me was…I can't explain it. Emmett told me I was being paranoid, but I ended up being right about him."

"What do you mean?"

Sydney hadn't thought about Emmett's brother in a long while. Her encounters with Danny Dawson had thankfully been few, but just thinking about them chilled her, as if a strong wind blew away all the warmth of the moment.

"At first, it was little things. The first time we met, he shook my hand but held it too long, staring at me like he was starving and I was a steak dinner. He would make lewd comments about how I looked or my sex life with Emmett, and then laugh it off like he was joking. Emmett didn't seem to care, but he respected my request not to be left alone with him.

"Then one afternoon, I came home from an errand, and Danny was waiting inside the apartment. I don't know how he got in. I told him Emmett wasn't home, but he said he was there to see me. He told me all the things he wanted to do to me. I reminded him I was with Emmett, but he just ignored me. The more he talked, the more scared I was. He planned to rape me, and he wanted me to know exactly what he was going to do and how he was going to do it."

"He got off on scaring you."

"He did. And just when I thought he was all talk, he grabbed me and forced down on the floor. He tried to kiss me and grope me. I fought him off. He was surprisingly strong, but I went for all the soft spots—his eyes, his groin, whatever. He seemed to thrive on it. He just laughed. Emmett walked in on us wrestling on the floor. I screamed for him to help me. He watched us for what seemed like forever, and then suddenly Danny climbed off of me. He just leered at me and left. Emmett walked him out like it was just any other visit.

"When Emmett came back, he was angry. He accused me of seducing Danny. He blackened my eye and busted my lip to punish me. It was the last time I ever saw Danny when Emmett wasn't around."

"That's messed up."

"It was all messed up, but something about their relationship was beyond messed up. It was almost unnatural."

"I'm sorry you had to live through that."

"Me, too. I'm sorry you've been caught in the middle of all my baggage."

He dropped a kiss to her hair. His hand caressed her cheek as he rested his forehead against hers. "I'm sorry you had to go through that, baby. But it made you strong. You're beautiful and brave. To be with you means being with all of you, baggage and all. That's what I want — to be with you."

She fisted the fabric of his t-shirt, her breaths quickening. She lifted her chin until her mouth hovered over his. His breath brushed against her face as faint as butterfly kisses on her skin. A tingle started at the nape of her neck and surged through her body, reaching the ends of her fingers and the tips of her toes.

"You are a dangerous woman, Sydney Reede," he growled before his mouth captured hers.

He nibbled at her lips until she gasped. Tilting his head, he deepened the kiss, devouring her mouth. Their tongues tangled in a dance all their own. Her arms snaked around his neck, pulling him flush against her, her leg slinging across his hip. Delicious heat burned her from the inside out. Just when she thought her lungs would burst with the need to breathe, he pulled away to trail kisses along her jaw and down her neck. He liked the hollow space above her collarbone, and she gasped at the flood of desire filling her.

"Cole!"

She could feel his smile against her skin. "I want you, Sydney. I want you all to myself. I want to take my time and taste every inch of your skin."

"I want you too," she whispered, still trying to catch her breath against his tender onslaught.

"Let's get out of here. I don't care if we have to take a security detail with us. I'll make them keep a perimeter watch all night if it means having time alone with you."

She surprised herself by giggling. "I'm sure they'll enjoy spending all night outside, but I don't care if they're outside or inside. As long as you and I are locked away just the two of us, that's all I want."

"Damn, I've dreamed of having you in my bed, naked, your hair spread across my pillow. As much as I don't want to let you go now, we need to go make our goodbyes so I can get you home."

Sydney rose and gripped his hand to pull him up to his feet. She planted a kiss to the corner of his mouth before turning to head back inside. She flushed under the knowing smiles they received when they announced their departure, but Cole just dropped an arm around her shoulders and stared them down. Sydney hugged Kat in farewell before Rigger and Lex flanked them to escort them to the SUV.

"You sure about this?" He squeezed her hand as he whispered in her ear. They sat close together in the back seat with eyes only for each other as Lex drove to the safe house.

"That I want to be with you?" Her voice was just as low, and she could almost feel the intensity of his stare. "Yes. I have never been this sure of anything in my life."

"I don't ever want to push you into doing anything if you're not ready."

"I appreciate that. This is what I want. This is what I've wanted for a while now."

He kissed her briefly but firmly, and Sydney felt the electricity straight to her toes.

"Hey, you two. Save it until we get you home." Rigger stared at them through the rearview mirror, a shit-eating grin splitting his face.

Cole flipped the bodyguard off, confident the dim light from the streetlamps would illuminate his response. Rigger's chuckle confirmed that it did. Even as a blush stained her cheeks, Sydney couldn't stop her giggle at their antics. Not only was she growing close to Cole, but she was becoming attached to the KSI teams and investigators as if they were the family she didn't know she needed. If she could find a silver lining in her relationship with Emmett, it would be the people it brought into her life.

Butterflies fluttered in her stomach as they pulled in front of the safe house. She wanted Cole with all of her being, but since she hadn't been with anyone since Emmett, she stared to doubt that she could satisfy Cole. Emmett had treated sex as another method of manipulation. She'd long ago stopped finding any enjoyment in the physical act and was thankful when he stopped bedding her the last few months of their engagement. She knew being with Cole would be different, special. But would she be enough for him?

Before they went inside, Rigger and Lex cleared the house to make sure their security had not been breached. Cole held her in the circle of his arms, his eyes alert to their surroundings as they waited. Getting the all clear nod from Lex, they stepped inside.

"You go to the bedroom and freshen up. I'm going to talk to the guys for a few minutes, and then I'll join you." Cole kissed her briefly, but the contact sent a spark of electricity straight to her toes.

She smiled and retreated without bothering to ask what the men had to talk about. Tonight she was content to let them worry about guarding over her without asking to be kept in the loop. She was too preoccupied with what was to come once she and Cole were alone. Once she closed the bedroom door behind her, she crossed over to the dresser. She slid open the top drawer filled with her underthings and reached toward the back for a filmy piece of silk and lace.

She'd been surprised when she'd unpacked the suitcase Chloe had brought to her at the safe house and found the slinky negligee. It had been a birthday present from her friend, but it had stayed hidden in her dresser since she had no reason to wear it. What possessed Chloe to pack it, she didn't know, but now she felt like she needed the sexy lingerie to build her confidence. Her knees felt so weak, she was surprised they weren't knocking together.

Locking herself in the bathroom, she unplaited her hair and brushed the thick strands until they fell in shiny waves. She washed her face and grimaced at the freckles across her cheeks and nose. She wished she had makeup to cover them but refused to dwell on what she didn't have. She wanted to hurry and be in bed before Cole finished with Rigger and Lex.

She shed her clothes and slipped the negligee over her head.

The fabric fell over her body like liquid silk. The spaghetti straps settled on her shoulders. The neckline dipped into a deep V, trimmed with delicate lace that showcased her cleavage without making her feel uncomfortable. The hem floated just above her knees, the champagne-colored fabric hugging her curves. Even though she was used to sleeping in shorts and oversized t-shirts, she had to admit the gown made her feel sexy without being too risqué.

Sucking in a deep breath to calm her nerves, she stepped from the bathroom. She drew up short, a gasp escaping her throat. Cole sat on the edge of the bed, his boots and socks scattered on the floor next to him. She stared at his bare feet, wondering how a man's toes could be so sexy, when he stood and kicked his footwear under the bed. He approached with slow, purposeful strides that reminded her of the jungle cat he was nicknamed after. She almost bolted, but the intensity of his gaze kept her rooted to the spot.

He stopped in front of her, and Sydney couldn't draw a breath. His hands settled on each side of her neck, his thumbs caressing her cheeks.

"You're beautiful."

She swallowed the lump in her throat. His eyes fairly glowed with a bright fire and a promise of what was to come. His head started to lower, and panicked, she jerked away from his touch.

"I'm sorry. I, um…You're, um…I just…"

He placed a finger on her lips to silence her. "It's okay. I'm nervous too. We can take this as slow as we need to. Nothing has to happen tonight if you're not comfortable. I'd never pressure you. I hope you know that."

Her heart melted. She grabbed his finger and pulled his hand down. "You're nervous, too?"

He smiled. "Yes. I want it to be special for you. You've been through a lot. The last thing I want to do is rush this."

"You're not rushing anything. It's me. I haven't...I mean it's been a long time. What if—"

"Stop. There's no way that sex between us won't be hot as hell."

"It's been a while for me. I'm not sure I'm even very good at this."

"Oh, baby," he drawled. "All you have to do is feel. Let me worry about the rest."

He lifted her in his arms as if she weighed nothing and dropped her in the center of the bed. She giggled as she bounced a little before settling against the pillows. He loomed over her, his eyes roaming her body as if he wanted to devour her. She squirmed under his scrutiny, her hands smoothing her negligee against her thighs.

"You're beautiful," he breathed, his tone almost reverent as he studied her.

Words escaped her. She couldn't look away from the desire burning in his eyes and the slight curve of his lips. She'd never considered herself to be beautiful. If not for her red hair, she'd call herself plain. But with the way Cole spoke to her and looked at her, she believed him. And she was thrilled that he found her beautiful.

He reached over his shoulder to grab the neck of his shirt, pulling it over his head in one swift motion. She was faced with the hard lines of his chest and his golden skin. A sprinkling of hair covered his pecs before falling in a single line to disappear under the waistband of his jeans. She reached out, but her palm hovered over his chest. She was almost afraid to touch him, as if he was a dream that would disappear under her fingertips.

"Touch me, Sydney."

His gentle command was all she needed. She ran her fingers over his chest, and then his arms, before settling on his shoulders. His own hand stroked her hair, and then his finger caressed her cheek. He lowered his head and captured her lips. She buried her fingers in his hair as she surrendered to the kiss. He gently pulled her hair, tilting her head to gain better access to her mouth. The kiss built in intensity, setting her blood on fire.

She barely registered his hands on her legs until they slid under the hem of her gown. The silky fabric glided across her thighs, raising goose bumps on her skin. It pooled just under her breasts as his hands hovered over her stomach. His touch was light, but Sydney thought she'd die from the pleasure of it. He ended their kiss, staring into her eyes as his lips curved in a wicked grin. Before her foggy brain could register what he was doing, he moved down.

He kissed the expanse of her stomach. Sydney didn't have a chance to feel embarrassed at the flabby weight she carried around her middle. She wiggled at the onslaught of passion his kisses evoked. He ran a finger along the edges of her panties, and she feared she would either faint or die from the overwhelming desire without ever knowing what it would feel like to have him inside her.

He slid her underwear down her legs, the movement deliberate and slow.

"Cole," she moaned, wishing he would move faster. She needed him to bring the release she desperately wanted.

He tossed her panties to the side and kissed his way up her legs, moving from one to the other until he reached her core. He nuzzled her and dropped a warm kiss to her center. She bucked, crying out her pleasure. He stood and shucked his jeans and boxer briefs in one fluid motion. He reached for her gown, and she helped him pull it over her head. They were bare before each other. Her breath left her in a rush.

He was ripped, his broad shoulders and muscular chest tapering in a trim waist and thick trunk-like legs. His thick erection rose to meet his belly, and all her fears and doubts fled. All she could think about was feeling him next to her, on top of her, inside of her. She reached for him, bringing him down for a kiss. She poured all of her feelings, all of her passion, into the kiss. She nipped at his lips, then smoothed them with her tongue. His hand kneaded her breast, rolling her nipple between his thumb and forefinger. She responded by thrusting her tongue in his mouth, dancing with his tongue, relishing how close she felt to him.

Cole broke away, his chest heaving as he caught his breath. "I wanted to take my time. I wanted to know every inch of your delectable body. But I don't think I can last. I need to be inside you."

"Don't wait," she gasped. "I need you. Please."

He left her long enough to grab a condom from his jeans pocket and rolled it on. Then his body covered hers, weighing her down in the most delicious way. She wrapped her arms around his neck and her legs around his waist. He lined himself up at her entrance and thrust inside her. She gasped at the exquisite combination of pleasure and pain. He stilled, allowing her body to adjust to him.

"God, Syd. You're so tight."

"I need you to move."

"I don't want to hurt you."

"You won't. I promise. Please, Cole. I need this."

He kissed her and grinned. "Whatever you want."

So he moved, the friction unleashing Sydney's passion. Her fingers dug into his back as her world shifted on its axis. She was caught up in a whirlwind of pleasure and held on for dear life. He picked up the pace, the sounds of their bodies connecting filling the room. She cried out as passion swirled within her.

"Cole! Oh, Cole! Please don't stop!"

Never slowing down, he reached between them to massage her clit. The intensity of the contact sent her over the edge. Her orgasm rocked her, shattering her reality until there were only her and Cole and this moment. His release soon followed hers, and they rode out the force of their orgasms until they were both spent. Without breaking their contact, Cole rolled them until he laid on his back with Sydney cradled against his chest. She purred at the feel of his fingers gliding through her hair.

"That was…intense."

He chuckled. "Yes, it was. I hope I didn't hurt you."

She raised her head and lightly kissed his lips. "You were amazing. Everything about tonight was amazing. Eating and laughing with your friends, talking with you in the moonlight, and this. It was special. You are special to me."

She worried she may have shared too much. They talked about their lives without actually talking about what they felt for each other. She chewed her bottom lip as she waited to see if she ruined the moment. He touched her chin until she released her lip, then he kissed the bruised flesh.

"You are special to me too, Syd. Now relax. I want us both well-rested when we do this again."

She grinned and settled against him. In a matter of moments, she fell asleep, feeling safe in Cole's arms.

Chapter Twenty

Fathomless black eyes glared at her. Thin lips twisted in a sinister leer as large hands reached for her. Her mind told her to run, but her feet were glued to the ground. She opened her mouth to scream, to call for help. No sound came from her throat. The hands loomed larger as they drew closer. She stretched up to defend herself, but she couldn't reach him. His hands grasped her throat and squeezed. She couldn't draw in breath. Her lungs burned. Spots appeared before her eyes, and she realized with a startling clarity that death was imminent.

"You are mine, Sydney. You are mine."

His voice held a steel edge. It would be the last thing she would hear. His craggy face the last thing she would remember.

Sydney woke with a start, her heart pounding in her chest. A sheen of sweat beaded on her forehead and upper lip, and the sheet wrapped tightly around her body as if she'd been tossing and turning. She sucked in cool air as she tried to orient herself to the real world after the vividness of her dream.

She turned her head as Cole stirred next to her. Laying on his back, he faced her, exhaling soft breaths through his mouth. Her head was on one muscular arm while his other one rested across his stomach. Her eyes focused on his lashes fanning across his cheeks, softening the rugged plains of his face. The sight eased her panic and evened her breathing. With careful movements, she rose from the bed, pausing whenever he stirred to see if he would wake. She finally tiptoed into the bathroom, lightly closing the door behind her.

Once alone, she allowed her tumultuous thoughts to run free. She stared at her reflection and grimaced. Her freckles shined under the harsh light, and her red hair was a riotous mess about her shoulders. Her mouth was plump and swollen, evidence of the night she'd spent with Cole. A smile curved her lips as she recalled just how thoroughly he worshiped her body last night and how she'd enjoyed learning his—every hard plain and curved muscle and rough scar. His form was perfect with its imperfections, and the image of him standing over her, gloriously naked, would forever be burned in her memory.

And then the dream upset her sense of peace. She'd left Cole's side to escape the unease settling in the pit of her stomach, but the brief flashes of her dream wouldn't stop replaying in her mind. Eventually, Cole would come for her, checking to make sure she didn't regret sleeping with him. She never wanted him to doubt how much she wanted him, how amazing his body felt covering her, skin to skin.

The night had been the best of her life, and she wanted nothing more than to have a repeat in the light of day. Too bad her brain had other ideas.

She reached to twist the hot water spigot in the shower and added enough cold to keep her skin from burning. Stepping under the shower spray, she closed her eyes as the water sluiced over her body, steam quickly filling the room. As much as she wanted to forget, she drifted back into the recesses of her memory, recalling what she could of the dream. Fear and panic started to build in her chest, but she powered through, knowing she'd never shake off its impact until she remembered what details she could.

She had no idea how long she stood there, her eyes closed, the relaxing effect of the shower doing its job. A pair of strong arms snaked across her middle, and she was pulled against the familiar, solid strength of Cole's body. She hadn't heard him enter the bathroom, but she wasn't startled by his sudden presence, either. She relaxed into his embrace. The evidence of his morning arousal nestled against her back, and her blood pulsed in her veins. She tilted her head, her eyes still closed, and offered her lips.

The kiss was soft. His lips brushed against hers with the faintest of touches. She sighed, and he took advantage of her parted mouth to deepen the kiss. His tongue swept her mouth, tasting the sweetness she had to give. Without breaking contact, she turned until her breasts were pressed against his chest. She whimpered when he ended the kiss. He grinned, his hand cradling her cheek. Her eyes moved from watching water droplets slide over his skin to meet his own intense gaze, the amber irises glowing with desire.

"Good morning." His voice held an early morning gruffness that caused her to shiver even under the warm spray of the shower.

"Good morning." She wrapped her arms around his neck and nestled her cheek against his chest.

"I had hoped to find you in my arms when I woke this morning. I had visions of kissing you out of a deep sleep, but instead I found that side of the bed cold."

"I...needed to think. A shower always helps me center my thoughts."

His brow furrowed. "Everything all right?"

She smiled as her thumb caressed the space between his brows until the lines smoothed. "Oh, yeah. Everything is just fine."

She had no idea she could infuse the sexy drawl into her voice, but she delighted in his answering grin. She expected him to take her back to the bedroom. Instead, he turned her around. Before she could question him, he reached for a bottle of two-in-one shampoo and conditioner. He filled his palm with the white liquid, replaced the bottle on the shelf then rubbed his hands together until the liquid lathered.

When his hands buried in her hair, she closed her eyes and moaned. His fingers deftly worked the lather through her thick tresses. She didn't have the heart to tell him how much she hated using two-in-ones on her thick hair, not when his gentle ministrations felt so good.

He pulled down the shower nozzle and thoroughly rinsed the soap from her hair, the heavy strands falling slick and straight down her back. His finger followed the line of her hair down the delicate crease of her back and along the curve of her backside. Her breath caught in her throat. His light touch was exquisite torture, but she stood perfectly still, not wanting him to stop.

Replacing the shower head, he reached for a bottle of body wash, repeating what he'd done with the shampoo. This time, his hands massaged the soap into her skin, starting with her shoulders then trailing down her arms. When he fondled her breasts, she moaned and breathed deep. A woodsy aroma that was all Cole invaded her senses.

"I'm sorry I don't have something that smells more fruity or flowery."

She giggled. "I don't care. This is perfect."

His hands traveled down her sides. Sydney thought she would explode from pleasure as he kneaded her backside before caressing the apex between her legs. She could hear him kneeling behind her to massage each thigh and then each calf. She never knew a shower could feel so erotic, and she'd never be able to take one again without being turned on.

By the time he rinsed the soap from her body, Sydney was near her breaking point. "Cole," she groaned.

She heard a tear and glanced over her shoulder to see him roll a condom over his impressive erection. His hands gripped her shoulders to turn her slowly. He kissed her hard, backing her against the shower wall. He lifted her, and her legs instinctively wrapped around his waist. He broke the kiss just as she felt his cock nudge her entrance.

"Look at me."

Her eyes flew open, immediately entranced by the smoldering depths of his own. He rested his forehead against hers as he thrust inside her. She gasped as her body adjusted to him, and then she groaned at the pleasure exploding within her. His pace was slow at first, teasing her oversensitive libido. When his thrusts sped up, the intensity built. She gripped his shoulders, her nails biting into his skin as she wondered if the mounting ecstasy would be too much for her to bear.

Her orgasm hit her with the force of a freight train. Blinding light flashed before her eyes as she cried out his name. She threw her head forward to rest on his shoulder, grounding herself against the onslaught of emotion that coursed through her. He growled through his own release, and they rode the high together, clinging to each other for dear life.

Sydney fell limp against him, thankful for his strength to keep her from collapsing against the shower floor. She ran her hands up and down his back as he brought his panting under control. He slipped out of her and steadied her on her feet. He lowered his head to kiss her, his lips lingering, before he turned off the water and helped her step from the shower. Without a word, he toweled her dry from her hair down to her toes before hastily doing the same to himself. Then he lifted her in his arms. He carried her to the bed and settled her on his lap, his back against the simple wooden headboard.

Sydney wrapped herself around him, peace settling over her. His hands roamed over her back, his caresses lulling her into contentment.

"Cole," she mumbled against his neck, his pulse beating against her lips.

"Yeah, baby?"

"I wish we didn't have to go to work."

He chuckled, and she loved feeling the vibration of his chest against hers.

"We don't have to. It's Saturday. We can spend the entire day right here, just the two of us."

She shook her head. "I'd love that, but I need to go to work."

He stayed quiet long enough that she started to wonder if he was ignoring her. She opened her mouth to repeat herself when he spoke first.

"You have a lead, don't you?"

"Maybe. I don't know for sure. It could be nothing."

"But your gut is telling you something. Is that why you got out of bed?"

"Yes. I had a dream, and it got me to thinking. I'd rather not say any more until I know if there's something worth saying."

He nudged her lightly with his shoulder until she raised her head to look at him. "What is your gut telling you?"

She sighed. "What if I'm wrong? I don't want to let everyone down."

"What is your gut telling you?"

"That I need to check it out. That it could be the lead we need."

He kissed her. "The only way you can let anyone down is not trusting your gut. Even if it's nothing, we have to rule out leads before we can pinpoint the one we need. Get dressed, sweetheart. You've got work to do."

Sydney pushed away from the computer, reaching for the eye drops she kept nearby. She wouldn't allow herself to look at the clock on her screen because she didn't want to know how long she'd been working. The kinks in her body and her dry eyes were enough evidence of how much time had passed. The more she researched, the more questions she raised that kept her investigating one source after another.

She was proving her hunch to be true, but the knowledge wasn't making her feel any better. If anything, she was realizing just how much danger they were facing with this case.

The door to the command center swished open. "Never fear," Chloe dramatically announced as she breezed into the room. "I deliver sustenance."

The rich aroma of strong coffee and baked goods brought a tired smile to Sydney's face. "You have beignets. They smell amazing, but why are you here? Shouldn't you be at work?"

Chloe set the bakery box on the table next to Sydney before settling in a chair, her own to-go cup of coffee in her hand. "My morning meeting got canceled, so I thought I'd come by and see you in action."

Sydney sipped her coffee. "Cole called you."

"He did. He said you guys got here before the sun came up, and you've been working non-stop since. He's worried about you. He said you have a lead, but you won't tell him what it is. Should we be worried?"

"Actually, yes. I didn't want to tell the team until I knew for sure, but I found Emmett's partner. And I think he's the reason Emmett is harassing me again."

"What?" Chloe leaned forwarded, her eyes wide. "How is that possible?"

Sydney sighed. "It's a long story. I wasn't even sure I was right until I came in to do some digging."

"When are you briefing the team?"

"As soon as Cole can get everyone together. They need to know exactly what we're up against. They've been trying to bring down Emmett without all of the information."

"Then I'm staying. I should hear this too."

"That's not nec—"

"Don't. I've been under protection this whole time because they're afraid Emmett will hurt me to get to you. I deserve to know what you've found."

"All this time, I didn't think I could have anything useful to bring to this investigation. But after talking to Cole last night, it's like whatever was blocking my memory was lifted. He never batted an eye when I told him. He just encouraged me to trust my instincts and brought me here to do what I needed to do."

"He's a good man. As much as I hate to admit it, they all seem to be."

"Even Sam?" Sydney couldn't resist teasing her friend about her bodyguard, especially when Chloe made a point to give him a hard time.

"Yes, even Sam. But if you say anything, I'll deny it to my last breath. It would just boost his already overinflated ego, and I sure as hell don't need to deal with that."

"Your secret is safe with me. I'm just glad to hear that you don't think I'm crazy for trusting them."

"No. Not anymore. They're going above and beyond to protect you, so they can't be all bad. And I can see Cole makes you happy. You deserve that. But I promise, if he hurts you in any way, I'll castrate the SOB."

Sydney rolled her eyes. "Please don't do that. I kind of like that part of him, so I'd be sad to see it go."

Chloe choked on her sip of coffee, eliciting a coughing fit. "Oh, my God. Sydney Reede, are you telling me that you sealed the deal with Cole? When? How was it? I need details. How have we been sitting here this whole time, and you never brought this up until now. Way to bury the lead."

"I'm not telling you any details, but you're right. He makes me happy. So all I'll tell you is that last night was perfect. And this morning was hot."

Sydney's cheeks flushed, and Chloe cackled. "Oh, no. I'm not letting you off the hook. Let's get the team in here for the briefing. Then you and I are sneaking off somewhere for some girl talk."

Sydney didn't have the heart to tell Chloe the girl talk would likely have to wait once the news about Emmett's case came to light.

Chapter Twenty-One

Sydney stood with her back to one large screen that occupied the entire wall of the KSI command center. Her heart pounded in her chest, her stomach rolling with unease. She sensed Chloe and Cole sending her looks of reassurance, but she couldn't face them. She kept her eyes focused on a point on the back wall, trying to ignore all the faces in the room.

She pressed a button on a small remote controller in her hand. Without glancing behind her, she knew the screen showed a larger-than-life image of the man she dreamed of last night.

"This is Daniel Dawson, the man I believe to be Emmett Carter's partner in all of his criminal activities. Emmett introduced Danny to me as his foster brother, but other than living in the same group home as teenagers, they never lived with a foster family to my knowledge. I haven't seen Danny in years. I've actually only met him a few times, but it was enough for me to know he has evil inside of him. I wouldn't be surprised if all of their crimes are his idea, and Emmett is along for the ride."

"I've done deep background checks into Carter," Kat reminded her. "I never came across any connection with Danny Dawson."

"He's been off the grid for years. I had to get...creative, but he's involved."

"What do you mean, creative?" Jay eyed her skeptically.

"Just bear with me, and I'll explain. Emmett was put into the foster care system when he was fourteen. His father had just died, and his mother signed over her parental rights to the state, claiming she couldn't care for him on her own. I accessed his records. His social worker believed Emmett suffered from severe abandonment issues, and that resulted in him misbehaving enough that no foster home would accept him. So he went to a state group home.

"Emmett told me once when we were dating about how much he was bullied at the group home. His file confirms it. The abuse was bad until Danny stepped in. Emmett's social worker made a note in his file, speculating that Emmett befriended Danny out of survival. The others at the group home steered clear of Danny. They were all afraid of him. Even then, people could see that something about him was off."

"I'm guessing since you're telling us all of this that it's relevant to the case. So I have to ask—what was in it for Dawson? Why befriend that wimp Carter when he already ruled the group home?" Wings' tone held its typical sarcasm, but his question had merit. She'd wondered the same.

"I accessed Danny's records as well. His social workers all said he was a loner. He had been in the system since he was an infant. He'd been placed in more foster homes than you can count, but they never worked out. The foster parents were either abusive or neglected him, or Danny exhibited behavior that forced the foster parents to put him back in the system."

"What kind of behavior?" Cole asked.

"Danny abused their pets, played cruel practical jokes on the other children, vandalized property, stole from the homes—you name it. No one ever caught him red-handed doing any of this, but all indications pointed to him as the culprit. According to the group home's records, even the most sainted of foster parents had a difficult time with Danny, and some even said they were afraid of him. By the time Danny was thirteen, the group home stopped trying to arrange foster care or adoption for him.

"He seemed to thrive on intimidating others, both at the group home and at school. His friendship with Emmett was completely out of character. There was an evaluation from an employee at the group home that said she hoped Emmett would be a good influence on Danny. The opposite was actually true. Emmett became Danny's sidekick in terrorizing the others.

"Danny and Emmett ran away from the group home when they were seventeen. There's no record of either of them for years. No employment records or tax records, no driver's licenses, no bank accounts, not even an arrest report."

"They were likely living on the street, probably stealing whatever they needed," Jay speculated absently.

Sydney nodded. "The next time there's any record of Emmett was when he was employed by the investment firm where I met him. He started at an entry level job and quickly worked his way up to an executive position."

"The company never checked his credentials," Kat spoke up. "His resume stated that he had an MBA and had worked for a smaller investment group. I checked into that when we first started investigating. There's no record of him attending college anywhere."

Sydney took a deep breath, since the next part of her presentation involved her own experiences with Danny.

"I had just moved in with Emmett when I first met Danny. I thought it was odd that in the year we dated, Emmett never told me about or had me meet his best friend. Once I met Danny, I wished I hadn't. The way he looked at me gave me the creeps. It's hard to explain, but if the boogie man was a real person, he would be Danny Dawson. Afterward, I told Emmett how I felt and he assured me I'd never be left alone with Danny. This was before Emmett became abusive. I had no reason not to believe him."

"Something tells me Dawson didn't leave you alone," Tristin

spoke up, and Sydney watched Cole's hands curl into tight fists, the only indication that he knew the rest of her story.

Sydney shared with the group what she'd told Cole earlier that evening. She wasn't sure how she managed to retell the memory again without falling apart. Her heart pounded in her ears, drowning out the silence that descended once she finished.

Chloe immediately rose to stand next to Sydney, placing a reassuring arm around her friend's shoulders. She didn't speak, but Sydney drew strength from her friend.

"Danny and Emmett have a tight relationship. They look out for each other. Emmett is an abuser, but Danny is the one I'm afraid of. I hadn't thought of him in a while, but when I started remembering all the things Emmett told me about his days at the group home, I remembered Danny. I wasn't even sure if he was still in Emmett's life until I did some digging."

"And what did you find?" Cole asked.

"Danny's mother gave him up for adoption at birth. He was illegitimate, and she managed to conceal her pregnancy up until the moment she gave birth. There was no father of record on Danny's birth certificate, and he changed his name sometime along the way."

Sydney hit the switch on her remote, and the image of a beautiful woman with shocking white-blond hair and arresting brown eyes popped on the screen next to Dawson's image.

"Daniel Dawson Morgan was born to Cecilia Morgan, who later became Cecilia Rappaport."

"Oh, my God! I know her!" Chloe stood gaping at the screen.

"Who the hell is Cecilia Rappaport?" Wings bellowed.

"She's a very wealthy woman who would give her fortune to be accepted into the country club crowd. But considering how she came into her money, it won't happen until some of the older families start dying off. She used to work for James Rappaport, and the two had an affair while his wife was dying from pancreatic cancer. Not four months after he buried his wife, he married Cecilia. While he was alive, everyone within his circle tolerated her, but he died of a heart attack a few years ago. After that, she's resorted to crashing all sorts of events because she doesn't receive an invitation. I swear she's donated half her fortune to as many charities as she can find, hoping to win people over. It's not worked, but that doesn't stop her from trying. Are you telling me this guy is Cecilia and James' son?"

"Yes. James never claimed him, and I'm guessing she left his name off the birth certificate to protect him. I'm also guessing she thought she would lose him if she kept the baby, so I think that's why she signed away her parental rights when Danny was a baby. When Danny became an adult, he legally dropped his last name and started going by Danny Dawson."

"Didn't Emmett try to go into business with Cecilia?" Chloe asked.

"Yes, he used to stalk her any chance he got to convince her to invest in whatever scheme he had going. She'd always turn him down, and he'd be enraged. I don't know if Emmett knew of her connection to Danny, but it seemed too big of a coincidence for me not to wonder."

"We always thought Carter knew someone with connections who could cover up his crimes. Would she have enough power to make that happen?" Jay took a couple of steps closer, his gaze focused on the screen, his jaw tense.

"Actually, it's entirely possible," Chloe answered. "James had a lot of power. I heard rumors that he had the mayor and a couple of city councilmen in his back pocket. Whenever he wanted to purchase some land or build something, they would help him get around the ordinances and give him some business incentives. It's possible Cecilia maintained those same connections."

"You mean, connections like these?" Sydney clicked the control again, and grainy images of Cecilia Rappaport appeared. She was obviously at a hotel just outside of town, but the crowd had to study the images before they recognized who she was with.

"Well, that's the mayor with her in that one picture. Who's the other guy?" Tristin squinted as if that would help him see the image clearly.

"Damn," Jay hissed. "That's the sheriff. There's our leak."

Sam moved forward, his face a mask of rage. "You mean, he's the one who blew my cover and almost got me killed?"

Jay faced his friend and nodded gravely in his direction. "The DEA looped him in on all of the operations in case we needed backup. He could have shared that information in some pillow talk, and Cecilia could have shared it with Carter and Dawson."

"I want him, Jay," Sam roared. "I want him taken down with the rest of them. The bastard almost got me killed."

"There's just one problem," Zane interjected, and every eye in the room turned in his direction. "It's all circumstantial. None of it proves Carter's ties to human trafficking or drug trafficking. None of it proves what he did to Jay's sister."

"But it shows what he wants with me," Sydney said. "He knew if I told you about Danny, you'd eventually find out about Danny's mother, and it all would start falling down around them."

"How do we piece this all together? Even if we know what he wants with you, how do we turn that into evidence to take him down?" Tristin mused.

"It won't be easy," Jay admitted. "They've known about us this whole time, so they know about our investigation. They've stayed one step ahead of us because they've seen us coming. Now they know Sydney's with us. They'll get desperate, and that means they're more dangerous than before."

"So what are you saying?" Cole's eyes narrowed as he regarded the team leader.

"I'm saying we've got to get ahead of him if we have any hope of bringing him down. We need a plan."

Jay took a position next to Sydney. She felt shaky from all she'd shared, so she gladly moved to the side to let the team leader take control.

"We can't waste any time. Kat, we need you and Sydney to gather all the intel you can find on Dawson, Rappaport and Carter. No detail is too small. Tryst, we need Brick, Einstein and Isobel to get in here now. I want them and Sam running down known associates. Alpha Team, we're going back through everything we know. Now that we've identified Carter's partners, I want to comb through our case for clues that may not have made sense before. There could be a link we dismissed earlier because we couldn't tie it to anything.

"Rigger and Lex, Delta Team is taking over protection detail. Coordinate with Jordan. I want to track everyone as they come and go. If no one has a reason to leave, then they don't leave. No intel gets shared outside of KSI. We're on lockdown until further notice. We're plugging this leak."

Chloe cleared her throat. "Um, wait a minute. When you say lockdown, you don't mean me, right? I have a job outside of here, remember?"

"Sorry, Chloe, but yeah, I mean you, too. We can try and set you up with a work space inside KSI, but it's too easy for Carter to get to you outside of here, even with a protection detail. It sounds extreme, but we can't underestimate him. It's how he's beaten us so far."

"But what about showering? Eating? Sleeping? I mean, do you really think it makes sense for all of us to stay here 24/7?"

"We'll figure it out. This is the way it has to be."

Sydney reached out to squeeze Chloe's hand. "You could actually help us. You know Cecilia and Emmett and the society crowd they're a part of. We could use your insight."

"Fine, I'll stay. I'm sick of Emmett and his creepy brother hurting my best friend and God knows how many others. I want to help, so you can go in and kick their sicko asses."

Sydney couldn't hold back the grin that split her face. Everyone at KSI had yet to witness just how deep her friend's fierceness and inner strength ran, but they were about to get a ringside seat.

"Let's get to work," Tristin ordered.

"Everyone has their assignments. Take ten to get refreshed, and then get back at it. I'm with Chloe on this. I'm ready to kick ass and put these guys away for good."

"Roger that," Zane agreed, and the group dispersed.

Chloe returned to Sydney's side and enveloped her in a hug. "You okay?" her friend whispered in her ear.

"Yeah," Sydney breathed. "I'm fine. Talking about it is supposed to be therapeutic, right?"

Chloe pulled back to study her friend's face. "Bullshit. Talking about it is like reliving it, and what you went through would have shattered the strongest of women."

"Not you," Sydney fought the tears stinging the back of her eyes.

"You're stronger than me. I put on a good show, but you – there's nothing about you that's a show. You're real, and you're the bravest soul I've ever met. And I'm not the only one who sees it."

Chloe cut her eyes, and Sydney shifted her gaze to see Cole hovering nearby. His nervous energy was palpable, but he still gave the two women privacy.

"He's amazing. I trust him, and I never thought I could trust a man after the pain Emmett put me through. Cole's different."

"He is, and unless I'm wrong, which we both know I never am, he's crazy about you. I like him."

Cole captured her gaze, and her heart began to race. "I do too."

She was unaware of Chloe stepping away as Cole came to her side. He didn't touch her, but his eyes caressed her face.

"You're amazing."

Sydney's heart flipped over as a blush stained her pale cheeks. "I don't know about that. I'm just glad I'm finally able to contribute something to this case. It's about time I earned my keep around here," she joked.

"You don't have to prove yourself to us. Especially to me. You're one of us, and you have just as much right to be here as I do."

"Thank you," was all she could bring herself to say.

Electricity sparked between them, and as often happened when the two of them were together, everyone and everything in the room faded away until she was only aware of the man in front of her. The beautiful man with the breadth and handsomeness of a mythical god, the courage and protectiveness of a knight in shining armor, and the sincerity and romance of her dream man. She yearned to be alone with him. She craved his touch and his kiss.

As if sensing the direction of her thoughts, his warm palm cupped her cheek. His head lowered slowly. Sydney's breath caught in her throat. His firm lips lightly brushed her cheek and hovered until she thought her heart would pound through her chest.

"I have to go. If you need me, call or text me. I'll be there. Always."

"I know."

His smile warmed her from the toes up. He raised his head, gave her cheek one final caress and then turned to follow the other team members as they left the command center. She slowed her breathing, willing her heart to return to normal rhythm as she watched him walk away. She could no longer deny that Cole Atwood hadn't just won her respect and her trust. He'd captured her heart.

Chapter Twenty-Two

Adrenaline pumped through Cole's veins, and anticipation set his nerves on edge. After hours of strategy planning with the Alpha Team, he felt the familiar thrill that came when he had a mission with his old SEAL buddies. He finally felt a part of a team again.

They were close to capturing Carter. Cole could feel it. Once Carter was out of the picture, he and Sydney could finally explore what was going on between them.

"You good, Panther?" Jay appeared at his side.

"Ready for this to be over."

"It will be soon. We're close." Jay allowed his stare to drift to where Zane reclined in the conference room chair, staring at a laptop screen while BB worked. "You and Zane cool?"

Cole followed his team leader's gaze. He could pretend not to know what Jay referred to, but he respected the man too much. "Sydney belongs with me. He knows that."

"I just don't want my team to be at war because of a woman. Especially when we're supposed to be protecting her."

"No worries, Jay. We're good. So how did you know he had feelings for Syd?"

"He told me." Jay crossed his arms across his chest. "He figured if he didn't, you would."

Cole couldn't hide the surprise from his face, which put a smirk on Jay's.

"I know. He's a private guy, but he wanted to let me know what was going on. He said he talked to you about it."

Cole nodded. "As long as he doesn't make a play for her, we have no problems. And if his feelings for Sydney means he does everything within his power to protect her, then I'm fine with that."

Jay gave a curt nod. "Fair enough. But make no mistake, if this becomes a problem for the team, I won't hesitate to bench you both. Your friendship with Tryst won't save you. The team comes first. Understood?"

"Copy that."

Jay fell silent, staring ahead at nothing in particular.

"You good, Jay?"

"No," he surprised Cole by admitting it. "My head's in the game. But now that we're this close to taking Carter down, I wish Addie could be here to see it."

"Your sister?"

"Yeah. Her name was Addison, but my parents and I always called her Addie. Until after she was kidnapped. She got away from him, but she never escaped him, man. Evidently, Carter started calling her Addie, so just hearing the nickname caused her a PTSD reaction. He killed all that was good within her. I want him to pay."

"Sorry, man. For what it's worth, I want to make him pay as much for your sister as for Sydney."

Jay slapped a hand to Cole's back. He opened his mouth to speak just as BB shouted for everyone's attention.

"Guys, we've got a problem!"

The group gathered around the conference table, and the hard expression on BB's face charged the atmosphere in the room.

"My contact at the police station just forwarded me some intel on a case he thinks could be linked to our investigation. They discovered the victim's body early this morning. Female, strangled and left in a wooded area just outside of town. Jogger stumbled across the body around dusk yesterday." BB went to work at his laptop, and soon a photo filled the screen in front of them.

Cole's blood ran cold. His eyes narrowed. The woman's image stared at them with wide blue eyes, her auburn hair falling to her shoulders. Her face was long but with freckles dotting her nose and cheeks.

"Adrienne Masters was reported missing by her roommate the day after Panther and Sydney had their accident. Adrienne was a pediatric nurse, and she was working a late shift at the same hospital where Panther and Sydney were treated. She never made it home from her shift, so her roommate reported it right away. Her car was still in the hospital parking lot. No trace of her. No signs of a struggle. Security footage revealed nothing."

"She could be Sydney's twin." A muscle in Cole's jaw bulged as he clenched his teeth.

"Carter took the nurse when he couldn't get to Syd." Zane's fist slammed into the conference table.

Cole felt his own anger boiling over, but he was too paralyzed to express it. Carter had been watching the hospital. He killed someone else because he couldn't have the one he wanted—Sydney.

"Jay," he murmured.

"I know. If Carter kidnapped and killed the woman because she reminded him of Sydney, it could mean he's ready to make a play for her again."

"Oh my God!"

Sydney's voice was barely a whisper, but it washed over Cole as if a bucket of ice cold water was dumped over him. His head whipped around to see her, Chloe and Kat standing in the doorway of the war room. Sydney stared at the photo on the screen, her face drained of all color. He swiftly moved to envelop her in his arms, shielding her from the screen. Her slender frame was shaking. A sob escaped her throat.

"He killed her. He hurt her because of me." Her voice was muffled, but he heard every word.

He buried his face in her hair, pulling her tighter against him. "None of this is your fault. We'll get him."

She raised her face. The torment in her eyes broke his heart. "I can't handle this. He's hurting people because of me. Why? He doesn't care about me. Why is he doing this?"

"He's crazy, and he's a bastard. But we will take him down—I swear."

She pulled away. "I need some air."

She fled from the war room before he could stop her. Chloe caught his gaze and nodded her intention to follow her friend.

"Make sure their security detail is close," Cole ordered Kat.

She nodded and disappeared. Cole shot a piercing stare at Tristin. "Don't make me a liar."

"We'll get him."

"Do we think it's a coincidence he just so happened to run across a nurse who looked like Sydney while she was at the hospital? That's awfully convenient," Wings spoke up.

BB shrugged. "It could be he never planned to kidnap Adrienne until he saw her. When he couldn't have Sydney, Adrienne provided the next best thing. Crazier things have happened."

"Maybe it's both," Zane theorized. "He could have stalked Adrienne before the accident, but when he couldn't get his hands on Syd, he kidnapped Adrienne instead."

"Why he took her is irrelevant at this point," Jay said. "Every woman he's taken before now has ended up as part of his trafficking ring. This one he killed. He's escalating."

The revelation sent a chill over the room. Tristin finally cleared his throat.

"Do you think this is Dawson and not Carter? From what Sydney said, this seems more like Dawson's MO."

"We need to find them. Now." Cole ran a frustrated hand through his hair. "I'm going to check on Syd. I suddenly need some air too."

He headed out of the war room, but one look in the command center told him Sydney and Chloe weren't there. Cole wandered down the hallway toward the investigators' offices but still saw no sign of the two friends. When he crossed paths with Isobel, he had her check the ladies' room only to find it empty. Though Sydney said she needed air, he hoped she had the wherewithal not to actually step outside, but when he couldn't find her, he had no other choice but to check with Jordan downstairs.

"They went out the side door."

Before he could say more, Cole set off for another part of the building, one he'd never explored before. He found the side exit of the building as Jordan directed. His gut rolled and burned, a sensation he wanted to shrug off but couldn't. Something was off. He slammed through the door and recognized the alley that ran between the KSI building and the office building next door.

All around him was eerily quiet. The sun rose high enough to cast the alley into shadows. Sydney and Chloe weren't here, but his gut still burned. Instinctively, he reached for his gun. He moved with catlike steps further into the alley, scanning his surroundings.

He pulled out his phone and called Sydney's number. A distant ringing reached his ears, and he lowered his phone to listen. The ringing was punctuated by a strange gurgling noise. Cole whipped around with his gun aimed down the alley. The he saw it—the combat boot visible from around the corner from the back of the building.

He moved stealthily, pausing to check behind every shadowy nook for anyone waiting to get the drop on him. Clearing the alley as he walked, he finally reached the end and turned the corner ready to shoot if necessary.

All was clear. Except for the bulky frame of Brick, sprawled out on the pavement, bleeding out from a wound to his chest.

Cole holstered his gun and dropped to his knees by the investigator's side. He whipped out his cell and dialed Tristin. Switching on the speakerphone, he placed it on the pavement as he assessed the brawny man's condition. He shuddered to think what went down for someone to take out a guy of Brick's size. He immediately whipped off his shirt and applied pressure to the man's wounds.

"Panther, where are you? Is Syd all right?"

"Brick's down. Syd and Chloe are MIA. Call 9-1-1, and if we have anyone with medic training, we need them in the alley behind the building. Now!"

Cole could hear pandemonium going on in the background before the call ended, but he focused on Brick. He had no idea how to assess the severity of the man's injury. All he knew to do was put pressure on the wound to try and stop the flow of blood pooling around him. A moan escaped the big man's throat.

"Brick, what happened? Were Syd and Chloe out here with you?"

"S-sor-sorry, man." Brick gasped, as if breathing was a chore. "H-he f-foo-fooled me. Took them. V-van w-w-waiting."

Icy fingers of dread tickled down Cole's spine. "Who? Who fooled you?"

"Y-you h-h-have to f-find them," Brick managed before losing consciousness.

The loud thud of the door to the KSI building being slammed open told Cole his back-up arrived. "Down here," he called.

In no time, he was surrounded by his Alpha Team members, Tristin and Isobel, who carried with her a first aid kit. Cole wasn't sure how much help the kit was going to be with a wound as severe as Brick's, but he was relieved to have someone else try to help the man.

"What the hell?" All color drained from Tristin's face. "Is he alive?"

"Yes, but it's bad. We need that ambulance."

Isobel's mouth was set in a thin, firm line as she applied gauze to Brick's wound. The man never stirred. He still had a pulse, but Cole thought his pallor already looked like that of a corpse. In no time, blood soaked the gauze, and Isobel worked quickly to replace it.

"I'll flag down the ambo and show the paramedics where to come," BB offered, taking off at a dead run back down the alley.

"He's going to need blood if he's going to make it to the hospital. He's losing it way too fast." Isobel barely glanced at any of them, her attention on Brick.

"He'll make it." Jay stared down at his friend. "You hear me, Brick? You're going to pull through this. Hang in there."

As the paramedics made their way down the alley, Jay turned to his team. "Wings, you and Zane sweep the area. BB, check with Jordan. We need security footage to find out what went down. I want to know why he wasn't alerted to what happened here."

The men moved to follow orders after one last look at their friend.

"Panther, what happened?" Tristin watched them do their work, his expression tight with concern for his friend.

"I was looking for Sydney and Chloe. They weren't in the building, but I remembered Syd said she needed air. Jordan saw them on the monitors come out the side entrance. I knew something was off, especially when I came out and they weren't anywhere around. I tried calling Syd's cell, but it's somewhere in the alley. I found Brick while I was looking for it."

Tristin nodded as he watched the paramedics hoist Brick onto a gurney and hurry him down the alley. "I'm riding to the hospital with Brick. Whatever you need, use it to find them. Keep me in the loop."

"Copy that. Same to you about Brick."

Tristin left as Wings and Zane jogged up.

"We found Syd and Chloe's cell phones," Wings told Jay. "There are some tire treads as if a vehicle tore out of here in a hurry. I took a pic and sent it to Kat to run it through the system. It's too early in the morning for any witnesses to be around to see anything."

"I want to see the security footage. We've got cameras everywhere, so we had to pick up something."

The group made their way back to the building entrance down the alley. Wings flashed a key card at the scanner on the door and swung it open with the entry light shined green. Their heavy footfalls sounded like a herd of elephants charging through the KSI building as they double-timed up the stairwell to the command center.

"Panther, was Brick unconscious when you found him?" Jay led the group down the hallway. His expression was grim, his shoulders tense.

"At first, but he came around when I tried to stop the bleeding. Said he was sorry. There was a van waiting, and Syd and Chloe were taken. He said he was fooled, but I'm not sure what he meant. Either way, I don't have to see the security footage to know this is Carter. He's got them, and I plan to move heaven and earth to get them back."

"I know, Panther. We'll find them. Right now, we have to figure out what happened, so we can track them down. I just can't believe they got the drop on Brick. He's one of the best, plus he's a damn beast!"

They burst through the glass doors but drew up short when Kat turned watery eyes toward them.

"I have the security footage cued up. Travis is on his way to help, and I have a nurse friend at the hospital who promised to call with updates on Brick," Kat told Jay quickly.

"You've seen the footage?"

She nodded, a tear falling from the corner of her eye. She turned back to her computer and tapped her keyboard. The KSI security footage from the alley began to play, and every eye in the room was riveted to the screen.

The footage picked up where Sydney had crashed through the building exit into the alley. She stumbled over to the wall of the building next door. Leaning her weight against the wall, she wrapped her slender arms around her middle, sobs obviously wracking her body though no sound filtered through the video.

Chloe wasn't far behind her, but didn't immediately rush to her side. She stood in front of her friend, talking as Sydney wept. They were alone in the alley for several minutes before Brick and Einstein followed them.

"Einstein was there too?" BB voiced the question everyone was thinking. "Where is he? Did they take him too?"

No one answered him, and he didn't expect them to. The video continued to roll. The women never acknowledged the two investigators, and their conversation was obviously becoming heated, their gestures wild. Brick and Einstein retreated toward the back of the alley to keep watch.

Without a word, Kat toggled the screen to pull up the video from the back of the building. Obviously keeping his attention on the women in front of him, Brick failed to notice Einstein moving too close, his blade at the ready. Brick turned, and Einstein moved quickly. Three quick thrusts into Brick's chest had the man falling to the ground. Einstein stepped backward a couple of times, his eyes on his partner as the bigger man lay bleeding. Then he turned to run back down the alley.

"Son of a bitch!" Jay exploded.

Kat toggled once more back to the footage at the side of the building. A black, nondescript van pulled into the alley as the women talked to Einstein. He had sheathed his knife and held a gun on the women, gesturing for them to approach the van. Two men dressed all in black, masks obscuring their faces, jumped from the van to drag the women inside.

The women didn't go easily. They struggled against their kidnappers, and Sydney dropped to her knees, sweeping her leg out to knock the thug after her off his feet.

"Good girl," Zane said under his breath, and Cole wished he could bask in pride for how well Sydney used her self-defense techniques under pressure. But the more of the footage he watched, the more he felt fear settle in his bones.

Before Sydney could do more to escape her kidnappers, Einstein jerked Chloe from her assailant's arms, secured her to his body so she could no longer fight, and held his gun to her temple. The threat to her friend obviously shook Sydney enough to stop fighting. She was the first to climb into the van. The masked men followed, and Einstein threw Chloe inside before sliding the van door closed. Einstein rode shotgun while another guy drove like a bat out of hell down the alley.

The gravity of the situation hung heavy in the command center, sucking all of the air from the room. Several seconds passed before Jay broke the silence.

"We need a BOLO on the van."

"Done. We also placed a call to our friends at the gang task force with the police department. They ran the van's plate, and the van was reported stolen from a used car lot two days ago," Kat said quietly.

"Did we get a clear shot of any of the kidnappers?"

"Our cameras never caught their faces, but the van headed west out of the alley. We found footage from a traffic cam about a block away that caught an image of the driver without his mask. We're running it through facial recognition, but no matches so far."

"I can't believe it," BB spoke up. "We were wrong. Our leak was Einstein. How could we have missed that?"

"No, we were right about the sheriff being a leak." Jay's words were clipped passing through his clenched teeth. "Carter wouldn't have known to turn Einstein until he realized who we were and why we were involved. We just underestimated Carter's influence. We need a full dossier on Einstein. I want to know how he managed to fool us all into believing he was one of us."

Kat nodded. "I've called in Travis. I figured we could use all hands on deck right now."

The gym owner was also a talented computer analyst who filled in at KSI on occasion. Once a law enforcement officer, Travis had the training to keep a cool head when situations became tense or dicey.

"Good idea," Jay agreed. "Have you already brought him up to speed?"

"Yes. He's already planning to dig for information on Einstein as soon as he gets here. In the meantime, I already messaged you the address to his apartment. And I also sent Lex and Rigger to the hospital to watch over Brick and Tristin just in case."

Adam "Rock" Davis stepped from the shadows of the command center with his Delta teammate Dallas "Tex" Wittier at his side. The Delta Team leader held Jay's gaze, the two exchanging a silent communication only they understood.

"The Delta Team is ready to assist. I have Arrow helping Jordan place motion sensors around the perimeter, and Rigger and Lex are reporting in every half hour from the hospital. Tex and I can check out the traitor's apartment."

Jay nodded. "Thanks. Go and call me with updates. Talk to some of the neighbors while you're there. I'm hoping learning more about his comings and goings, so we can get a lead on where they took Sydney and Chloe."

As the men left the command center, Jay continued. "Do we have any other way to track Sydney and Chloe besides their cell phones? What about Einstein's phone?"

"We tried to ping Einstein's cell, but he's dumped it. BB has already changed the access codes for the building, and we have the office staff reissuing new keycards. We also cut off Einstein's access to the KSI network, and we're scrubbing his computer and any other tech stuff in his possession to see if we can find his connection to Emmett Carter," Kat answered.

"How did Jordan miss what was going on?" Cole demanded. "He monitors the security feeds from the lobby, right?"

Kat's eyes flashed sympathetically in his direction. "The cameras continuously record the footage, but the monitors in the lobby rotate the display between the interior and exterior cameras. I doubt Einstein planned his attack around the feed rotations since it seemed he acted in the moment. Either he got lucky enough to avoid detection, or Jordan was distracted and missed it flashing on the screen. He's adding the motion sensors as an extra precaution so we can't be ambushed again."

"I appreciate the effort, but we need all hands on deck. I doubt there will be another surprise attack since now Carter has what he wants," Jay said.

"Shit!" Cole exploded, running his hands through his hair as he paced.

"I can take Arrow with me to go to Einstein's girlfriend's place. It makes sense we should talk to her too," Isobel spoke up, stunning everyone.

"I didn't know he had a girlfriend," Wings responded.

"Yeah, he wanted us to think he was a player, but I saw him meet up with her outside of Torch one night. I got curious, so I followed him. They wound up at her place."

No one considered it strange that the investigator had followed her colleague, or if they did, they kept the observation to themselves. Cole was beginning to realize Isobel's curiosity was part of what made her a great investigator. In this case, he was grateful her instincts afforded them another lead.

"Makes sense. Go. Check in as soon as you find out anything."

"I'll go with her," Cole volunteered. "I need to do something, or I'll go crazy."

"You need to get cleaned up. Tryst has a shower in his office. Use that. I've got some spare clothes in my office I can loan you."

Cole was confused until he looked down at his clothes. He'd been so caught up in finding Sydney, he failed to register the amount of Brick's blood staining his shirt and tactical pants. Spots even marred the surface of his boots. He stared at the stains, his mind spinning with the worst case scenario for Sydney and Chloe.

"Any luck picking the van up on traffic cams?" BB's question broke through Cole's fog, returning his focus to the case.

"We lost it just outside of town. The area is too rural for traffic cams. We're hoping the BOLO the police department put out will net us some leads, but if there's a leak within our network, who knows if something will make it back to us," Kat said.

"Do a property search," Jay told her. "Check for anything in Carter and Dawson's names or anything their known associates own. They have to have a place where they're taking the women.

Carter wants Sydney for something, so he's going to move her somewhere for her to be useful."

"Right. We'll get looking. And anything else we can do, just say so. The idea of Sydney and Chloe being with this guy…"

Kat's voice trailed off, leaving a heavy silence weighing on the room. Cole tried not to think of what Carter was doing to Sydney, but the possibilities ran through his mind like a movie reel. What if Jay was wrong, and Carter had already disposed of Sydney and Chloe? What if Carter sold her and Chloe before they could get to them? What if he killed them? He would never see the woman he loved again.

He'd known for some time he loved Sydney even if he'd never said the words out loud or even admitted it to himself before now. He didn't care he'd only met her a short time ago. He didn't care there was still a lot about her he needed to know. He felt what he felt. There was no point denying it. He loved her, and he let a madman kidnap her.

Cole tamped down the panic setting him on edge.

Hang on, Syd. I'm coming. I swear I'm going to find you.

Chapter Twenty-Three

"Syd. Syd. Wake up. Please wake up."

The frantic voice broke through the fog clouding Sydney's brain. Her head pounded, but she used every ounce of her will-power to force her lids open. She stared right into her best friend's terrified face.

"Where?" was all she managed to say. Her throat and mouth felt like cotton. What she wouldn't give for a sip of water.

"I don't know. We have to figure out how to get out of here."

As Sydney rose from the cold concrete slab she lay on, she felt as if she moved through molasses. Sitting up made pain settle directly behind her eyes, and the room swirled around her. She reached out to grab Chloe's arm to steady herself. Closing her eyes again, she waited for the overwhelming sensation to pass.

"They drugged us with something."

Chloe's words stirred Sydney's memory. The van. The alley. Brick. Einstein. The redheaded nurse. It all jumbled in Sydney's mind, and she fought to make sense of the images.

"My head kills." She cradled her forehead in her hand. "I can barely make sense of what happened."

"Einstein screwed us all over. Bastard delivered us right to your damn ex."

She groaned. "It's my fault. I shouldn't have gone outside. I made us easy targets. I was just so…"

"You were upset, Syd. After what you've gone through, it's understandable. I'm, um, sorry for what I said. I was only trying to help."

Their argument came flooding back, intensifying the pounding in her head. After she fled the war room, she'd hurried down the stairs and through the maze of hallways on the first floor at KSI until she found a door leading outside. She hadn't realized Chloe was on her heels until they were in the alley. Sydney had been hysterical, so Chloe gripped her arms, forcing her friend to face her directly.

"Get a hold of yourself, Syd, and get your head out of your ass. This is no longer all about you. This is affecting all of us, and we need you to get yourself together and do your job."

As if someone had flipped a switch, Sydney's chaotic emotions went from hysteria to full-blown anger. She knew Chloe only grumbled at her to get her under control, but suddenly, Sydney was tired of Chloe calling her on the carpet. She was tired of Emmett using her as a reason to hurt other people. She was tired of having her every move watched. She was just tired.

Einstein and Brick burst through the door into the alley, but Sydney barely acknowledged them. She turned her anger to her friend, jerking free of Chloe's hold as she squared off against her.

"Where do you get off talking to me this way? I'm the one this is happening to. I'm the one who's having to live with all of this. You think it's easy to keep my shit together with a mad-man coming after me? You know nothing of what I'm feeling or what I need! You're just here so you can put on your superhero cape and come to the rescue of your messed-up friend and feel important. I'm just some kind of charity case for you, and I'm sick of it. You don't like the way I'm acting? Well, you can just get the hell out of here."

Neither saw what went down at the back of the alley or saw Einstein approach them with a gun in his hand until he shouted at them.

"Shut up! Now!"

She and Chloe instinctively hovered close together as the man they thought was protecting them loomed over them menacingly. Their confrontation was forgotten in light of the new and unexpected threat. Sydney stole a glance around the big man to see Brick's large boot extending from the back of the building, where he laid on the ground out of sight. The gravity of their situation hit her like a sledgehammer to the gut.

"What the hell!" Chloe had seemed ready to confront Einstein, but Sydney held her back.

"What did you do to Brick?" Sydney had asked just as an unknown van pulled into the alley.

Einstein's responding smile was devoid of emotion.

"Syd, we have to go!" Chloe's warning had come too late.

Men in masks jumped from the van and dragged them inside. The women struggled against them. Sydney had employed all of the self-defense moves Zane drilled into her, but all the fight went out of her when Einstein gripped Chloe and placed the gun to her temple.

Once they were in the van, their hands and feet were zip-tied. One of the masked men rode in the back with them while the other drove. Einstein sat in the front passenger seat, his watchful eyes darting from the road to the back where they sat. Sydney felt hatred like she never knew before.

"How could you work for someone like Emmett?" She never expected a straight answer but needed to ask all the same.

Einstein regarded her with blatant disdain. "I work for myself. I choose what I want to do based on the fattest paycheck I can get. It's nothing personal."

"Nothing personal?" Chloe screamed. "You piece of shit! You just admitted to prostituting yourself out to a guy who gets his jollies from kidnapping and abusing women. Not exactly something I'd be bragging about if I were you, Einstein." She spat out his nickname as if expelling something foul.

Sydney couldn't remember beyond that point, so she figured that's when they were drugged into unconsciousness. She shook her head gently to clear her mind.

"We can't focus on what happened now. You're right. We have to figure out a way to escape. Or at least contact Cole to let him know what happened."

"Do you think Brick's okay?"

She grimaced. "I don't know. I don't know what Einstein did to him. I'd like to think he just knocked him out since we didn't hear any gunshots. I can't let my mind consider the other possibilities. Not when we need to keep our wits about us."

"I swear to God, I'm so mad right now, if Emmett comes in here, I think I could take him out by myself."

"Well, hold on to your anger, but don't underestimate Emmett. It's been my mistake the entire time I've known him."

Sydney forced herself to study the small room they were in—cement floor, block walls and no windows with one heavy metal door as their only means of escape.

"I checked the door already. It's locked. I couldn't hear anything outside. I don't think there are any cameras in here, but who knows for sure."

"I don't have my phone."

"Remember? They tossed them before shoving us in the van."

"So Cole and the team can't track us."

"It's on us. Are you up for it?"

Sydney sighed. "Looks like I'll have to be. I tried using all the tricks Zane taught me, but they didn't work in the alley. I don't know if they'll work now. We'll be outnumbered, and we don't even know if Emmett's here. We don't know where we are. If we escape, where will we go?"

"We'll figure it out. Together. I just know we can't stay put."

Sydney nodded. "What do you think they have in mind for us?"

"It can't be anything good. Emmett's done nothing but hurt you, and I don't see that changing now. He has no use for me either, so I don't have high hopes that he brought us here for any reason other than punishing us."

"Then we stay together. There's power in numbers. Stand up. We have to assess our injuries so we'll know what we're able to do when they come for us."

Sydney scrambled to her feet, fighting against the wave of nausea that almost brought her to her knees. Chloe stared at her curiously, keeping her seat on the floor. "What do you mean?"

"I'm not going down without a fight. I promised myself I would fight for my life instead of allowing Emmett to hurt me again. I will fight for you too. I know it seems pointless, but it's all we have."

Chloe hesitated a heartbeat before rising to her feet. Her eyes closed for a few seconds as she gained her equilibrium. Then she focused a fierce stare on her friend. "Tell me what to do."

"Are you okay?"

Chloe started to nod but stopped. "Just dizzy. My head hurts like a son of a bitch, but it's nothing I can't deal with. What about you?"

"The same. I'll have to power through. I may throw up from the effort, but I'll just make sure to aim at the bad guys."

A strangled chuckle escaped Chloe's throat. "I swear I don't know how you can hold your shit together, but I sure am glad you're here with me. I'm not going to lie. I'm scared. I don't want to be killed, but then there's also the very real possibility they'll sell us since that's what they do. I can't be someone's slave. I'd rather die."

Sydney sobered up, her eyes holding her friend's gaze. "They won't sell us. Emmett needs me for something, and then he'll be ready to be rid of me. I think he kidnapped you to use as leverage to get me to do what he wants. He knows I'll do whatever he asks just so he won't hurt you."

Chloe reached for her friend's hands, grasping them tightly. "Then here's our vow, and you have to agree to this with me. We don't give in. No matter what. We don't allow them to manipulate or get a hold over us, even if it ends badly. I don't want you to give in to Emmett because of me, and I know you don't want the same thing from me. He'll expect us to, though, and I say for once in his sorry life, we shock him by doing the unexpected. You with me?"

Sydney swallowed, not sure she could hold true to the vow if it meant her friend would be hurt or killed. But they had to accept the truth of their situation. She had no doubt Cole and the Alpha Team were moving heaven and earth to find them, but the likelihood of the guys getting to them in time was slim to none. The sooner she accepted her fate, the better off they both would be. Strangely enough, the realization gave her renewed strength.

The time had come to fight. Sydney was ready for it. She'd prepared for it.

"I'm with you."

Chloe nodded slowly. "Now, what's our plan?"

So the women took the next few precious minutes they had to plot their plan for survival, knowing, without admitting it out loud, they actually planned their final stand.

"You guys are not going to believe this," Isobel announced dramatically as she led the way into the command center, Arrow following close behind.

Cole immediately stopped his pacing and faced her. He kept wishing he'd gone with them to question Einstein's girlfriend just to have something to do. He hated feeling helpless, but he'd battled the emotion for the last hour. His training taught him how to remain calm and calculated in crisis situations, but the images of what Emmett Carter was doing to Sydney had just about sent him over the edge.

"What did you find out?" Jay demanded.

"Einstein's girlfriend is pissed, which was lucky for us. He broke up with her about a month ago. Instead of telling her, he just cheated on her with two women at once. The ass."

Cole could no longer wait to know what they'd found out. "What intel did she give you?"

"A lot. Why didn't Tryst tell us he hired Einstein away from Tarrant Security?"

The security firm's name had Cole's head whipping around to stare at Jay, his body stiffening. Tarrant Security was the firm that had tried to hire him before he was approached by Tristin to work at KSI. When he realized Tarrant was more of a mercenary group, he'd quickly turned them down and never heard from them again. For the company's name to come up now was unsettling.

"He didn't work there long. His first job with them went wrong, and Tryst approached him about a change. He seemed grateful for the opportunity," Jay explained.

"He chased the money," Arrow said. "Penny, his ex, said he couldn't stop talking about how Tryst paid much better than Tarrant, so the choice to change jobs was a no-brainer. Then, she said about six months ago, Tarrant started calling him again. There was one guy he would meet with off and on. She was waiting for Einstein to say he was going back to Tarrant, and she was surprised when he never did."

"It was Dawson, Jay," Isobel said. "The guy who kept coming around. Penny described him, so we showed her the picture Syd sent to us. Positive ID."

"What does Danny Dawson have to do with Tarrant? Does he

work for them?" Jay demanded.

"Penny said she never knew his real name, but Einstein always called him 'the boss.' So yeah, I'd say he works for them. That just tells me Tarrant is dirtier than we thought."

"You think they're the ones who took Syd and Chloe?" Cole asked.

Arrow nodded. "That's what we're thinking. Those guys moved with too much precision not to have some type of training. But they're hired hands only. If we go after Tarrant with all we've got, they'll likely hang Dawson and Einstein out to dry."

"I wouldn't count on it."

Five sets of eyes shifted in unison to stare at Travis Knight, who sat at a computer monitor with dark-framed glasses perched on the end of his nose. "Dawson doesn't work for Tarrant. He owns the company."

Jay moved closer to stare at the computer monitor over Travis' shoulder. "That can't be right. Marcus Tarrant is the CEO. The company carries his name."

"According to tax records, Marcus is just the CEO, not the owner. The owner is listed as Phoenix Enterprises, which is essentially a shell company. It took some digging, but I managed to find where Phoenix Enterprises traces back to Daniel Rappaport, who we now know is Danny Dawson. Tax records also show Einstein has never left Tarrant's employ. He would take on odd jobs for them during his down time from KSI. He was playing both companies against each other."

"And guess who is a client of Tarrant Security?" Kat piped up from her terminal. "Cecilia Rappaport. The company supplies her security detail when she travels, but from what I can tell, Einstein was never on her security detail."

"But it's a huge coincidence, isn't it? How they're all tied to this one company, which is our biggest competition for contracts?" Arrow returned dryly.

"Damn," Jay swore. "This is getting more complicated by the minute. Are there any ties between the cartel or Emmett Carter and Tarrant?"

"Not that I've found," Travis replied. "But Phoenix Enterprises owns a lot of real estate, everything from warehouses to homes. One of those warehouses – one on the east end of town – was burned to the ground a couple of weeks ago. Supposedly, it was empty, but the cause of the fire is suspected to be a meth lab explosion."

"A warehouse would be a good place to hide someone you don't want to be found," Cole pointed out.

"Keep checking on properties. Anything isolated would be a good place to stash someone," Jay ordered.

Fingers flew over keyboards, setting Cole's nerves on edge.

"Jay, any word on Brick and Tryst?"

"Brick is in surgery. His injuries are massive, and he was still unconscious when they arrived at the hospital. Tryst said the surgery will probably take a while, but he'll keep us posted. I should probably call and update Tryst on our progress."

"I've got something!" Cole started as Kat shouted. "Oh, my God. Cole! Jay! This is it! It has to be!"

Cole was the first to reach her side. A satellite aerial map filled the screen. He followed her finger where it pointed to a white structure in the middle of the remote area. "What am I looking at?"

"The Lansing compound."

"Wait," Arrow said as he came up behind Cole. "Lansing? The place where that religious freak held his followers hostage a year ago? The one the FBI raided?"

"The very one. Watch what happens when I switch to the infrared satellite view."

Before Cole's eyes, with one click of the mouse, the map shifted to show a series of red dots lighting up the structure. His sharp gaze zeroed in on two particular dots, very close together but set apart from the rest. His heart slammed against his chest before plummeting to the pit of his stomach. Kat was right. This was it. And the two isolated dots had to be Chloe and Sydney.

"Dawson bought the compound owned by a religious fanatic who tried to convince his flock to commit mass suicide?" Jay said dryly. "What a sick son of a bitch."

"Danny Dawson doesn't own it," Megan corrected him. "Cecilia Rappaport does."

"What the hell…" Cole could barely wrap his head around all of the twists and turns they were uncovering with this case.

"I figured since Travis was focusing on Dawson and Phoenix, I would run a separate property search on Rappaport. Since Dawson used her last name to set up his shell company, it made sense he might use it to purchase property that wouldn't trace back to him. Between her and her late husband, she owns quite a bit, but this just jumped out at me. It's not every day you find out about someone who buys an abandoned religious compound.

Cole caught Jay's eye. "This is it, Jay. I feel it."

The team leader nodded once. "Let's get everybody to the war room. BB is already there setting up our arsenal and communications. Kat, call in everyone who is out in the field. Tell them to drop what they're doing and get here ASAP. We've got a rescue to plan."

When everyone hustled to get the team back to home base, Cole released a long breath.

Hang in there, Syd. We're coming.

Chapter Twenty-Four

Sydney stared at the hands on Chloe's watch, wishing they would stop ticking away the seconds of their captivity. The two friends had been in their prison for hours with no contact with anyone outside of each other. They prepared a plan to protect themselves, knowing the time would come. But they were forced to wait and as time slipped away, Sydney's resolve grew faint.

Their dizziness had lessened during that time, but their headaches persistently reminded them of what had happened in the alley. The gravity of the situation weighed heavily in the silence stretching between them as they settled on the floor. Sydney's mind went from thoughts of Cole to memories of Brick's body lying in the alley. She prayed more than once he'd only been knocked out cold. She refused to consider a more terrible scenario.

"So are you going to marry Cole or what?" Chloe suddenly asked, breaking the stillness of the stuffy room. A thin line of perspiration had started to form on her upper lip.

Sydney stared at her wide-eyed.

"I know," Chloe continued. "I'm going stir crazy here, so I'm imagining we have a plate of Tony's tacos in front of us, we're in our yoga pants and t-shirts, and we're gossiping. Humor me, please."

Sydney gave her an indulgent smile. "I don't know. I love him, but we haven't known each other long. I haven't even told him how I really feel."

"What? What the crap, Syd? What are you waiting for? The guy is crazy about you."

"I think so too, and it's not like I haven't wanted to. It just hasn't felt like the right time to talk about it. And what if I'm wrong about the way he feels?"

Chloe snorted. "Puh-leeze. I know I'm not wrong about how he feels about you, so you shouldn't worry about that. So as far as excuses go, that one sucks."

"But you can't deny everything about our relationship is complicated."

"Yes, but your life has always been complicated. So that excuse sucks too."

Sydney's mouth set in a somber line. "He's not like any guy I've ever met. Not that there have been many guys, and they didn't really set the bar high. But Cole is one in a million. I'm scared of rushing things and losing him. I mean, what if he's only attracted to me because I'm a damsel in distress and he has some hero complex or something? I've read it's a thing for guys sometimes."

Chloe shook her head. "It's possible, I guess, but I don't think so. He loves you too. I see it in how he looks at you and how he acts around you. It's not a hero thing for him."

"When I'm with him, I don't feel these doubts. I trust him, and I feel safe and comfortable with him. We've talked about so much stuff, and he listens to what I have to say. It's like I've known him my whole life. But I don't want to make the wrong choice."

The two friends studied each other for several moments. Sydney wondered if she saw a hint of tears glistening in her friend's eyes.

"I'm jealous," Chloe admitted. "I'd have to be blind not to see the chemistry between you two. It's the real deal. I can't say you are destined to be together forever, but I'd be lying if I said I didn't want what you two have."

"You've always said you're married to your career."

"And I'm tired of it."

"What you do is important, Chloe. And you're good at it. You just need the right person to share it with. I can fix you up with one of the other Alpha Team members. Zane is cute and brooding. Jay is a take-charge guy who would never be threatened by a self-assured woman. Then there's BB. He's so smart—"

"Stop!" Chloe raised a hand, palm facing out. "Do not fix me up with Cole's friends. I do not do fix-ups. You know that."

"Okay, okay. I'll back off. But I still think you need a guy. Not a hook-up. A guy who will appreciate you."

"Th—" Chloe was interrupted by the heavy metal door screeching open. Startled, they both stood to their feet.

The women unconsciously took a couple of steps back as they watched Einstein swagger into the room with Emmett and Danny Dawson following behind. Einstein secured the door with a loud bang and positioned himself in front of it. The smirk on his face made Sydney clench her fist with the urge to punch him in the throat. But for now, he wasn't the threat. The threat – or threats, as it were – circled around her and Chloe as vultures circling an animal carcass.

Emmett wore his signature designer suit, the linen jacket unbuttoned to reveal the expensive black dress shirt and matching leather belt holding up his slacks. His smile was meant to be disarming, but the coolness in his eyes chilled Sydney to the bone.

Danny's smile was predatory, his eyes focusing solely on Sydney. Instinctively, she reached to grasp Chloe's hand like a lifeline as they faced down their captors. Danny's hair was a longer than she remembered, but otherwise he was the same menacing man who'd attacked her all those years ago.

"Hello, Sydney," Emmett greeted her. "I've been waiting for this moment for longer than I like."

"So have I," Danny added, and those three words sent fear rippling through her body. With Emmett, she knew his moves and his triggers. Danny was an enigma, just as dangerous, if not more so.

"Well, forgive me for wishing I was anywhere but here." She figured the two of them sensed her fear, but she refused to show it.

Emmett cocked his head to the side as he regarded her. "Are you saying you haven't missed me? Well, now I'm hurt." Emmett's mocking tone drew a chuckle from his foster brother.

"I wish." Sydney's nerves were so frazzled, she felt ready to snap.

"Enough with the back talk, Sydney," Danny snapped at her, and she jumped in surprise. "Show some respect, or I'll have to teach you a lesson you won't like."

Her retort died on her tongue. She tightened her grip on Chloe's hand and felt her friend's reassuring squeeze in return. She had to pull herself together if she hoped to make her stand against them.

"Relax, Dan. We have time to put them in their place. Sydney's transgressions are going to require a great deal of…punishment. But she has a job to do first. We can't lose sight of that." Emmett's tone was calm and smooth – the same tone he used when trying to woo a new investor.

"Cut the shit, Emmett. Your whole 'Godfather' routine is just making you look like a fool," Chloe raged.

Before either woman could react, Emmett rushed up to Chloe and backhanded her left cheek with enough force to send her sprawling to the floor.

Sydney gasped and dropped to Chloe's side. Her heart twisted at the sight of the blood trickling from the side of her friend's mouth. Her cheek was an ugly red and already starting to swell.

Danny and Emmett's laughter joined to echo in the room, an evil noise worthy of any psycho-slasher movie.

"Are you all right?" Sydney's hand reached to touch her friend's injury, but instead hovered over Chloe's cheek.

"I'm fine. He hits like a girl." Chloe pierced Emmett with a burning stare.

"Shut up!" Emmett spat at her. "You'll only make your situation worse the more you talk."

Sydney snapped her head up to glare at her ex, hatred darkening her eyes to a stormy hue. "Why am I here? You've been rid of me for months. Why do you want me back now?"

"I don't *want* you now, and I didn't want you then. You're a means to an end. I had high hopes for you in the beginning, but you proved to be useless. Until now. Now you get to make up for all the times you disappointed me."

"What are you talking about?"

"Did you ever wonder why I chose you in the first place?"

"Chose me? You targeted me. Like you have all of the women you've kidnapped, abused and sold." She wasn't sure where her bravado sprang from, but she clung to it despite her warning to Chloe.

Emmett started to pace. His stride was slow, easy, with a grace she'd always considered unusual for a man. Each step brought him a whisper closer to her, and Sydney's nerves sizzled with unease.

"It was my idea," Danny finally spoke up.

"What?" Chloe demanded.

Emmett's grin sickened Sydney. She wanted to look away but forced herself to hold his stare.

"Poor little Sydney. You see, Dan decided you were the perfect one to help me learn. I wasn't convinced. I've never been fond of redheads. Dan convinced me that's what made you perfect. There was very little danger of me becoming attached to you."

"Is that what happened with Addison Colter? You became attached to her."

Sydney wasn't sure why she said that, and Emmett's visceral

reaction made her wish she could take her words back. From one breath to the next, Emmett loomed over her. His hand gripped her chin tight enough to leave bruises on her pale skin, holding her head immobile. She blinked rapidly to dispel the tears blurring her vision.

"You are not allowed to talk about her! You know nothing."

"Whoa. Wait." Danny was at his foster brother's side in an instant, pulling him away from Sydney.

She winced at the sting Emmett's grasp left behind. Her eyes narrowed as she watched the two brothers step away from her. Danny forced Emmett to stare into his eyes. She couldn't hear his whispered words, but she could detect the urgency behind them.

"Hell, can we just get on with this?"

Sydney wasn't sure Einstein meant for his words to be heard, but with the block walls amplifying every sound, the words carried as if he had shouted them.

Danny's reaction was to slowly reach for his side arm and pointed it at the man. Einstein hastily moved for his own gun, but Danny fired. Sydney watched in horror as a bullet pierced the center of Einstein's forehead, sending the big man crumbling to the floor. Blood pooled around him as Sydney and Chloe's screams reverberated against the walls.

With a calmness belying what he'd just done, Danny slipped his weapon into the waistband of his jeans and turned back to Emmett.

"Should we tell her what her new job is?"

Emmett's smile was sinister. Sydney tensed as her ex approached her, but he only leered at her, his hands at his side.

"You are going to upgrade our online security."

"You don't need me for that. You can hire any computer hacker to put up firewalls and security protocols."

"And risk them blackmailing us or going to the authorities? No, it has to be you."

"I'm not helping you sell innocent women or traffic drugs. If that means you kill me, then do it."

"That's not how this works," Danny drawled. "We plan to kill you, but only after you do your job. If you refuse, the punishment for you both will be much worse. I promise you'll wish you were dead."

"I don't care. I'm not helping you."

"You may not care about yourself, but we know sweet, sweet Chloe means too much to you. Right? I mean, she's like family. We know how important family is, don't we, brother?" Danny's eyes darkened, sending a chill down her spine.

"Of course, brother." Emmett eyed Sydney with an evil humor gleaming in his eyes. "You will be falling all over yourself to do exactly what we ask. To deny us will have serious consequences for Chloe. You don't want that, do you?"

"Go to hell!" Chloe shouted at him, spitting at him, though her saliva landed to the concrete floor instead of his expensive loafers.

Danny glared at her. "Been there, sweetheart. I have no trouble taking you there with me."

"You can't force me to do this. Whatever happens, I can't help you get away with selling women as sex slaves. It's sick."

Danny and Emmett exchanged a look that sent her stomach plummeting to her feet. Danny grasped Chloe's hair and yanked her to her feet. Emmett grabbed Sydney by her arm to do the same. Chloe cried out, receiving another backhand to her face.

"We'll see how quickly you change your mind once you see what we have planned for Chloe," Emmett told her, his voice low but loud enough for both women to hear him. "I don't think you'll deny me for very long."

"I hope she does." Danny's lecherous stare swept Chloe from head to toe. Sydney suddenly felt defiled and in need of a shower, and she wasn't the one on the receiving end of his attention. "As fiery as this one is, it'll be fun breaking her."

"You touch me, asshole, and I'll rip your dick off," Chloe threatened in a low tone, which only seemed to fuel the sexual fire in Danny's eyes.

"Oh, yeah, I'm going enjoy this."

Danny dragged Chloe over to the door and pounded his fist against the steel. Her struggles against his grip were for naught. He managed to avoid her arms as they lashed out at him. The door swung open to allow two muscled men dressed all in black to storm their way in.

"No!" Sydney cried, panic rising to choke her. "Leave her alone! Don't touch her!"

"Take her," Danny ordered the men. "Hold her in my room, and don't let her out of your sight. And do not lay a hand on her. Not yet anyway. She's all mine."

One man hoisted Chloe over his shoulder in a fireman's carry. Her protests and punches to his back had little effect on him as he moved down the hall.

"Let her go," Sydney screamed and lunged after them, only to have Emmett pull her back and toss her to the floor.

Danny stopped the second man from following his partner. "Get rid of him," he ordered, indicating Einstein's corpse with a jerk of his head. The man dragged the body from the room as if it was as mundane as taking out the garbage.

"I swear to God, Emmett. If you hurt her, I will kill you myself." Rage and fear for her friend battled within her.

A chilling laugh rumbled through the room. Sydney raised her eyes to stare at Danny as he strode back toward her. With a slight nod from Danny, Emmett jerked her to her feet, pulling her tightly against him. Her arms were pinned behind her against her ex's body. His arms held her securely for Danny's inspection. Her breath caught in her chest, and her eyes widened.

Danny ran a finger down her cheek to trace the curve of her throat before circling her breast. Sydney began to shake uncontrollably – whether from fear or from anger, she couldn't be sure.

"Such fire. I always knew you had it in you, hidden under that sweet innocence. I do love fire in my women. It makes breaking them so satisfying. Emmett was making progress in breaking you when he decided to let you go. I was against it. I wanted to have my time with you. Looks like I'll have my chance after all."

He opened his hand to grab her breast, kneading the pliable flesh through her shirt. She recoiled and spit in his face. He slapped her, the force jerking her head so her temple smacked against Emmett's collarbone.

"The sooner you work with us, the better off you'll be. She's all yours, Emmett. I'm sure you know just how to persuade her to take care of our unfinished business. But make no mistake, Sydney, I'm coming back for you. Just the thought makes me hard. I think now I'll spend some time with your pretty friend."

She opened her mouth to protest, and then she felt Emmett's breath, hot and sticky in her ear. "You belong to us. Forget your Navy SEAL because you will not be seeing him again."

Danny laughed, a soulless sound that would haunt her. "Try not to break her spirit too much, brother. Leave a little for me."

He strode to the door and left her alone with Emmett. *Stay calm,* she told herself. *You can do this. You can get away and get to Chloe. You can't let Danny hurt her.*

She tried to recall all the lessons Zane had drilled into her during their self-defense sessions. The first rule Zane repeated was not to panic. The second was to fight if she could. If not, lull her attacker into a false sense of security before doing something to catch him by surprise. She stopped her struggling and forced her expression to soften.

"You're not like him, you know," she told Emmett. "Why would you let him drag you into all of this? With all of your investments and partnerships, you don't need to follow Danny into his shady businesses."

Emmett released her and shoved her roughly back to the floor. "What makes you think he did? Poor little naïve Sydney. God, you are an idiot!"

He started pacing, and Sydney knew what was in store for her. He would rant and rail at her and then hit her until she lost consciousness. It was a scene she'd lived through more than once. She had precious little time before he let loose on her. Her mind worked quickly.

"Dan is the only person to ever understand me. We're alike in a lot of ways. I saw that when we were kids. I knew we'd make the perfect team, and I was right. If anyone tried to push us around, we eliminated them. People always said we would never amount to anything. I knew they were wrong. And look at us. We have the kind of power people only dream of."

"It's not power. Abusing people, treating them like they're worthless, that's not power. That's insecurity. You're scared people won't take you seriously, so you hurt them first. You think demeaning people makes you look good. You're a coward, Emmett. Nothing you do will change that."

He loomed over her, his face a solid mask of fury. "You shut up!"

"Fat chance of that!"

She pushed her frame upward, her head connecting with the bottom of Emmett's chin. Her world dipped as her ears started to ring, but the move accomplished what she'd hoped. Emmett's head snapped backward, a resounding crack resonating in the room. He stumbled, and Sydney used his moment of weakness to her advantage. Pure adrenaline pumping through her body, she shoved him to the side. She rushed frantically toward the door. Her only thought was to get to Chloe before Danny could hurt her.

"You bitch!"

Emmett's scream caused her to falter for a moment, but she pushed on. She reached out to grab the handle on the door, praying she wouldn't find it locked.

Suddenly, the door burst open, the impact sending her sprawling to the ground. Men dressed in camouflage brandishing automatic weapons rushed into the room, deafened by Sydney's high-pitched scream of terror.

Chapter Twenty-Five

Cole watched the Alpha and Delta teams equip themselves with weapons, bulletproof vests and ear pieces, trying to tap down his fear. Sydney had been in Carter's clutches for hours, and he couldn't stop the images of what her ex was doing to her while they tried to get a plan together. He knew the time they've taken to strategize was necessary, but he grew more anxious with every second ticking by.

They all assembled in the KSI war room, listening intently as Jay outlined every detail of the rescue operation. Not only were the teams well versed in the details of Plan A but also with Plans B and C. The rule of thumb was to prepare for everything to go wrong with Plan A, as it typically did, and though Cole was ready to roll out, he understood how critical it was to have every contingency accounted for.

Isobel and Sam had insisted on joining in the rescue op since they'd been involved in Sydney and Chloe's protection from the get-go. Cole could sense the urgency humming between everyone involved. He didn't know Einstein as well as the others, but he could understand their feelings of betrayal and anger at having one of their own turn on them.

"Leave nothing to chance," Jay ordered his teammates. "These people know we're after them, and they've had inside intel on our playbook. Cunning and stealth are our only plays. I get this is personal for all of us, but now's not the time for vengeance. Sydney and Chloe are counting on us. Stay alert and stay in contact."

"If they know we're coming, won't they evacuate?" Rock asked.

"They don't know we've discovered their location. That's why Alpha is going in by air to hopefully catch them off guard and prevent our targets from slipping away. By the time we're in place, Delta and the investigators should be ready to move in from the ground. We're going in without any law enforcement support since we don't know who to trust. Tristin will clear the way. The only objective here is the rescue of the hostages by any means necessary. Understood?"

Cole resisted the urge to cringe each time Jay referred to Sydney and Chloe as hostages. He'd never been involved in an op that felt so personal. As the teams readied to leave, many of them slapped his back as they passed in a show of support. He figured when Jay approached him, he would make the same gesture, but the team leader surprised him.

"I meant what I said. Now's not the time to settle a score. Get it together or stay behind."

Cole narrowed his eyes. "No way are you benching me. You have as much at stake here as I do."

Jay nodded. "After what he did to Addison, part of me wants to put a bullet in his head and leave him in the desert for the animals to pick apart. I've got to keep that locked down. When a personal agenda is involved, an op can get sloppy. That can't happen today."

Cole stepped closer to his team leader. "I can keep my feelings out of an op. But once Syd and Chloe are safe, make no mistake, Carter is *mine*."

"We're on the same page. Carter has to pay, but though the world would be better off if he's eliminated during the op, I want him alive, so we can use him to take down his whole operation."

"He can't get away this time," Cole reiterated. "He has to be out of Sydney's life for good."

"One way or another, he will be," Jay vowed. "Let's move."

Cole didn't ask how KSI had access to a stealth chopper. He was just grateful to have it for their approach to the compound. If his mind wasn't consumed with thoughts of Sydney, he could have appreciated Wings' expertise piloting. When he was behind the controls, gone was his wiseass attitude. In its place was a professional determined to have his team's back with air support.

Cole stayed quiet during the flight, mentally preparing himself for what they would find once they landed. He closed his eyes, and an image of Sydney—her fiery hair tamed in a braid, her eyes wide and trusting, her smile sweet—set his heart to pounding.

Hang on, baby. We're coming. Don't let that bastard hurt you or Chloe.

The words played on repeat in his head. Oddly enough, focusing on that mantra kept him calm. He needed to be grounded going into this op. Sydney's life depended on it.

They hovered over the compound to get an aerial view of what they were dealing with. Jay used his ear wig to communicate with Rock on the number of guards walking the perimeter and to coordinate the air and land attack. Adrenaline rushed through his system when he heard Jay yell to Wings, "We've got the green light from Rock! Touch down!"

Wings lowered the chopper until they could jump onto the roof. The team moved as a unit as they rappelled down the building, sounds of gunfire exploding around them. With one giant swing on his rappelling cord, Zane gained entry by busting through a window, surprising two hulky guards inside armed with automatic weapons. Cole was hot on his heels, and together they took out the targets with rapid fire.

The others entered the same way, and Jay took the lead. Using hand signals, he communicated with the team to follow his direction. The floor plans they'd studied in the war room familiarized them enough with the compound's layout, and they made quick work of clearing the area. The rest of the rescue team were keeping the guards occupied with an attack at the front, so the Alpha Team were able to make their way through the maze of hallways without running into too many of the armed targets.

The compound seemed to be one endless maze, but their steps were directed by Travis, who communicated with them through their ear coms from where he sat back in the KSI command center.

"While you were in the air, the heat signatures alerted us to a change," Travis warned them. "Three more people entered the room where we suspected they're holding Sydney and Chloe. Then two more came in, and if my guess is right, they took one of the ladies and moved her to another room down the hall. The original room still has two heat signatures, but I think one of them is a target, not a hostage. The room is coming up on your left."

"Sydney's there," Cole muttered through the coms. His gut screamed at him that she was close and was likely in that room. And she was likely with Carter. No one questioned how he knew this to be true, and he couldn't have explained his certainty if he tried.

As they approached the door, Jay and Cole flanked the steel barrier as the others assumed an attack position. BB suddenly appeared with a battering ram. On Jay's mark, BB crashed through the door and backed out of the way of the others. They stormed into the room with guns at the ready only to be welcomed by a shrill scream.

In one sweeping assessment, Cole saw Carter clutching his face as he backed away from them, and Sydney laid on the floor, her arms up to shield her as the scream ripped from her throat.

"I got her," he shouted.

The others moved forward, shouting for Emmett to raise his

hands and drop to his knees. Cole dropped to Sydney's side just as he heard Emmett shout.

"Stay back, or I'll shoot her in the head."

Cole glanced over his shoulder to see Emmett brandishing a gun, his eyes wide and frantic. The gun was pointed directly at Sydney, and she released another piercing scream. Cole folded his body over her, his Kevlar vest shielding the both of them from any pot shots Emmett would take.

He heard gunfire and braced himself for the impact only to feel nothing. He heard a scream and risked a look. Emmett clutched a hand to his shoulder as blood poured from a bullet wound. With a nudge to the back of Emmett's knees, Jay forced the man down to the ground and secured his hands with a zip tie.

Moving his rifle to rest against his back, he drew her closer to his body.

"Syd, it's us. It's me. It's Cole. I've got you. You're safe now."

His heart broke as she trembled in his arms. Her arms trapped between them, she rested her fists against his chest as he cradled her head.

"Target secure," he heard Jay shout.

Cole looked over his shoulder, relishing the site of Carter with his hands secured behind him as his teammates circled him. Carter glared at him even as BB secured his hands behind his back with a zip tie. Cole wished the man would attempt to escape just so his teammates could take him out, but he would be satisfied with the man wasting away in a prison.

"Cole?" Sydney's voice brought his attention back to her. "Oh, God, Cole. Please! They took Chloe. Down the hall. She was screaming... Oh, my God! I don't hear her screaming. What if they—"

Immediately he whipped his head to find his teammates. "Chloe's one of the heat signatures in the other room."

"On it." Zane and Jay hurried from the room, their guns raised.

Cole could hear Travis communicating directions to them through the coms, and he reached up to pull his mic from his ear. He didn't need the distraction as he assessed Sydney's condition.

"It's okay, baby. Zane and Jay will find her. Are you all right? Did he hurt you?"

He pulled back to peer into her face, where a bruise darkened the skin on her swollen cheek. Cole placed his palm gently against it, his eyes softening even as his anger raged inside. "He hit you."

"I fought him, Cole. I tried to remember everything you and Zane taught me. I wasn't sure if you would get here in time or not, but I fought anyway. I knew you would want me to fight." Her words tumbled from her mouth, and her eyes were wild with hysteria.

"Did he—" Cole almost couldn't bring himself to ask the question, but they needed to know. "Did he do anything else besides hit you?"

She vehemently shook her head. Tears welled up in her eyes. "I didn't know if I'd ever see you again. I knew you'd look for me, but I wasn't sure if you'd get here in time."

"Always, Syd. I will always come for you. You ready to get out of here?"

"No! No, Cole. I'm not leaving without Chloe. I'm not!"

She wiggled in his arms and pushed against him. Cole tightened his hold. He didn't know what shape Chloe would be in when his team got to her, and the longer Sydney stayed in the compound, the more danger she was in. As far as he knew, the teams were at the front still fighting to take down the guards as they gained entry. He needed Sydney to be away from all of it in case their side lost the upper hand. He shifted his weight to lift her into his arms.

"Cole, please. I can't leave her."

Cole ignored her pleas. He shot a glance at BB, who signaled him to proceed. He stepped from the room to the sounds of gunshots and froze.

"Chloe," Sydney whimpered.

"Keep moving, Panther. You've got a clear line to the chopper," BB said.

"Carter?"

"I got him. I'm going after Jay and Zane."

Cole needed no other encouragement. With quick steps, he moved back the way they came, intent on escaping.

"Travis said the exit is up ahead to the right," BB shouted once he realized Cole was no longer wearing his ear wig.

Cole moved quickly, taking the woman he loved as far away from danger as he could get her. Her arms had snaked around his neck, and she held on with a firm grip. He burst through the exit, relieved to find Wings on the ground waiting for them.

"They have Chloe. Zane's bringing her to the plane," Wings told them as they climbed into the chopper.

When Sydney didn't respond to the news, Cole suspected she was going into shock. He gently settled her on a seat at the back of the helicopter.

"We need Isobel," Cole told the pilot, and Wings immediately relayed the info over the ear wig.

"She's on her way. You should put your com back in."

The grave tone of Wings' voice chilled him. He reached to replace the device, and the cacophony bouncing against his ear drum told him pandemonium was breaking loose inside the compound.

Zane, Jay and BB suddenly boarded the chopper. He saw Zane carrying his own bundle and realized Chloe rested in the man's arms. When he placed her in a seat away from where he and Sydney were, he realized she had not fared as well as Sydney. Zane gave Wings the go-ahead to take off before moving to where Cole knelt beside Sydney. Zane stared down at her resting against the seat, her eyes closed as tears trailed a path down her cheeks.

"Wheels up!" Wings shouted as the chopper lifted into the air.

Cole took advantage of the noise from the plane's engines to question Zane, but the man started talking before Cole could say a word. Zane spoke low, careful that Sydney didn't overhear, and the coms picked up his words easily.

"Dawson and another guard had Chloe in the other room. He beat and raped her. The bastard was zipping up his pants when we burst in. I took him out with a single shot. Jay got the guard who was about to take a turn with her, but more were heading our way after hearing the shots. Sam and Isobel showed up to help us take them down, and we took a minute to dress Chloe as best as we could. Jay sent us back to the chopper and stayed behind with BB to help the Deltas clean up."

Cole shut his eyes for a moment, his heart hurting for what Chloe and Sydney had gone through. He then pierced Zane with a hard stare. "It's not over for them. Carter is still breathing."

"Carter is going down, Cole. They'll put him away for a long time, and Sydney will be free of him."

He looked down at his woman to realize her eyes were now open. Her gaze locked on her friend as Isobel treated Chloe's injuries.

"Syd—" Cole began.

He reached for her head to offer comfort, but she gently pushed him away. On wobbly legs, she used the other seats to balance herself so she could cross the chopper to her friend.

Sydney fell to the floor beside Chloe. Her vivacious friend turned vacant eyes to face her. Sydney tried not to react to the blood matting Chloe's hair at her temple, to the nasty bruise already darkening the skin around her eye, or to the cut on her lip. Chloe's blouse hung open, her bra torn to reveal her breasts, but she made no move to cover herself. Her feet were bare, but she still wore her jeans.

"Chloe," Sydney managed to whisper before her voice broke.

A hand suddenly reached over Sydney's shoulder, offering a shirt for Chloe to wear. Since Isobel still worked on Chloe's head wound, Sydney just spread the shirt over her friend to cover her. Sydney wanted to offer some kind of comfort, but words failed her.

Chloe shocked her by grasping her hand. "Are you okay?"

Sydney nodded, her heart breaking. Even hurting, Chloe was still looking out for her. A sob wracked Sydney's body.

Chloe suddenly withdrew her hand and sat up straighter. She leaned forward, away from Isobel's ministrations, until she was inches away from Sydney's face. "No," Chloe ordered her vehemently. "Do not fall apart. We survived, and Emmett will rot for what he's done. We survived. You have your life back. No tears. Promise me. No tears."

Sydney reached up to swipe away her tears, but paused. "He only hit me, Chloe. What Danny did to you…" Her voice trailed off.

Tears welled up in Chloe's eyes, but the woman stubbornly refused to let them fall. "I can't cry. If I cry, they win. If I cry, then it's real. I can't handle it if it's real. I can't."

"They didn't win, and you can handle anything. You're a badass, remember?" Sydney said the first thing that came to mind, even though the words felt wrong passing through her lips.

"H-h-he raped me. I fought, but he r-raped me. Nothing I did stopped him. That's not badass." Chloe's voice was monotone. Her eyes closed to shut out everything around her.

"He's dead, Chloe," Isobel told her firmly, never pausing in her ministrations. Chloe's lids lifted, and her stare focused on the woman she barely knew. "Dawson can't hurt you anymore. And Sydney's right. You'll survive this because you have her and the rest of us in your corner. You're a strong woman, and you will fight to get through this and prove that bastard did not break you. That is, in fact, what makes you a badass."

Sydney didn't know Isobel well, but the woman's words endeared her to Sydney's heart. She wanted to hug her, but somehow she knew the gesture would only embarrass Isobel. Instead, she reclaimed Chloe's hand and decided no more words were needed.

Once Isobel finished offering first aid to Chloe, she and Sydney helped the battered woman don the shirt one of the guys had handed them. The t-shirt dwarfed Chloe's slender frame, but she hugged the material close to her body.

"Sydney, I need to examine you, too," Isobel told her softly.

"I'm fine, Isobel. Really. He slapped my cheek, but I'm pretty sure nothing's broken. I just want to sit with Chloe. Will you sit with us?"

"Of course."

They settled into seats around Chloe. After a few moments of silence, Sydney heard Chloe mutter something. She leaned closer to hear her friend quietly repeating, "I am a badass. I am a badass."

Sydney squeezed her friend's hand before seeking out Cole with her eyes. He watched them from his seat across the chopper. Concern was etched in his features, and she offered him a slight smile, hoping he would take it as an indication she was okay.

His golden eyes softened, and she was grateful he understood her need to be with her friend. Sydney allowed the warmth from his gaze to seep into her limbs.

The events of the last day were almost too much for her to process, so she focused only on the mantra Chloe repeated again and again.

I am a badass.

Chapter Twenty-Six

Sydney woke slowly, blinking several times as she tried to identify the faint noises around her. Just as she remembered she was in a hospital, the memories of her abduction and rescue came rushing back to her. She raised her hand to stare at the IV, and her muscles protested the movement. A low groan escaped her lips.

Cole's handsome face appeared in her line of sight, and she felt him envelope her other hand. "Are you all right? Do I need to get a doctor?"

Sydney couldn't respond right away, so taken was she with seeing his face. Even with stubble darkening his jaw and his bloodshot eyes, he looked beautiful – her knight with a rugged exterior instead of armor. After Emmett kidnapped her, she had resigned herself to the possibility she might not see Cole again. She had no idea how he'd found her, but for the first time in her life, she felt as though fate had looked out for her. Her eyes drank in the slope of his nose and cheekbones, the golden hues in his eyes, and the kissable curve of his mouth. His mouth curved into a smile, his eyes gleaming with a rich glow.

His lips brushed across hers with feather-like touches that pushed her discomfort far from her mind. A small whimper of protest passed her lips when he raised his head. His smile widened into a grin, flashing his white teeth, his eyes darkening with desire.

"Wrong time and wrong place. But soon. Very soon."

Cole dragged a chair closer to her bedside and sat, leaning forward to keep the contact with her hand. "Now, let's talk about something else before you tempt me to lose my control. Answer my question. Are you all right?"

"How's Chloe? I want to see her. Do you think the doctor would let me be with her?"

"I don't know if you can stay with her, sweetheart, but I'll take you to see her."

"You didn't answer my question. How is she?"

"It's hard to say. Kat and Isobel have been with her. She's… she's not really talking to anyone. She let the doctors do all the necessary exams, but she's just lying in her bed now. I'm not even sure if she's slept. She has to be in pain, but she's refusing to take pain meds unless it's ibuprofen. Nothing stronger. Kat said a counselor has been in to see her, and Chloe was polite but didn't open up to her."

"Her injuries—how serious are they?"

"Nothing life-threatening. Physically she'll be fine in a few days."

Physically, she'll be fine… Sydney heard what Cole didn't say. Psychologically and emotionally, Chloe's healing wouldn't come in just a few days.

"I want to see her, Cole. She may not talk to me either, but I want to be with her. Even if it's just a few minutes."

"The doctor wants you to rest up, but I think I can sneak you down there to visit. I know she'll be glad to see you."

"I just can't…I never wanted her to experience anything like that. It's all my fault."

He placed a hand on her cheek. "No, honey, it's not. None of this is on you. Put the blame where it belongs – on Carter and Dawson. Now, it's your turn to answer my question. Are you all right?"

"Yes," she told him, but sighed when he raised a quizzical brow. "I'm tired. Sore. I feel like my whole body is bruised, which makes no sense since Emmett only hit my face. I feel…overwhelmed and confused. It was all such a blur, like I was watching it happen to someone else, but it happened too fast for me to keep up with what was going on."

"You're still in shock. It's a normal reaction. That's why the doctor ordered no visitors for you and Chloe, so you could rest. But when you're up for it, there's a waiting room full of people who want to say hi."

"Really? But you're in here."

"Yeah, well, the doctor and nurses realized very quickly that I'm not going anywhere."

"Who else is here?"

"Everybody," he drawled. "Tryst was here already with Brick, so he just joined everyone else. Kat, Zane, Jay, BB, Wings, the Delta team, Isobel, and even Sam have essentially taken over the waiting room. They didn't want to leave until they could see for themselves you and Chloe were okay."

Her jaw dropped. "They don't have to stay. They've done so much. They have to be tired. You, too. You all should go home."

"I'm not leaving. Neither are they. That's how it is when one of us is hurt or sick or in trouble. Take it or leave it."

She smiled. "I'll take it. I'll definitely take it."

"It's good to see you awake. I've been impatient to see those amazing blue eyes since you were admitted for observation."

"You think my eyes are amazing? Maybe you need to take another look at yours. I've never seen eyes that color in my life. I dr…" Her voice broke off, and her cheeks flushed a color deep enough to rival her red hair.

"You what?"

"Nothing. Tell me what I've missed while I was out of it."

His eyes narrowed. "Syd. Tell me."

She nibbled her lower lip, knowing she couldn't deny him but embarrassed to share something so personal. "I dream about you, okay? I dream about your eyes. A lot."

His grin returned, and the very eyes she talked about brightened to a warm amber. "Good to know."

Her lids closed. "Please, take my mind off my embarrassing confession and tell me what I've missed."

He chuckled. "It doesn't matter. You're supposed to be resting. You're safe, and you don't have anything to worry about anything anymore."

She pierced him with a stare. "Tell me. I deserve to know."

He squeezed her hand lightly. She held his gaze and waited. No way was she going to let him get away with not answering her question.

"Our ambush paid off. We secured the compound and took Carter and most of his crew into custody. A few of his guards were taken out during the raid. Dawson is dead, thanks to Zane. All of the hostages were freed and are getting medical treatment."

"Hostages? You mean, there were more people there besides me and Chloe?"

He nodded gravely. "Four other women were being held in different rooms of the compound. They had to be sedated before we could bring them here. They were too traumatized to understand we were the good guys. Local law enforcement is trying to track down their identities and notify their families."

"Oh, my God. Those poor women. Is there anything we can do for them? If I had my laptop, I could help search for their families."

"It's already being done, sweetheart. They're getting all the help they need. You need to focus on yourself."

"What about our team? Is everyone all right?"

"Tex took a bullet to the vest. He's fine, but he'll have a nasty bruise for a while. Rigger had his shoulder dislocated during a fight, so he's in a sling for a few weeks. The rest are fine. Just worried about you and Chloe."

She sighed. "So what's next? Do they have enough evidence for Emmett to go to prison?"

"Jay turned Carter over to the FBI. Last I heard, they issued search warrants for Carter and Dawson's homes and other properties. Tryst said they're hoping the women we rescued will recover enough to testify, but I think Cecilia Rappaport may agree to testify for a reduced sentence for her involvement."

"Her involvement? So she was part of this?"

"I don't know the whole story, but yeah, it looks that way. We also found Einstein's body shoved into a room with a gunshot wound."

"Danny shot him," Sydney explained.

"Good. 'Cause Einstein left Brick for dead in that alley."

"How is Brick? I prayed he was okay. I couldn't let myself believe he died in the alley."

"We got to him before that happened. Isobel did what she could for him until the ambulance arrived. He had to have surgery, but the doc told Tryst he should recover. He's out of commission for a while though, but he's glad to be alive."

"I'm so glad. I can't believe he was hurt trying to protect me. I wish I could understand why Einstein would turn on everyone like that."

"It doesn't matter at this point. You will probably have to give a statement about everything, but Tryst has managed to hold them off for a day or two."

"I'll make sure to thank him for that. Do you think I can visit Chloe now?"

"You don't want to sleep some more first?"

She shook her head gingerly. "Please. I want to be with her."

He sighed and dropped a gentle kiss to her forehead. "Let me see what I can do."

Cole rose and left the room. Sydney closed her eyes, slowing her breathing to relax her aching body. Her mind, however, refused to shut down. She imagined her best friend lying in a hospital room identical to hers, alone and broken and in pain. If Chloe hadn't involved herself in Sydney's mess, she would never have been with her at KSI to be kidnapped. Despite what Cole had told her, she couldn't help but feel at fault for what her best friend endured.

"It's not your fault."

She wasn't aware that she was crying until she heard the voice coming from the doorway. Swiping the moisture clinging to her face, she scowled at Zane, who leaned against the closed door of her room.

"You should knock before entering into someone's hospital room."

He smiled, not at all ashamed. "Panther asked me to come and sit with you while he talks with Tryst and the doc. How are you feeling?"

She opened her mouth only to close it firmly. She'd started to say she was fine, but she knew Zane would see through the platitude as easily as Cole had. "Not great, but better than Chloe, I'm thinking."

"Stop blaming yourself for what happened to her. That's on Dawson, and he paid for that with his life. It's also on Carter, and he's going to pay by spending the rest of his life rotting in prison. None of what those two assholes did is your fault."

"They wouldn't have come after her if not for me."

"They didn't have to take her. Einstein could have dropped her in the alley like he did with Brick. They could have taken you and only you, but they decided to use her as leverage. Stop blaming yourself."

She quieted. Zane always shot straight with her, even if his words were tough to hear, or brutal to her psyche.

"I'm glad you're all right," he said softly as he walked closer to the bed.

"Thanks. And thanks for coming for me, and for… you know, for what you did to rescue Chloe. I'm sorry you had to do that."

"It's not the first time. I know you probably don't want to know that about me, but I'm an Army sharpshooter. It comes with the territory. Dawson was an evil SOB who needed to be eliminated. I won't lose sleep about it."

"I should be sorry it had to come to that, but I'm not. He would have haunted me and Chloe for the rest of our lives if he were still around. I have mixed emotions about Emmett's fate. I'm glad he'll pay for what he did to us and to all of the women he's kidnapped and sold to sickos, but part of me wishes Jay would have killed him the way you killed Danny."

Zane sat in the chair Cole had vacated, and he reached for her hand. Sydney felt comforted by the gesture, but it failed to give her the warmth she experienced when Cole touched her.

"I get that. But the way it played out is for the best. We wouldn't have taken them down and rescued the other hostages if not for your intel on Dawson. It's good to have you as part of the team, Syd."

She smiled. "It's good to be a part of the team, Houdini."

Releasing her hand, he leaned back against the chair with a dramatic eye roll. "We need to talk about this nickname. Can't you think of something better than Houdini?"

She chuckled then winced when it caused her aching body to protest. Cole stepped back into the room in time to witness her reaction.

"I sent you in here to keep her company, not cause her pain," Cole growled.

"Stand down, Panther. It's not what it looks like. We were just talking."

"Yeah, well, sorry to cut it short, but Syd and I have somewhere to be." He opened the door to allow a nurse to step inside with a wheelchair. "Chloe's awake. You'll have to keep your visit short, but the doc said he thought seeing you might help her. You up for a short ride down the hall?"

"Yes," she said as she struggled to sit up.

After the nurse took the IV bag off the pole next to her bed, Cole lifted her from the bed to gently place her in the wheelchair. Despite his careful movements, Sydney still needed a minute to fight the dizziness sweeping through her. She finally gave the signal for the nurse to proceed, and Cole and Zane flanked her as they headed to Chloe's room.

Sydney tried to prepare herself for what she would see walking into her friend's room, but she had to fight a fresh rush of tears. Chloe's hair lay limply about her shoulders. She sat up in the bed but stared unseeingly at the television, unaware of the people or activity around her. The room was dim, adding a melancholy aura.

"Just a few minutes, Miss Reede," the nurse reminded her before slipping from the room, Cole and Zane following suit.

Sydney rested her hand on her friend's arm, surprised when Chloe didn't react. She longed for her friend to utter some type of smart ass remark or to stare at her with anger. The stoic, catatonic expression on Chloe's face broke Sydney's heart.

"I thought of all these things I would say to you when I saw you. Now that I'm here, I realize how stupid it all sounds. But I wish I had something to say, instead of just rambling on like I am now."

"You don't have to say anything."

And so Sydney didn't. She sat by her friend's bedside quietly, hoping to give Chloe the support she needed. Whether Chloe liked it or not, she was in her corner to stay.

After a few minutes, the nurse returned. "It's time to go back to your room, Miss Reede."

"Just a few more moments, please," Sydney implored and was relieved when the nurse relented.

"You should go, Syd. You need to rest," Chloe said in a flat tone.

"I've been resting. In fact, I just woke up. Evidently whatever they used to knock us out had some wicked side effects."

Chloe didn't reply. Sydney breathed deep and exhaled softly. "I wanted to see you. I wanted to see for myself how you were doing. I think everyone is trying to be positive for my sake when all I want to know is the truth."

"And do you feel better now? Now that you've seen me lying here all broken?"

Chloe's harsh tone was like a knife to Sydney's chest. She squeezed her friend's hand a bit harder.

"Would *you* feel better if the roles were reversed? You can try to push me away, but I'm not going anywhere. I know all of those tricks. I used to do them with you after we first met, remember?"

Silence stretched between them again. Sydney guessed her friend thought ignoring her would force her to go away. She refused to let Chloe retreat into herself. An odd noise broke the silence of the room. Sydney's eyes adjusted to the dim lighting enough for her to see the tears rolling down her friend's face.

"Oh, Chlo," she whispered, not bothering to stop the flow of her own tears.

"I never knew, Sydney. I was so stupid. I thought I was your rescuer. I would singlehandedly show you that you could have a better life without Emmett. I never understood what you went through with him. I never knew how it felt…"

Chloe's voice broke. Sydney wanted to rise and embrace her friend so they could cry together, but she didn't trust herself to get out of the wheelchair without becoming dizzy and falling.

The nurse returned, immediately concerned to see the two friends upset. "That's it. It's time for you to leave, Miss Reede. You two need to be resting, not making each other cry."

This time Chloe raised a hand to stop the nurse. "Please, no. Just a few more minutes, please. Just a few more."

Sydney knew the nurse wanted to protest, but something in Chloe's plea must have changed her mind. She placed a box of tissue between them on Chloe's bed before exiting the room again.

"It's my fault," Chloe mumbled.

"That's not true."

"Yes, it is. If I hadn't mouthed off to him the way I did, it would have been different. We said we wouldn't show our fear. We didn't want them to have the satisfaction, but if I had kept my mouth shut, then they would never have separated us and he would never have…"

"Wrong. I lie to myself like that all the time. I blame myself for what happened to you and to Brick. Even when Emmett and I were together, I believed if I had just been more docile or said the right thing or wore the right clothes, then Emmett would be happy with me and never hurt me. But Emmett and Danny cared nothing for what I did, or what you did, or what any of their victims did. They were evil men who believed control came from belittling and abusing someone else. They had plans for us, Chloe, or they never would have taken us. And nothing we could have said or done would have changed those plans. So stop blaming yourself for what happened, and I'll try to stop blaming myself too."

"I'm sorry."

"Oh, Chlo, I should be the one who's sorry. You were only involved in this mess because you were trying to help me. And you did. In so many ways. And you'll help me more. And I'll help you. It's how we work. It's why we're great friends. We'll get through this. It'll take time, but we'll come out of this stronger. It's who we are."

Sydney wasn't sure if Chloe found strength or comfort from her words, but she would repeat them as often as it took for her friend to believe them. And for her to believe them herself.

The nurse returned to take Sydney back to her room and refused to listen to any more protests.

"Want me to stay?" Sydney asked, ready to do battle if it came to that.

Chloe shook her head. "It's okay. Go back to your room and rest. I just need some time. By myself."

Sydney sensed Chloe wasn't just talking about that moment. She was asking for time to deal with her ordeal on her own. As the nurse wheeled her back to her room, she vowed she wouldn't let Chloe push her away. The two of them would deal with this together and find their way to the happy life they both deserved.

Epilogue

One month later...

Sydney stepped through the door and immediately smiled as she breathed in a mixture of incredible aromas. Each day when she came home, she fell more in love with the quaint house. After living in apartments most of her adult life, to actually have a house, no matter how small, was a joy she never expected. And those days when she would find Cole Atwood waiting for her only added to the peaceful life she was becoming accustomed to.

As was her habit, she secured the door behind her, flipping the deadbolt without a second thought. She settled her messenger bag on the nearby table and her keys on a hook on the wall above it. Hours spent in front of computer terminals left kinks in her neck, shoulders and lower back. She longed to sink in a tub full of hot, bubbly water until the skin on her fingers and toes wrinkled.

But first things first.

She followed her nose to the kitchen. Small but functional, the room was one of her favorites. Not because she enjoyed cooking or even knew how to make more than instant macaroni and cheese, it was because her man enjoyed cooking and often preferred her kitchen to his own.

Her man. Her smile widened. Watching the big, bad Navy SEAL toiling in her kitchen—sautéing vegetables in a pan, preparing sauces, and chopping ingredients on the counter—was a sight that never grew old.

She leaned against the doorway to study him. A line of sweat formed on his upper lip and his forehead. A navy t-shirt stretched taunt across his muscular chest and arms, his jeans hanging loosely on his trim hips. As he turned from the counter to the stove top, she saw he was barefoot, and desire pooled in her belly. She never realized she had such a foot fetish until she saw Cole in his bare feet.

"Welcome home," he drawled, letting her know he'd been aware of her presence the whole time.

Sydney didn't move. Instead her smile widened, and she continued to enjoy the view. His dark hair looked mussed despite the short cut. His rugged features were relaxed as he continued to create something she was sure would be the best meal she'd ever put in her mouth. His creations usually were.

"It's good to be home." She crossed her arms just under her breasts. "Something smells wonderful."

"Tilapia with a tomato cream sauce, sautéed vegetables, and roasted potatoes. You hungry?"

"Yes, but I just might be more tired than I am hungry."

Lowering the temperature on one of the stove top burners, he wiped his hands on a dishtowel and returned it to the counter. Then he turned, his beefy arms outstretched. Without hesitation, she pushed off the door frame and walked straight into his embrace. Her arms snaked around his middle, her head resting on his chest. His lips planted a whisper of a kiss to her hair. Whenever she heard the word contentment, this was the image she had in her mind – the peace and security of being in Cole's arms.

"I missed you."

The Alpha Team had just finished a ten-day op overseas, and Tryst had given the team members much-needed time off. Sydney, on the other hand, had been assigned as the tech support for the Delta Team's latest mission. Since being hired at KSI, Sydney almost exclusively worked for the Delta Team. From time to time, she did assist the private investigators in routine cases, and she still worked for her own private cyber security clients. She juggled a lot and stayed busy, but she loved it. The only drawback was how little time she and Cole spent together.

"I missed you, too, baby," he drawled, sending goosebumps down her arms. "How's the case going?"

She pulled away just enough to raise her lips to meet his in a quick but searing kiss. "It's done. The team is heading home tomorrow. I actually had time to visit Chloe at work today. I needed to run some diagnostics on the server at the marketing firm, and Kat said I could take some time this afternoon to do that."

"How is she?"

The light in her eyes clouded over. Before she could reply, he leaned down to kiss her softly. "We can talk over dinner. It's almost ready."

She nodded. "I'll get some plates."

In short order, they worked side by side to have their dinner plated, and they sat down at the small table in the open space beside the kitchen. She wasted no time in sampling tonight's meal, releasing a moan as the delicious flavors exploded on her tongue. She caught Cole watching her intently.

"What?"

"You're beautiful."

She felt a flutter in her tummy, a flush heating her cheeks. "I'm eating like a death row prisoner with his last meal, and you find that beautiful."

He grinned. "I said *you* are beautiful. Your eating habits are a different story."

She playfully punched his arm. "Ha, ha. Enough about me. What did you do today?"

He talked about his day and the plans he had for them for tomorrow since neither of them were working. When she'd polished off her food and sat back, Cole turned the conversation to more serious conversation.

"Tell me about your visit with Chloe."

She sighed and started twisting her fork between her fingers. Her eyes stared unseeingly at her hand as she spoke.

"She pretends nothing has changed. It's like she leaves the house every morning wearing this mask so people won't suspect how she's really feeling. She acts fierce and tough, and ready to take on the world. But I see it in her eyes. They're empty. There's none of her fire or zest for life shining in them. She refuses to talk to me about the rape. She says it's in the past, and it accomplishes nothing by dwelling on it."

Sydney paused as she considered the changes she'd seen in her best friend since their abduction. Chloe continued to lose herself in work, but once she was off the clock, she shut herself away at home, never going out or talking with anyone. Chloe was going through the motions of her life, refusing to let anyone see the pain she was in.

"I asked her how the therapy sessions were going, but she wouldn't say much. I've sort of expected her to stop going, but she still keeps her appointments. I just wish she would talk to me. It's like she's trying to protect me from what happened to her."

"That's what she does. The whole time you've been friends, she's done everything she could to protect you. She strikes me as someone who doesn't like to relinquish control and doesn't want to be a victim."

"You're right. She doesn't. I just wish she'd let me be there for her, though. Our friendship is more than her supporting me all the time. It's a two-way street."

"Maybe you can plan to have a Taco Tuesday soon."

"I actually invited her to dinner tonight, but she said she was eating with Sam and Monica."

Cole raised a brow. "Wow. I mean I knew she and Sam started to be friends when he was her bodyguard. I just didn't realize she was acquainted with Monica or was hanging out with them."

"After Monica brought Aiden to the hospital to visit, it's like their little family is Chloe's refuge," Sydney explained, smiling as she thought of Sam and his girlfriend's little boy. "I never thought Chloe was a fan of kids. She always said she had no interest in settling down and starting a family, but when it comes to Aidan, she lights up whenever she sees him or talks about him. I think they see how good he has been for her, so they've made a point to invite her over quite a bit. I'm glad too. At least she is connecting with someone."

He covered her hand in his. "Come here."

She stared at him a moment before pushing her chair back. She stood and moved over to sit in his lap, tucking her head under his chin. Her ear rested against his chest where his heart beat a soothing rhythm. In the days following her kidnapping, she'd come to rely on that rhythm to be her beacon in the storm.

Her life had ceased being the same since the day when Emmett and Danny had kidnapped her and Chloe. She'd stayed with her friend following their release from the hospital, but after only a few days, it became apparent to her that the longer she stayed, the more Chloe pulled away from her. Sydney had turned to Kat and Isobel for support, and they convinced her to give her space. As much as she knew their advice was sound, she still missed her best friend.

Cole had talked to her about moving in with him, but Sydney yearned to be on her own. After living with her parents, then a college roommate and then Emmett, she was ready for something that was totally hers, where she set her own routine and did things her own way. Cole accepted her decision without argument, and Sydney fell even more in love with him.

Cole had been the one to find the quaint little house where she now lived. She had been looking for an apartment, but the moment she saw the house, she knew this was where she belonged.

The only upset to her new normal were those times when reality crashed into her life. She had requested regular updates on Emmett's arrest and impending sentencing, but each time she heard them, her memories threw her into a funk of what ifs and guilt. Footage of Emmett's arrest stayed at the top of news reports for weeks with Cecilia Rappaport's involvement making it fodder for tabloids.

Sydney also kept tabs on the four women who were being held at the compound with her and Chloe. Two of them were reunited with their families. One was identified as a known prostitute who had no family to speak of. The last still remained unidentified. She struggled the most, only telling authorities her first name and not much else. Her doctors suspected her trauma blocked her memory. Sydney did her own searching whenever she could, but so far she'd hadn't been any luckier than the authorities in identifying the woman.

The physical searches of homes and properties resulted in very little evidence, but the FBI continued to investigate. For now, the case against Emmett rested on what was discovered at the compound as well as the testimonies of Cecilia Rappaport and a couple of the drug cartel members who were the muscle guarding the compound. It was enough to convict her ex, but Sydney couldn't help but wonder if someone had stepped up to continue the drug trade and human trafficking.

"Talk to me, baby."

She shivered as Cole's deep voice trailed down her spine like a sensual caress, pulling her from her wayward thoughts. "I would much rather sit here with your arms around me than to talk anymore."

"And I would rather you talk than worry about Chloe in silence. I'm here for you, Syd. Whatever you need."

Sydney smiled, his words causing her heart to do a backflip. "I know. I appreciate it more than you know. Do you ever think about that night at the charity benefit? So much has happened since then."

"Standing outside the ballroom was the first time I looked into your gorgeous eyes. I was a goner."

She raised her head to peer into his handsome face. "A goner? No way. A hysterical female barreled into your arms and then ran away from you. No way were you a goner. You just had a hero complex that couldn't resist a damsel in distress."

Despite the teasing glint in her eyes, Cole's brow furrowed. She couldn't tell if she irritated him with the comment or if he was playing along.

"Hero complex? Really?"

Then his long fingers found the sensitive spot along her ribs. With a shrill yelp, she struggled to leap to her feet to escape the tickling, but he followed her retreat. Sydney twisted from his grasp and ran to the living room with Cole fast on her heels. Her laughter carried through the house, and Cole grinned at the sound. Finally wrapping his hands firmly around her waist, he lifted her from her feet and dropped her to the couch. With catlike speed, he covered her body with his, his legs holding his weight so he wouldn't crush her.

Sydney's laughter faded into a chuckle that disappeared in her throat as she caught the intensity of his gaze. His hand brushed a lock of auburn hair from her face, his touch feather light. Her breath hitched in her throat. Cole lowered his head until his mouth was mere inches from her, his breath warm against her face. His scent—

musky and masculine—swirled around her, intoxicating her more than the wine she had with dinner.

"I need you to know..." He stopped as his eyes searched hers intently. "I'm not good with words, but I want you to know what I said is true. The moment I saw you, I knew I wanted to be there for you always. I could tell you were someone special. I never knew just how much you would affect my life, but I have not been the same. I love you, Sydney. I'm in this for the long haul. I get that you need time, and that's okay. I'll wait for as long as it takes, but I mean for you and me to be together forever."

Tears stung the back of her eyes. She wiggled her arm free from where it was trapped against his body. Her palm cupped his cheek, enjoying the feel of its rugged contours against her skin. Her thumb traced his lips, her heartbeat increasing its pace. Cole froze, her soft touch lighting a fire in his blood.

"I love you, Cole. Not because you rescued me. Not because you protected me. But because you empower me. You make me feel special and safe. You show me what a relationship with a real man is like. If you're in this for the long haul, then so am I."

He released a pent-up breath, his smile slow but brilliant. The golden hue of his eyes captivated her.

"Ah, baby, I love you."

A thrill zipped through her body, and her heart pounded loud enough to echo in her ears. His lips captured hers in a kiss that slowed time, the world around them fading. All that remained was the two of them, their bodies touching from lips to toes, their love pouring into a kiss rivaling any they experienced so far.

Finally he lifted his head, and Sydney whimpered at the loss in contact. "I'm not going home tonight, Syd."

Since Sydney's release from the hospital, he'd forced himself to move slowly, to take his time until she was certain he would never treat her like the other men in her life had. He could no longer wait to move their relationship forward. She'd gotten under his skin like no woman ever had, and he was ready to show her just how much she affected him.

"I don't want you to," she whispered.

His heart skidded in his chest. He searched her face for signs she might regret her words. All he saw was love and desire.

"You deserve better than me. You deserve somebody who can lay the world at your feet. If I was a better man, I'd let you go so you could find that someone. But, God help me, I can't. The idea of you finding happiness with someone else kills me. I need you like I need air to breathe. So as long as you will have me, I swear I'll do all I can to be the man you deserve."

She placed her fingertips against his lips, swallowing the lump in her throat and blinked away tears.

"I don't need someone to lay the world at my feet. All I need is you, by my side, loving me. I don't know yet what the future looks like for us, but I know, without a doubt, I want you in it. I made a mistake with Emmett, but something beautiful came out of all of it – my love for you. I can't feel sorry about that. I can only swear to you not a day will go by when I won't tell you how much I love you and how thankful I am that you rescued me from my past."

Cole was done talking. He swept Sydney up in his arms and carried her to her room. Their movements became frantic as they undressed each other, but once Sydney stood before him, Cole stood transfixed. The dim lighting of the bedroom cast an ethereal glow around her. Her skin translucent, her brilliant hair falling over her shoulders to caress her full breasts, her eyes the color of the ocean – it all took his breath away.

"You're making me nervous."

Cole drew her flush against him. "Don't be nervous, baby.

You're just so beautiful, I had to take a moment."

She melted into his arms, her own encircling his neck. "I love you, Cole."

"I love you, Syd."

He crushed her mouth with his and lifted her until her lithe legs wrapped around his waist. He moved until they fell to the bed, never breaking contact. Their hands were everywhere, touching and exploring each other. Need welled up within him in a frenzy, and Cole knew he had to claim Sydney now.

"Hold on."

He scrambled off the bed to search his pants pocket for a condom. In short order, he covered his cock and was back in his spot above her. He held her gaze as he entered her with one swift motion.

"Oh, Cole!" A shudder wracked her body. Her hands gripped his lower back, urging him even closer.

Cole felt his control snap. His thrusts sped up until all he could focus on was the feel of her lush body around his and the sweet sounds of her moans. His release came like a tidal wave as her own pleasure crashed over her. They clung to each other as they rode the high of their orgasms.

When he finally stilled, the intensity of their coupling fading, his body relaxed on top of hers. He needed to roll his weight off of her, but he was zapped of all strength. Her hands began to caress his back, her nails lightly stroking his skin.

Cole suddenly knew what true contentment felt like. And Sydney knew her heart had found a safe place to land.

Author's Note

Thank you for taking the time to read Knight's Rescue. This book was actually the first one I wrote in this series, so it definitely holds a special place in my heart. I loved telling Cole and Sydney's story, and I hope you loved it as well.

If you enjoyed Knight's Rescue, please consider leaving a review on any or all of these platforms: Amazon, Goodreads and Bookbub.

About This Author

Shelley Justice is a Southern belle who lives with her husband and two children in Alabama. Her love for the written word inspired her to start writing when she was thirteen years old, and she's been living in her imagination and crafting stories ever since. In addition to being a bookworm, she is a self-proclaimed TV addict with a special affinity for dramas. She also loves romantic movies, especially of the black-and-white variety.

www.shelleyjustice.com
https://linktr.ee/authorshelleyjustice

Acknowledgments

I offer my biggest thanks to my family. I could never have made my dream come true without your support and encouragement. I love you more than you'll ever know.

Thank you to my ride-or-die, Christie, for being my source of support, my sounding board and my voice of reason when doubt and insecurity rear their ugly heads.

To my author sisters—Emily, Colleen and Maryann—thank you for offering advice, for answering my endless number of questions and for talking all things writing with me. You guys are the best!

To my editor, Carolyn, and my proofreader, Susan, thank you for catching all the things I miss and for making my stories better. You guys are awesome!

To my amazing graphic designer, Clarise, thank you for producing amazing covers that are better than I imagined.

To my growing reader community, saying thank you doesn't seem enough when it comes to have encouraging and supportive you've been. You are making this journey one to remember.

More From This Author

Read more from Author
SHELLEY JUSTICE

KNIGHTS OF KSI SERIES

Available on Amazon
Read for Free with Kindle Unlimited

KNIGHT'S HAVEN
Book One

KNIGHT'S RESCUE
Book Two

KNIGHT'S TEMPTATION
Book Three

KNIGHT'S JOURNEY
Book Four

KNIGHT'S HOLIDAY
Book Five

KNIGHT'S DESIRE
Book Six

KNIGHT'S FALL
Book Seven

KNIGHT'S SEDUCTION
Book Eight
Releases 2023

KNIGHT'S HONOR
Book Nine
Releases 2023

Made in the USA
Coppell, TX
25 March 2023